Sweet Giselle

Sweet Giselle

Karen Williams

www.urbanbooks.net

Urban Books, LLC
78 East Industry Court
Deer Park, NY 11729

ISBN 13: 978-1-60162-489-5
ISBN 10: 1-60162-489-1

First Printing April 2012
Printed in the United States of America

10 9 8 7 6 5 4 3 2 1

This is a work of fiction. Any references or similarities to actual events, real people, living, or dead, or to real locales are intended to give the novel a sense of reality. Any similarity in other names, characters, places, and incidents is entirely coincidental.

Distributed by Kensington Publishing Corp.
Submit Wholesale Orders to:
Kensington Publishing Corp.
C/O Penguin Group (USA) Inc.
Attention: Order Processing
405 Murray Hill Parkway
East Rutherford, NJ 07073-2316
Phone: 1-800-526-0275
Fax: 1-800-227-9604

Dedication

This novel is dedicated to my children . . . Whom I breathe for and would stop in an instant for you two.

Acknowledgments

I'm back! Let's see, it started with *Harlem on Lock*. Then there was *The People Vs. Cashmere, Dirty to the Grave, Thug in Me, Around the Way Girls 7, Even Sinners Still Have Souls,* and *Aphrodisiacs: Erotic Short Stories.* And I have been out for only three years! God is good all the time! And now we are at *Sweet Giselle.* Ahh. (*Exhaling.*) I'm absolutely ecstatic to finally bring this story to light! I so enjoyed writing it! It's funny that each time I finish a story, I get all emotional and teary eyed. For me these characters live in my world as I write their story. And when I end the story, I have to say good-bye to them. And then I move on to new characters, so it always works out.

I'm so happy and blessed to be able to do what I love, and that is these stories. What puts the icing on the cake for me is to know that people out there enjoy them. With a full-time job and two kids, it is not always easy, but it's the passion and, as my creative writing professor Mr. Dominguez always said, "the burning in the belly to write" that keeps me up at night and wakes me up early in the morning to get it done, and no matter how tired I am, I am truly enjoying every minute of writing. I'm also excited to announce that I will be writing as Braya Spice. My first novel under this name is called *Dear Drama.* Look for it in 2012!

I want to thank my beautiful children, Adara and Bralynn. You guys are my world and why I get my grind on day to day. Thanks to my mother and my sister Crystal.

Acknowledgments

To my nieces, Mikayla and Maydison; my nephews Omari and Jeff Jr.; my cousins Donnie, Jabrez, Devin, and Mu-Mu; and my goddaughter La'naya. Hey to Tammy, Shauntae, Ray, Eric, Christina, and Terry.

Thanks to my friends Sheryl, Roxetta, Lenzie, Christina, Kimberly, Linda, Tracy, Christina, Talamontes, Pam, Carla, Sewiaa, Ronisha RIP, Tina, Shumeka, Valerie Hoyt, Tara, Pearlean, Maxine, Dena, Barbara, Henrietta, Candis, VI, Phillipo, Latonya, Leigh and Vanilla, Yvonne Gayner, Sandra V., Sandra T., Ivy, Daphne and Lydia, Mrs. Pope, Rob, and Thomas. Thanks LaNesha for being a third eye and reading over the finished product! Hey, Netta!

My author buddies Mondell Pope, Aleta Williams, Terra Little, Terry L. Wroten: Ayo. A'ight! Y'all should know by now I'm corny!

Thanks to Carl and Natalie!

Thanks to my editor, Kevin Dwyer. I can honestly say you are making me a better and more polished writer.

Thanks to all my fans that have supported me. So many have reached out and told me how my stories have impacted them. Knowing this truly inspires me to write my heart out and give all I can give in my works. I know as an author I write with purpose. I often say, with each book, that I'm either making a statement or I'm asking a question. In stories like *Harlem on Lock, The People Vs. Cashmere,* and *Around the Way Girls 7,* I strived to be the voice for young girls who don't have one. These young girls that walk our streets every day, enduring horrific circumstances, are often swept under the rug. The young girls that view themselves as damaged or flawed, I want them to know that they are not. And that they can still persevere, despite what they have gone through. In *The People Vs. Cashmere,* Ms. Hope always told the girls not to be defined by their

Acknowledgments

pain. For those that don't know Ms. Hope was a real person: me. Those teaching in *The People Vs. Cashmere* were mine.

With stories like *Thug in Me* and *Even Sinners Still Have Souls,* I pushed the power of hope and holding on when every single card in your deck is inexpicably stacked against you. I say it again: hope is a powerful thing when you have nothing else. Hope can be all you need to keep going, to keep fighting, to climb your way out. Trust me, I know firsthand. In *Dirty to the Grave* I wanted to explore the dark side of our culture. Immorality crosses all races and all genders. For me this is evident in this novel. It also explores the idea that how you're nurtured, and how you're loved from conception shapes the person you become.

Essentially, I want my stories to inform, entertain, and evoke something in my readers. I have also often been asked why there is so much tragedy in my stories. This says it best: pain and struggle make strength apparent.

Anyhoo, I hope I didn't leave anyone out. If I did, and you were instrumental in my life, I thank you!

Feel free to visit me at:
www.AuthorKarenWilliams.com and on Facebook.

Enjoy

Prologue

"No! Don't shoot him please!" I begged.

I looked at my husband's horrified face as he pointed his gun at Bryce's head.

Bryce simply sat back, coughing up blood.

My husband looked from me to Bryce, then back at me, the whole time not lowering the gun. "Are you begging me not to kill this man, Giselle?"

I swallowed hard and tried to speak. My arms were spread wide, but nothing, no words, came out of my mouth. I dropped my hands to my sides as sobs hit me.

My husband started crying, too. Huge sobs escaped his body. The sobs were because he knew the truth. So why did he want to hear it?

Yes, I loved Bryce. I loved him more than I loved my husband, more than I loved myself, and surely, more than I loved my life. Which was pretty screwed up right fucking now! I was staring at the man I'd thought I would love forever, and fearing that the man I wanted to love forever was going to die.

"Pull the trigger, muthafucka. Get this shit over with," Bryce said.

My husband yelled out in rage and rushed toward Bryce. "Shut the fuck up!" He started to beat Bryce in the face with his gun.

I rushed forward, threw myself on my husband's back, and pounded him in his head with my fists. "Get off of him!"

He easily tossed me off his back. I flew back, lost my balance, and banged my knee as I hit the floor making a loud thud. My teeth clenched as pain shot up my leg. I was still hurting from the earlier beating my husband had put on me. I didn't know how much more pain I could bear.

My husband turned to me. He looked so hurt that I was protecting Bryce. "You want him, Giselle? Huh? You love him? Baby, just tell me the truth."

I closed my eyes briefly. Never in my wildest dreams did I think I would find myself in this situation. But it was my husband's bullshit that had got me caught up with Bryce to begin with. Neither of us had planned for this. Too many lives had been lost. Shit had gone too far, and I wanted to end it. All the pain now, the violence, the deaths. If I could end it . . . I knew I had to start with the truth.

"Giselle."

I opened my eyes and stared at my husband. His lips were trembling, and his eyes were bloodshot. "As much as this shit is going to hurt me to hear, baby, I need to know the truth." He took a deep breath. "Do you love this man?"

"Yes. I love him."

His whole face crumbled. Now he was bawling. "You were my baby." His voice lowered. "Sweet Giselle."

I started crying again, because when he said my name, it reminded me of the past. When I was his sweet, fragile, and naive wife. I was a wife who adored and looked up to her husband. I almost worshipped him. I thought he was perfection, the ultimate man. I didn't have any of those types of feelings for him anymore. He was just pitiful and pathetic to me. I almost felt sorry for him. More retaliation from him would change nothing. At the end of the day, even if he did kill Bryce, I still would not love him or want to be with him ever again. The things I found out about him were what had destroyed my love and my utter worship of him.

Suddenly my husband turned his focus back on Bryce. And before I could stop him, he fired.

Chapter 1

Before the Madness

February 13, 2011 . . .

I let the clips out of my sandy-colored hair so it swirled around me and down my back in luxurious curls. I could not get Crystal, my stylist, to do my hair tonight, so I got it done the night before and wrapped it up. She'd said something about her schedule being booked because it was so close to Valentine's Day. My baby had told me that he would hire a stylist to come to our home, but I wasn't parting with Crystal for any reason, because no one could do a weave like her or whatever I wanted, for that matter. But since my husband had paid for me to get hair implants a few years ago, I no longer wore weaves. And my hair now hung as far down as my lower back. I stared at myself in the mirror. I admired my beauty. My perfect brown skin. Skin that was kissed by the sun. I was so golden. Yes, golden.

I giggled to myself as my eyes passed over my Bambi-shaped brown eyes, my lips, which were the size of Angelina Jolie's. I had a set of dimples, which my brother also had. My teeth were straight and white, thanks to my hubby. Truthfully, there was nothing wrong with my teeth before, except for my gap, but my husband was a perfectionist. Plus, he had the dough, so why not be perfect? Now, my body was another thing. I had the plumpness in all the right places. Size thirty-four C breasts, with rich, dark nipples. My waist was small. My hips spanned, and my butt was round. My body was toned, thanks to hitting the gym my husband Giovanni had made for me in our lavish mansion. I had also gotten lipo on my inner thighs. My plastic surgeon was at my disposal. Giovanni always said, "Anything for my sweet Giselle." Then, whenever he said it, he gave me a look like he wanted to fuck my brains out, and I loved that shit! I loved, loved, loved my husband.

Tonight he was taking me somewhere special for our four-year anniversary.

I couldn't wait to put on the three-carat earrings and matching tennis bracelet Giovanni had bought for me. He had laid them on the nightstand, with a note that read, "This is just the beginning." I knew that as Giovanni's wife, I lived a life that most women fantasized about. My baby was rich, handsome, and affluent. We hung out with doctors, lawyers, celebrities, and self-made millionaires. It seemed like my baby knew everyone. Once a week my husband went to the shooting range with the Westwood chief of police, and the chief would often come over for dinner with his wife, Vanna. One summer we vacationed with them in Puerto Vallarta. I knew no man was as special and as loved as my husband.

I put my La Perla bra and matching thong on, the whole time admiring my body in the mirror. Some of the changes my husband had suggested, such as the hair implants, and the lipo on my thighs. Before him I had never worn thongs or gotten a Brazilian wax, but he insisted that I do these things. It was like he wanted to make me into the woman of his dreams in every way. Physically, mentally, and sexually. He always took time out of his busy schedule to tell me and show me how desirable I was to him. He made me feel super special.

Womanly. It was truly amazing what had transpired in these last five years. . . .

2006, The beginning . . .

I had just graduated from Carson High School and was looking forward to enjoying my summer before I went off to college. I wasn't tripping on going to a big college or out of state like some of my friends. I was cool going to Cal State, Dominguez Hills. I mean, I lived right across the street from it, in Stevenson's Village. It would be silly to go anywhere else. Plus, I loved my family and didn't want to be too far from my seventeen-year-old brother, Brandon. Yes, seventeen! There was only a year difference between us. I was born in January, and he was born that following year, in October. I guess my daddy did not follow that six-week rule after my mother gave birth.

I knew I needed to make sure my brother stayed on track because my parents were always working. My mother and father worked at the oil refinery that was located in Carson, California. While my father had been there as long as I could remember, my mother stayed home until my brother and I were the legal age to stay home alone. Then she joined my father at the refinery. When my mother was home, she ran a tight ship. Everything was on a strict schedule. And she kept my brother and me in line, seriously. The tight ship she ran allowed our home to stay in order even when she went back to the workforce, because she had our asses seriously trained. Our homework was always done, the house was kept clean, and we never tried to run amok, no matter if my parents were home or out. They could take a trip to India and could rest assured we would handle our business. Within the first year of my mother working, we were able to purchase a house in Stevenson's Village, whereas before we stayed in some apartments by the South Bay Mall.

Although I loved both my parents to death, I didn't really have a super close relationship with them, but I had a lot of respect and love for both of them. The reason why I didn't feel close to them was that they were gone pretty much the majority of the day. I knew their absence at home wasn't because they didn't care or were selfish parents, totally uninvolved in their kids' lives. It was because they worked long hours to provide a foundation for us now, and for our future. And when they were home, they both preached about the importance of having a foundation. One thing about my mother and father was that they never turned making money down. My father could have a high-as-hell fever, but no matter what, he went to work and would work overtime if they offered it to him. My mother was the same. She went in for overtime on her birthday. Even as they got older, their work ethic never changed. So I knew I had to go to college. It was not an option for me. So did my brother. I told my brother time and time again, "As soon as you hit eighteen, you will bring your ass over to where I am."

He would always laugh and say, "Okay, Gissy. Whatever." That had been my nickname since he was one. He couldn't say "Giselle," so he would say "Gissy," and it stuck until he could pronounce my name properly. Sometimes he went back to calling me Gissy. Now he was my booski! I loved my brother to death. He was my closest friend, and no matter what I would always take care of him. He looked like he could be my twin. That was another thing we could thank our parents for: our good looks.

My mother, Alana, was super pretty and my daddy, Toby, was super handsome. I took my father's coloring and sandy hair, while my facial features came from my mother, along with her nice, tight body. My brother had the exact coloring and facial features as me, but with a sharper jawline, which he got from my father. The shape of my brother's face was long, like my father's, while I had my mother's oval-shaped face. We both had gaps in our teeth, which came from our pops. Brandon said all the girls called his gap sexy. I never agreed. He was six-three, with a muscular build. I never gave him compliments, because I didn't want his looks to go to his head and I didn't want him to think that all he needed was his looks to succeed in life.

I was always told I was beautiful, but I didn't want to rely on my looks to get by in life. I personally believed that once you did, you started selling your soul, and well, looks lasted for only so long, so after that what did you have? I refused to be in my fifties, expecting men to pay me for sex, like my friend Lexi, who was equally pretty and had been stripping since we were in high school so she could keep up with the Joneses. For the past six months, she had been answering sex ads on Craigslist for money. I had told her time and time again that there was more to life than selling her body. I'd asked her, "Aren't you afraid of catching something?" and "What would your mom think?" even though the majority of the time alcohol had her mother out of touch with reality. But her answer to any of my questions or my judgment was to put her hand in my face and say that she didn't wanna hear that shit.

Lexi had been my best friend since elementary. She lived right across from me. Lexi's mother and her mother's sister and two brothers never quite left the nest. Instead of doing what normal people did, like going to college, getting a good job, getting married, and having kids; they passed on the college, the job aspect, the getting married part, and instead had kids and lived off their parents. Matter of fact, Lexi's aunt Mona was working on her fourth baby. All while her three uncles moved their baby mamas in, with their kids in tow. And while Lexi's mother had only one kid, Lexi, she was drunk the majority of the time, and Lexi had pretty much been raised by her grandparents. But since her mother spent all her extra money on liquor, and her grandparents were retired and living on a fixed income, they could not afford the things that Lexi desired. So, she claimed, she did what she had to do. She would sometimes try to get me to answer ads or even post one.

"Come on, Giselle. Stop being goody fucking two-shoes. A lot of girls post or respond to ads for sex on Craigslist."

Not this girl, I thought. *Not now. Not ever!*

But then I learned at an early age in life to never say never. Who knew that eventually I would have to do the same thing that Lexi did?

My father was diagnosed with cancer during my first semester. When the cancer in my dad's body spread and he could no longer work, my mother started missing work left and right, partly due to caring for my daddy and partly due to being severely depressed about my dad being so sick. Their were days when she couldn't bring herself to get out of bed. I had no choice but to ask for a refund of my college tuition and give it to my mother to help with bills. I would watch people rushing to class and wish that I was one of them. I felt a duel of emotions. Anger, sadness, and disappointment. I was sad that my father was dying and I was pissed that I couldn't go to college. For the longest time it was all I had wanted and I had worked hard for the opportunity.

I wanted to be able to finally have independence and pick my own classes, to be able to hang out, join a sorority, and go to parties, wearing new, cute clothes. And now I was missing it. But I told myself that this would not be a permanent thing. That got rid of the anger and disappointment. But the sadness stayed, because I knew the situation with my father would not get better, only worse, until it resulted in death. I knew this not because I was negative, but because this was what the doctor said.

A few months into the semester of school, my father passed. I felt like in that moment when I lost my father, I lost my mother, too. Because now she never had the strength to get out of her bed. And she lost her job because of it. And then . . . we were in danger of losing our foundation. Our home. Month after month, we were missing our mortgage payments. We went begging to my grandparents. First, we went to my mother's parents. My mother's father was only a janitor, but he managed to give us about seven hundred to help. Then we called her mother, who had relocated to Georgia, and since remarried. After dealing with her dodging my brother and me for damn near a month, I managed to get her by calling on Lexi's phone. She answered only because she didn't recognize the number. She promised to send one grand and to call my mother. She did neither. My mother had always said that her mother was a bitch. I agreed. To know your only daughter had lost her husband and you didn't even bother to see how she was doing? What the hell? Then we tried my dad's mother. His dad had died seven years back, so she was our only hope. But she couldn't help us. She had used the last of her savings to bury our father and was living on Social Security in a retirement home. Still, she mailed us a check for eighty bucks, which came in handy. Both my brother and I got jobs to help, but it didn't help much. Minimum wage was not enough to cover all the bills. We were at risk of foreclosure. I mean, we became three months behind on our mortgage. I really wished that what my brother and I were making was enough to cover it, but it wasn't. We were really in hard times, and I had no idea what to do about it. When that question, what was I going to do? popped into my head, I always got nervous. So I kept busy to keep any questions out. Oneway or another they always crept back in.

"You know what you need to do." Lexi said one day.

I stared at her as she stared intently at her cell phone. She was on the Craigslist Web site, looking for a "date." I was lying across her bed in the crammed room she shared with four of her female cousins, ages thirteen, eleven, ten, and six. There were three more kids, who were all boys. They slept in the living room so all the parents had their privacy. The youngest, Trinity, opened the door and stepped inside.

She was too cute with her hair French braided, with blue and white beads on the end. Her hair was always braided to the side of her face to cover up a huge birthmark. Despite it, she was adorable and was going to be a very beautiful woman one day. I wished they showed her how to embrace her birthmark as a part of what made her unique. Not as something that took away from her beauty.

She smiled at me shyly, revealing her front snaggleteeth. "Hi, Giselle," she said breathlessly.

I waved and said, "Hi, Trinity."

Lexi yelled, "Get the fuck out, ugly cuz."

Trinity jumped at Lexi's yelling. Her face then looked super sad, and she rushed out of the room.

I gave Lexi a sharp look. "You didn't have to speak to her that way."

"Giselle! Look at this." She passed her phone to me, and I glanced at the text on the screen of her phone.

Beautiful ladies earn three thousand dollars a day for figure modeling. No portfolio needed. No experience needed. Not a strip club. Future positions also available, with opportunity to make more money. For further info, reply to the e-mail address below. Must be at least eighteen.

Before I could respond, Lexi snatched the phone back. "Shit, I'm about to reply to this shit right now!" She started pressing the keys on her phone madly.

"Don't be stupid, Lexi. You know damn well no one is going to pay you three thousand dollars to model."

She twisted her head in a circular motion, continuing to press keys. "I don't give a damn what they paying me three thousand dollars to do. Long as I ain't fucking no dog or donkey, I'm good!"

I burst out laughing at her stupidity.

She continued as if she didn't hear my laughter. "You want me to sign you up, too?" she asked as she continued pressing the keys on her phone.

I was silent at first. But to myself, I had to admit that the opportunity to make three thousand dollars was tempting. That was a lot of money, and although we owed much more on our house, the amount of money they were offering would help greatly. But I had to be real with myself. The offer did not sound like it was for modeling clothes or shoes. It sounded like nudity to me.

"Girl, you got obligations. The first one is that house. Remember, you're supposed to be going to college right now. Do you really think that your mom is going to snap out of the funk she's in, Giselle?" Lexi asked.

"Would you if you lost the love of your life?" I snapped angrily. I didn't like how she had referenced my mother. She was going through a lot. To tell the truth, my compassion for my mother was wearing thin with all the stress I was going through, but no one else had the right to speak about her.

She looked like she regretted the comment she made. "I'm sorry, girl. I didn't mean to say anything that would hurt your feelings."

My face softened at her apology. "It's okay."

"I know this is hard for you. Working at Big Burger, when you're supposed to be at college, going to pep rallies, checking out all the cuties and shit. I know it still hurts that your daddy is gone. But this is an opportunity to make your situation better. Three thousand dollars is a lot of money for working only a day. And it said that there is opportunity to make more money. Maybe you can pay your house mortgage down some and make more money to put toward college tuition and books."

Big Burger was a local burger joint that was actually on the same street as CSUDH. The manager gave me a job there working full-time as a cashier, while Brandon worked farther up the street, at M & Ms Soul Food, as a part-time busboy. It was hard for me, though. Working there and seeing all the college students coming in to buy food. I always got a sick feeling being there and always felt depressed. I was supposed to be in college and stopping in Big Burger for food, just like them.

I bit my bottom lip before asking, "What do you think they will have us do?"

"Take some naked pictures maybe. I mean, it says modeling." She studied me before saying, "But I'm sure there are going to be a lot of girls showing up there, so I doubt they have to put a gun to anybody's head, let alone force us to do what we don't want to do."

"True." I sighed. "I need some extra cash, Lexi, but I don't want to sell my soul. What do I do?"

"Girl, you not going to sell your soul. That will always be intact. You just giving a little bitty piece of yourself away. But eventually, you are going to do that, anyway. At least this way, you're getting something out of it. Come with me, and let's scope it out. In the end, if we're not cool with it, we can bounce."

That was easy for her to say. Her cherry had been exhausted long ago and she had paraded naked in front of a lot of men. I, however, was still a virgin and had never been naked in front of anything other than a mirror or my doctor. I was saving mine for that special guy, should he ever come along. And really, I promised my daddy I would wait until I was married. So the thought of posing for nude pictures was repulsive to me. Because no matter how the ad sounded, I knew it had something to do with nudity. But in the end I knew my family had fallen on desperate times. Without our house, none of us had a foundation. I took a deep breath before saying, "Go ahead and put me down, too." Although a voice in my head was shouting, *No! No!* I ignored it and gave her a nervous smile. But the thought of this had my stomach doing flip-flops. I bit my bottom lip, uneasy.

She gave me a sly look. "Girl, I already did."

I shoved her playfully. But inside, I was still feeling uneasy about this quick decision I had made, and I was severely doubting that it was a good one. Nothing that easy could possibly be good or simple.

Chapter 2

"Giselle? Giselle? You know you hear me calling you, girl." Brandon was knocking on my door.

I was hiding underneath my covers in my bed.

When I didn't respond, he barged in my room. "Don't you hear Lexi outside, honking for you?"

"Yeah. Don't go out there," I snapped. "Ignore her."

"What?" He pulled the covers off my face. "What are you doing now, crazy girl?"

"Stop!" I swatted his hands away and pulled the covers back over my face.

He laughed.

"And it's none of your business, Brandon. Get out! If she comes to the door, tell her I'm not here."

I had chickened out at the last minute on going with Lexi to that job that we both saw advertised on Craigslist. As much as I'd tried to talk myself into doing it, I just couldn't bring myself to. I was young, but I went by instinct. And my instinct said that that ad was bad news. I was working my ass to full capacity at work. I even worked overtime on the weekends. I didn't feel too bothered by it. Because even if I was off work, it was not like I had money to go out and do anything, anyway. I would put my two checks together and put them toward our house note. But I was always several hundred dollars short and was still trying to catch up. I tried not to look at the notices that we received, or I would feel totally helpless. Like there was no progress, no light at the end of the tunnel. We were still way behind. I didn't want to feel totally hopeless, because that would take away the little motivation that I had. And most of all, I didn't want Brandon to know how far behind we were. But, yes, we were far behind. Try eight grand far behind. But I could only do what I could do. Same for Brandon. What Brandon brought home, we put toward the utilities and food. We didn't even bother paying the two car notes. Before my father had passed, they were paying off their cars in a timely fashion, so they owed only about four grand a piece on their matching Benzes. And although I wanted to pay them, we just couldn't. It was a struggle just to pay what we paid and still not break even.

"Everything okay, Giselle?"

I turned on my side and pulled the covers off me, hoping that there was no stress present on my face. "Yes. Why?"

"Because you're hiding from your best friend, that's why."

"Naw. She wants me to go on a double date to Roscoe's with her and two guys. The guy she picked for me is fugly," I lied.

He chuckled. "A date? Chile, please. The only dates that chick goes on take place at Motel Six or in the back of a car. Ain't no fried chicken, waffles, or smothered potatoes getting ordered. But plenty of bodily fluids are getting exchanged."

I tossed one of my pillows at him.

He ducked, and the pillow landed on the floor, inches from him.

"Shut up, Brandon. That's none of your business. You worry about yourself, passing all your classes and getting your ass to work."

He ignored me. "Seriously. I don't even know why you hang out with her. You are known as a good girl, Giselle." He screwed up his handsome face so he looked ugly. "She's known as a rat."

"She's my friend, Brandon. And you know it's not good to judge people. Lexi wasn't as fortunate as we were as far as having good parents. She had a way harder life than we had. She has had to depend on herself."

He waved a hand at me like he was swatting away some flies, while saying, "Naw. Bullshit. Everything boils down to choices. She chooses to do that shit, Giselle. It's not like she is out on the street. She has a home. Her grandparents provide for her. It would be different if she was homeless or hungry. That heffa is just being materialistic. But in reality, she could go out and get a job, just like you and I did."

I didn't have time to analyze what my brother was saying. I had too much on my mind. Too much. Worrying about whether or not what my friend was doing was wrong was not going to make our situation any better.

"Why are you debating this with me? Why do you care?"

"I don't," His eyes locked with mine. "I'm not concerned about Lexi. I'm concerned about you."

"What?" I tossed a hand at him and looked down at my purple comforter.

"Why you looking away, Gissy?"

"Brandon, stop," Idly, I traced a purple embroidery star on my comforter.

He walked closer to me and placed my face in his hands and put his face close to mine. "I know you weren't thinking about doing that shit she does, were you?"

"Boy, move. *I'm* the older sister."

"I don't want to hear that shit."

I tried to snatch my face away, but Brandon wouldn't let me. "Get away." I shoved him, and his hands fell from my face and he lost his balance a little. He regained his composure and continued to stare at me.

"Why can't you answer the question, Giselle? You're my sister. Older or not. I know you think you know what is best. But if you were even thinking about doing something like that, then you've obviously proved that you don't know shit about shit."

I took a deep breath. "Yes, of course I've thought about it. Right now times are really hard for us. And Lexi makes money." I took a deep breath. "But in the end, as you see, I'm still here. So, I obviously didn't go through with it. I'm not going to go through with it, so don't worry about it. You just do your part around here, and I will do mine. And hopefully, something will give and I can start college, and as soon as you finish up your senior year, you can be right behind me. Everything is going to be okay. I'm going to hold it all together, so don't worry." I was convincing myself as I told him this. I still felt unsure that I could do so, though.

Based on the expression on his face, my words didn't do a good job of convincing him that eventually everything would work itself out. Or maybe he didn't believe me when I said I had no intention of doing what Lexi did. But still, he said, "Yeah, okay." He passed me another look and walked out of my room, closing the door behind him.

Things continued to go downhill from there. Brandon would say, "God was going hard in the paint on us." Brandon's birthday came. For Brandon's birthday, I put a little money aside, bought him a cake, some cologne, and invited a few of his friends over. He was just happy about the fact that he was legal. He and his friends danced the whole night. It was all I could do, because there was no way I could afford to send my brother to the prom or to his graduation. Since my brother had so many credits, he finished up early, anyhow, and told me not to worry about it. He had also taken a lot of advanced placement classes, so he would be ahead of the game in college . . . whenever he was able to go.

Then, once we got past my brother's birthday, there was Christmas, New Year's, and my birthday. I worked a double shift and came home to find that Brandon had his friends over and they were partying for me. They played Lil Jon's "Snap Yo Fingers" at least ten times, making me want to mentally snap. I couldn't enjoy myself.

"Come on, Gissy," Brandon said as he and his friends were clowning around and mimicking the "Snap Yo Fingers" dance.

"No. You guys have a good time. I have to go in early tomorrow, so I need to get some sleep, and I need to check on Mama." They were too busy dancing to even see that I was already making my way up the stairs.

Once I made it upstairs, I went to my mother's door and knocked. "Ma?" I tiptoed in the room just in case she was asleep, which was what she did for the major-ity of the day: sleep and sit, staring out into space. It killed me to see the woman that I had always known to be so strong and so vibrant withering away before my very eyes.

She was sitting in her La-Z-Boy recliner, rocking back and forth. Her back was to me, but due to the rocking back and forth, I knew she wasn't asleep.

"Mama, you need anything?"

The rocking stopped momentarily. I heard her whis-per, "No." Then the rocking continued. "Yes" and "no" were the only two words I had managed to get out of her since my daddy had died. I wished I knew some way to pull her out of the depression that she was in.

I took a deep breath. "All right. Good night, Mama."

I left the door slightly open. Then I walked to my room, hoping I could stop my mind from racing just enough so that I could get some sleep.

"Giselle, wake up! They're taking Mom and Dad's cars."

"Whaaa?" I thought I was still asleep and dreaming. But my brother continued to shake my shoulders, showing me I was wide awake.

"Did you hear me? They are taking both the cars."

I jumped off my bed and raced down the hallway, then down the stairs. I was going so fast that I fell on the bottom step. "Shit." I winced at the pain coming from one of my ankles. I slowly stood to my feet and limped outside. Once I got out the door and was standing on our porch, I saw that they were already loading up two tow trucks with my mother and father's cars.

"Wait!" I yelled. I hurried down the three porch steps. I rushed up to one of the men. He was loading my mother's car. "Excuse me."

He tried to pretend I wasn't there. But I wouldn't let him. I grabbed one of his arms, until he looked at me. I was lost, but I had to do something to get them to not take my parents' cars. They had put so much money into them. Seventy percent of the total balance due on the cars had been paid. They couldn't just take them! Then I reminded myself that they could, but I hoped they wouldn't if I explained.

"Sir, can you give me another month? Our father died, and my mother lost her—"

Snatching his arm away from me, the overweight His-
panic man said simply, "Not my problem."

"Please just listen to me!"

He waved a hand at me and walked away.

Wow. Just like that.

I started to approach the other man, an older black
man, who was loading my dad's car, but he had already
hopped in his truck.

I felt helpless. I couldn't do or say anything to get
them to not take my parents' cars. And most of all, I felt
scared. What if the house was next? True, I was paying
what I could, but the letters still hadn't stopped coming with the threats to foreclose. Maybe in a matter of a
few weeks or even days they would take the house away
from us. That terrified the shit out of me.

I broke down crying in the middle of the street. My
shoulders started to shake as I did. "I can't deal with
this," I whispered to myself. It was too hard. I was busting my ass, and still, I couldn't afford all these bills.
With only a high school diploma and no real job experience, I knew I was not going to find a job paying more
than the minimum wage I was making now. So what
was I going to do?

I wiped the tears off my face and dug out the new
ones that had formed in the corners of my eyes with
my nails, almost scratching my face. I then took a deep
breath to regain my composure. I knew regardless of
whether I could deal with it or not, I had to, because no
one else would. I was starting to resent my mother. If
she would get out of her self-pity, then maybe she could
put a stop to this!

I turned about to walk toward the front door, when
for the first time I noticed Brandon standing on the
porch steps. My brother's expression slowed my steps
a little bit. He looked just as lost as I was.

Chapter 3

Little by little the small control I had over things was going away. The way I handled all the stress of the finances, and my mother acting pretty much dead, was to try not to think about "what-ifs." Because I was just too damn busy to focus on fear or "what if this happened or that happened?" I felt that my time should be put to figuring out how to handle what we were dealing with, not fearing the worst. But when I wasn't strong enough to shove the bad thoughts and the dread that we would be on the streets out of my head, I made sure that I was nowhere near Brandon, because that fear always had me in tears. Ever since the cars were taken, I had been stressing nonstop. I didn't think I would be able to hold this together any longer. I had started having so much anxiety that I couldn't sleep at night, which made me exhausted at work and always sent me home with headaches. I was also filled with fear that it had me running back and forth to the bathroom. Which meant my nerves were being affected.

My boss took some serious pity on me. I guess he noticed how uncombed my hair was and the serious bags under my eyes and how slowly I was walking because of the strain in my back. It just wouldn't go away, despite how much Icy Hot I put on it. The ache felt like it was on fire.

One evening at work I was making a move to grab the broom to sweep up when he put a hand over mine. "Go home, Giselle."

"I'm not off until nine. Did I do something wrong?" I still had three hours to go. I hoped he wasn't letting me go permanently. I started to panic, thinking of what I could have possibly done to get fired.

"No, don't worry. I will still pay you as if you worked 'til nine. Just go home and get some rest. You need it."

I smiled. "Thanks, Roberto."

And even though I lived down the street, I was too tired to walk, so I called Lexi to see if she could pick me up. After going to the job advertised on Craigslist, she came back with so much dough, she was able to buy herself a little bucket car, and she was always rolling through Carson in it. It was a 1993 red Honda Civic. I was not going to lie. I was a little low-key jealous that she was mobile and I was still on the bus.

I dialed her number quickly and took a deep breath.

"Hello?"

I hoped she didn't have any plans and could come pick me up.

"Hey, Lexi. It's Giselle. You busy?"

"Nope. Just lying down. Why? What's up?"

"I'm super tired. So I was wondering if you could pick me up from work."

"What? You're finally getting off early for once."

"Yeah. My boss took pity on me."

"He should. He got you working like a slave. Hey, I'm kinda hungry. Are you?"

"A little bit."

"Let's go eat somewhere. My treat. And hang out."

"You sure you can afford it?"

"Girl, hell yeah. I got you. Let's go to The Pike."

"Okay."

"All right. Give me a few minutes, and I will be on my way."

I rushed in the bathroom with my purse. I pulled out my comb and tried to tame my tresses. My mother used to take me to get my hair done every two weeks before my father got sick and passed. I pulled it back into a ponytail.

I was wearing a pair of jeans, a black tank top, and some tennis shoes. I knew I should have gone home and changed but I didn't feel like it. I didn't want to walk in my house, period. It was far too depressing that my mother still had not snapped out of her depression and was utterly lifeless on a daily basis. It was like a dark cloud was hovering over our house and it never left. I knew my brother felt the same way. I knew I had to go back. Just not right now. I needed a long-overdue escape. Because the more pressure that came over me, the more enraged I became at the weakness I saw in my mother. Why should I have to deal with all of this? She was the mother. She had brought us into the world, and now it was like Brandon and I were the parents.

I heard a car honk, so I pulled off my work apron and rushed out. I was so grateful to Lexi for inviting me out somewhere. I didn't care if it was to Taco Bell. I made it to her car, opened the door on the passenger side, and hopped in.

"Hey, girl!" she said excitedly.

"Hey!" I said, just as excited. Since I had been working these long hours, Lexi and I had not been able to hang out like we used to. But I was relieved to see that it didn't feel funny or awkward. She seemed genuinely happy to see me. I felt the same.

Once I was comfortably inside, we both reached over and hugged each other.

"All right, let's roll." She let me go and started the car.

I quickly put on my seat belt.

She turned down Avalon and made a right on Albertoni and headed toward the 91 Freeway. She was bumping to 50 Cent's "I Get Money."

"So what's up, Giselle?" She hopped on the freeway heading east.

"Nothing much. Just working."

"How's your mother?"

"The same."

"Brandon?"

"Good."

"Cool." She started punching eighty while talking to me. "Well, girl, I'm so glad we get to hang tonight. I've been busy as hell, too. Ever since I went to that job you flaked out on me about."

"I'm sorry about that."

"Oh. It's cool." She slid over to the 710 South. "I wasn't playing, though. I went and made that muthafucking money!" She started laughing, forcing me to give a fake smile.

I started to ask her what she had to do, but I stopped myself. There was no reason for me to know, since I didn't do it and didn't plan on doing it. And she wasn't volunteering any information either. She just turned up her music and rapped along with 50 Cent.

We got off the freeway and turned down Pine Street. A few minutes later, she drove toward the parking center at The Pike.

"Where do you want to eat?" she asked. "We can go to Chili's, Outback, Sharky's. There's a Roscoe's down the street from here. Or we can order food out of Game-Works, bowl, and play games and shit."

She drove into the parking center.

"You're the big spender, so it's up to you," I joked.

"Well, I wanna see some niggas! You know me."

I laughed as she pulled her car into a spot. She then put the car in park and turned off the ignition. She turned the lights on in her car, and for the first time I noticed how fly Lexi looked. Her hair, layered around her face, was so silky and shiny. She had on this really pretty diamond bracelet and a matching ring, and her nails were done. When she hopped out of the car, I noticed she had on a pair of True Religion jeans and a cute powder blue tank top. They matched the powder blue Jordans she had on. She reached in the backseat for her purse. It was a Dooney & Bourke. It was the super cute one with the pink and blue hearts on it. She was wearing a tan-colored leather jacket. I looked so tacky in comparison.

So I told her, "You know what? I'm still tired, so let's just go sit down and eat, Lexi."

She zipped up her jacket and said," Okay."

We settled for Chili's.

After a twenty-minute wait, we were seated and given menus. I picked the crispy honey-chipotle chicken crispers and fries with a side of corn, while Lexi picked the steak fajitas and shrimp. She also ordered some tortilla soup for us both.

We were both silent while we sipped lemonade.

When the waitress sat our cups of soup in front of us, I couldn't resist anymore. I had to know what Lexi had done to get all the money she had. And most of all, I wanted to know how much she got. It was stupid to press the issue, since I didn't go. Spilled milk . . . but I have a habit of beating myself up for making the wrong choices in life, and at that moment, looking at all the stuff she had that my parents had always provided for me, except the car, I had to know that I made the right choice by not going with her. So before she could even get a scoop of her soup in her mouth, I asked, "What did you have to do, Lexi?"

She looked at me and burst out laughing. "I knew you wanted to know! What took you so long to ask?" She slid her spoon in her mouth.

I shrugged her question off. "What did you do?"

She chewed and swallowed quickly, while looking around to see if anyone was listening. Then she beckoned me closer and lowered her voice. "It was at this big-ass mansion, girl, in Westwood. And that place was so fly! Fly! I envy whoever the dude's lady is. Anyway, when I got there, they had eleven other girls there. So I was a little discouraged, because those bitches were all beautiful, so I just knew that my ass was going to get sent home. I mean, I ended up late. Thanks to a certain flake."

I gave her a remorseful look.

She smiled and continued, "Anyway, girl, the owner has a bomb-ass studio built in the mansion."

I didn't care about that. "So what happened?"

"They started us off with the first scene. We were pretending we were at a party. We all had on skimpy dresses, and we had to dance as if we were really having a good time. We were in the . . ." She paused. "South wing of the house. Yeah! That's what they called it. This seemed like a separate house and shit. The south wing was huge. Huge! There were five rooms inside, and each had a number on it. After we finished the first dancing scene, we were told to go to one of the rooms. Some rooms were assigned to more than one girl or more than one guy. Each room has a camera guy that films. It wasn't nothing complicated. No script. The camera guy tells you what to do. Real simple. Then you get paid."

I gasped. "What kind of scene?"

"If you could see your face!" she exclaimed, chuckling. She gobbled down some more soup before continuing. "You have a choice. You can take some nude pics and leave it at that, or you could up the ante. You can also be filmed. You can do a scene by yourself, masturbating with toys. You can do an oral scene. Either you give or receive or both. You can do a full intercourse scene or anal. You can even do a scene with a girl, two girls, two guys, a girl and a guy, or an orgy. You choose. They don't force you to do shit. There are way too many participants out there. But the more you do, the more money you get."

"What did you do?"

"Nothing hard-core. I posed naked in six nude shots. I got three-fifty for every shot. Then I did a scene by myself. That was as far as I was going to go. And I made forty-two hundred."

"In one day?"

"In one day, and I could have made more. But I didn't want to be greedy."

"Are you worried that someone will recognize you?"

"If you are such a lowlife that your form of entertainment is looking at porn and nude mags, then you just as bad as I am, and you gotta know you a lowlife, so you ain't going to confront me on shit. I'm just a young, pretty girl having fun and getting paid for it. Look at all them dumb broads on *Girls Gone Wild*. They don't even get paid for that shit, and they doing all kinds of crazy stuff on camera!"

I never thought about it like that. She had a point. But I would still be scared of someone who knew me seeing me in the films or in print.

The waitress brought our food and placed it in front of us. I hadn't even eaten my soup yet.

"They are always looking for pretty girls, Giselle," Lexi added.

"I don't know if I could do that. Not that I'm judging you, though."

"Girl, I wouldn't care if you were. I'm making my own money, and that's all that matters to me. I don't care what anyone has to say about it. Pretty soon I will be able to move out of my grandparents' house and get my own crib."

I didn't know what to say. So I ate my food, while Lexi rambled on about her new, fabulous life and job.

When I got home, I noticed that Brandon was not there. I figured he was probably out with his friends. He was eighteen now.

Normally, I would go check on my mother. But the last thing I wanted to see was her looking miserable. I simply went to my room. I just wanted to sleep. I was dog tired. Once there, I stripped down to my underwear and lay down on my bed. My mind raced and raced yet again before sleep took over.

The phone was ringing nonstop. I didn't feel like getting up, so I ignored it, hoping whoever the person was would just stop calling. But they wouldn't. I sucked my teeth and pulled my covers off, climbed out of my bed, and snatched up the phone in my room.

"What?" I snapped.

"Giselle. It's me, Brandon. I'm in jail!"

Chapter 4

I bit my nails nervously as I rode with Lexi over to Twin Towers. It was three o'clock in the morning when I got that phone call from my brother saying he had been arrested. After I hung up with him, I looked up his case online. It said he'd been arrested for a two-eleven. That was robbery, and his bail was set at two thousand. Just finding this out gave me a serious panic attack. Once I was able to calm myself down, I called Lexi and begged her to take me to see him during visiting hours. I was so upset after I got the call from him that I was unable to go back to sleep. Just the thought of him being locked up with murderers and rapists was too much. What if they killed or raped my brother? I cried and prayed that nothing hurt my brother while he was in there.

Once we got to the jail, it took us, like, forever to go inside. We waited for over two hours in that long line.

I was so relieved when I was able to sit in one of the booths and the inmates finally came out. Seeing my brother behind that mirror, in that jail garb, instantly had me sobbing.

He refused to look me in my eyes. But he snatched the phone and put it to his right ear.

"Brandon, what in God's name did you do?"

"Something stupid. But, look, I did it for us. We are doing so badly. I was just trying to help. I took some money out of the register at work."

"Brandon!" I exclaimed. "Why would you do that? We were doing okay."

That was when he finally looked at me. "Oh, we were? Last time I checked, we lost both our parents' cars and were on the verge of losing a house both of our parents worked hard to buy. And if that wasn't enough, you were going to do some shit that would have ruined your whole life and humiliated the both of us!" There was so much anger in his voice.

"Brandon, listen. I know it is hard for us. And you are right about everything you just said. But you don't have to do stuff like this. This could ruin your life. Your record, for God's sake." I feared that it already had. I feared that even if Brandon were to go to college and get a degree, he wouldn't be able to get a job with a dirty record.

"I know, Giselle." His eyes got watery. He wiped them quickly and looked around, I assumed to make sure no one else saw that he was crying. "I was tired of seeing you so stressed out. I hated that you couldn't start school. All Mom and Dad worked for was to make sure we had a future, a foundation. Daddy died because of it. Mom is walking death. And now, after all we've lost, we don't have a future."

I fought back tears, trying to be strong. "We will have a future! Brandon, I'm going to work on getting you out of here. I called a bail bond company. They told me I would need two thousand to bail you out. Since this is your first offense, hopefully, they will consider only giving you probation. Either way . . . Brandon, don't stress. Give me some time to work on this. Most of all, trust me."

"I do trust you. I love you. I hope to God you can get me out of here. I will never do something so stupid again."

I looked away so he didn't see the doubtful look in my eyes. I couldn't let him see it, because he was depending on me.

I was quiet the whole way back. Lexi rattled on and on, asking me what I was going to do. Truth was, I had no idea what to do.

As soon as we got into my house, I went straight for the phone. I planned to do the only thing I could . . . beg my grandparents to let me borrow the money or give me what they could for the bail.

"Girl, this house is disgusting!" Lexi exclaimed, looking at the messy living room." Let me help you out."

"Go ahead," I said while going up the stairs with the cordless phone in my hand. I dialed the number for my mother's mother first and walked toward my mother's room to check on her. Her bedroom was empty, so I walked to her bathroom.

When the phone just rang and rang, I sighed. My grandmother on my mother's side had picked now to not answer her phone. I knocked on my mother's bathroom door.

"Mom?"

I waited for her voice.

The phone continued to ring. I figured she knew it was me calling and was purposely avoiding answering the call.

"Mom?"

I opened the bathroom door.

Once my grandmother's answering machine came on, I waited for the beep, while scanning my mother's bathroom for her.

"Mom?"

Still no response.

I assumed my mother was in the tub. The phone beeped, allowing me to leave a message. I walked toward the tub while saying into the phone, "Hi, Granny. This is Giselle," I reached for the shower curtain. "I really need to talk. . . ." My voice trailed off at what I saw, and I dropped the phone and screamed at the top of my lungs.

My mother was in a tub filled with water and blood. I stared at the gaping wound on one of her wrists, where she had sliced through her vein. One look at her lifeless eyes told me she was dead.

"I know you are against doing this, Giselle. But, really, what else are you going to do? Your mother is dead. Your father is dead. It's all on you now. You got your little brother rotting away in jail. You need to get him out."

I wiped tears off my face at the mention of my mother. A few days had passed, and I still had not been able to get that image of her out of my head. She had committed suicide. She'd slit one of her wrists. Although I never shared this with Lexi, I felt responsible for her death. There was no telling if she had done it the night that Lexi and I had gone out. If I had checked on her, like I normally did, maybe I would have been able to save her. Brandon didn't even know. When he called, I pretended everything was okay. I didn't mention Mom was dead. I was not looking forward to telling him the truth. It was a truth that killed me softly. I would never see her again. First, I lost my father, and now my mother.

I couldn't get her eyes out of my head. She was the woman I had respected and looked up to all my life. The one I wanted to be like. And just like my daddy, I had lost her too soon. The thought that killed me the most was that she was so far gone that she wanted her life to end. The pain to end. And now, I would never be able to see her again. If by chance my brother and I did go to college and have families, the chairs for my parents would be empty. My future children would not have grandparents. I covered my face again with my hands as this new reality hit me and made me sob.

I thought back to how hard it was seeing them carry my mother's dead body out of our house. I closed my eyes briefly, shaking my head. This just didn't seem real, and it didn't seem right. Why did my parents have to be taken away? My brother and I were not bad kids. We weren't. We always did as we were told—while some of the worst kids in the world had their parents and didn't have to deal with a fraction of what my brother and I were dealing with. All the negative thoughts I had had about my mother since her depression came rushing into my head, making me feel like shit.

Lexi rubbed my hand. "It's going to be okay, girl. Your mother just couldn't hold on anymore. And now it's just you and your little bro."

Damn. I wished I could turn back time. I wished that I had tried to help my mother overcome her pain, her grief, her depression. I should have sat with her, done her hair, like when I was little. Tried to drag her out of the house. I should've kept telling her that I loved her, and maybe it would have helped. I could have pushed her out of the despair that she was in by playing some board games with her or watching her favorite shows with her. But instead, I was frustrated and gave her maybe a few minutes a day, brought her food and something to drink, checked on her briefly, and left it at that. And sometimes, out of annoyance with the mood she was in, I didn't bother. It was too late now to change any of this. She was gone. The reality of the shit was killing me because I felt responsible.

And now I had to continue to hold everything together. Again, I asked myself how I was going to tell my brother that Mom was dead. Would he blame me for it? Hate me? Feel the same guilt I felt? Who knew? But I knew that I needed him there with me to deal with this hurt. I told myself that if I had to show some nudity, I would just have to. It was to free my brother.

Case in point, Lexi managed to get me to roll with her to do some work. We were going back to that mansion where she had made all her money—even though I didn't want to do this. I really had no nerve. I just couldn't stop crying.

"We're almost there, Giselle. You are going to have to wipe your face."

I nodded and dried my eyes quickly.

We were in Westwood. I knew this only because Lexi had continued to talk about the house and where it was. I hadn't really paid much attention.

"I thought only white people could afford to live in these mansions. But, girl, the man is obviously about his business, because he is straight balling!" she exclaimed.

I really was not listening to what she said. My heart was aching for my mother. I asked myself again how I was going to tell Brandon about this.

"Here it is, girl."

There were two wide-framed iron gates that protected this huge estate, which seemed to never end. She pulled up to the gates. There was what looked to be a surveillance camera there. She paused and waited. Then the gates of the estate opened up wide enough for her to slide her car inside. She drove along a long stretch, like she was driving through a park.

"Girl, I told you this place was big."

I didn't reply.

It took her almost ten minutes to get to the back of the estate. She pulled into a spot and parked.

"Giselle, tell me that this place isn't tight."

I simply nodded.

"Did you see how big that swimming pool was?"

I wasn't paying attention to it. Any of it. But to this I nodded as well.

"Well, come on, girl. Let's go."

After we got out of the car, I followed after Lexi.

"Girl, come on!" I wasn't keeping up, so Lexi grabbed me by the hand and pulled me toward the door.

A huge black man who looked like he could be a security guard opened the door for us.

"Hey, Wingo!" Lexi greeted him excitedly.

His office seemed state of the art, with several video cameras. I could see the front of the house, where we drove into the parking structure, and other areas, which I assumed were the studio. There was a walkie-talkie in his office, and someone was speaking on it. He turned it off quickly.

"Hey, Lexi." He inspected me before saying, "You brought someone to work?" He kept eyeing me.

"Yes, and she is all about business."

I looked away from him.

"Well, I can see that she is fine. Damn. Sometimes I wish I was one of the actors."

"Wingo, you're crazy!"

"Let me see your ID."

I pulled it out and showed it to him.

He scanned it, handed it back to me, and said, "Walk her down to intake."

"Okay," Lexi said.

I slid my ID back into my pocket.

We walked out of the office and headed down a corridor. I followed after Lexi. She stopped in front of a door. There was a sign on the door that said KNOCK BEFORE ENTERING.

Lexi knocked, and a woman said, "Enter."

Lexi turned the doorknob, opened the door, and I followed after her. I was surprised to see an older lady seated behind a desk. She looked like she was old enough to be my mother. She had brown skin and cherub features, was chubby, and had on a pair of glasses. To her right, a slim, light-skinned girl was completely nude. A young-looking black man was taking pictures of her. He looked like he was the same age as Lexi and me and wore baggy jeans and a T-shirt.

I looked away, while Lexi and everybody else in the room acted like this was perfectly normal. I guess, given what I was about to do, it was.

"Hey, Nette!" Lexi exclaimed. She was treating these people like they were her friends. She was so comfortable with them. Maybe it wasn't all bad here.

"Hey, Miss Lexi. What you got going, girl?"

"Well, I came to put in some work today," Lexi sang. "And I brought someone who would like to try out. My friend Giselle."

Nette studied me. Her eyes scanned my body like the security guard had earlier. "You're very pretty, so there is no doubt that we can use you. Immediately. Today."

I nodded.

"But the question is, can she prove she is eighteen? Because you know how Giovanni feels about that. We aren't trying to get into trouble of any kind. No matter how pretty she is."

"Giselle, pull out your ID," Lexi ordered.

I slid my California ID out of my pocket and handed it to Nette.

"Thank you." Her eyes scanned my ID, and then she looked back at my face.

I looked away from her. I swallowed hard, trying to get the lump in my throat to go away. It wouldn't. It had been there since the police and ambulance arrived and took my mother away.

She stood and walked over to a copy machine. She made a copy of my ID and gave it back to me. Next, she gave me some forms on a clipboard and a pen. I knew that one of them was a 1099 form. There was also some type of release form.

"You can have a seat and fill that out quickly. Now, this does not guarantee work. But we always do intake and screening first. Ultimately, it is up to our producer, but like I said, I don't see any reason why he wouldn't use you. We need some fresh meat. We have been getting the same girls. So that was great of Lexi to bring you in."

I nodded. "Thank you."

"Okay. You're done," said the guy taking pictures of the girl. He handed her a short silk robe.

She silently put it on, then slipped her clothes and shoes in a bag.

The guy was doing something with the camera he had. He told her, "Go down the hall. First door on your right. Good luck."

"Thank you," the girl said excitedly before rushing out the door.

Nette picked up the phone and pressed an intercom button.

A man's husky voice chimed in. "Yes?"

"You got a girl coming your way, Percy," she said and quickly hung up.

Lexi sat down next to me. "She told me the same thing when I came in, and you know I worked."

I nodded and filled out the forms, surprised at how professional this all was. When I was done, I brought them back to Nette.

She scanned them quickly and then placed them all in a manila folder. She wrote my name on the tab and said, "Okay. Go ahead and strip down so we can get some pictures from you for our file. Sean will be taking the pictures of you, like he did the other young lady."

I was a little slow to respond when she said that part. I was not comfortable with the idea of stripping down in front of anyone. I knew I had to do this, though. But the thought made me super uncomfortable.

"Honey, if you're afraid to do this now, then you can't possibly work." That was Nette.

Lexi jumped in quick. "She's definitely ready to work."

"Okay. Well, you have to hurry. We do have more people coming in," Nette said. "This is preliminary. After these shots, you have to be screened by the producer."

I was puzzled by that, since she had said she needed new faces. I figured it was just a way to put pressure on me. I knew I needed to do this. I took a deep breath and began stripping out of my clothes and shoes. When I was completely nude, I stood there, embarrassed, as the camera guy stared at all my curves.

It wasn't until Nette cleared her throat that he picked up the camera.

I kept my eyes closed at he took his shots, until he commanded me to open them. "I need to see your eyes."

I tried to look at the white wall past his frame and past the camera in his hand. After several shots, he told me the same thing he'd told the young woman. He handed me a robe, and as I put it on, Lexi went into one of the cabinets in the room and pulled out a bag to place my things in.

I tied the silk sash on the robe and stared down at my feet.

"You're done," he said.

"Okay, Lexi can show her where to go," said Nette. "Good luck, pretty lady. I hope this is a wonderful start to us working together. There is something special about you. Something tells me I'm going to see you again . . . in some way." I watched her hand Lexi a wad of hundred dollar bills. "And this is your finder's fee."

Lexi had left out the part about how she was going to get paid for bringing me here. But I was too focused on following through with this. I tried to give Nette a smile, but I knew it was so tight, it probably looked like I grimaced. So I gave a wave and followed Lexi out the door.

Once we reached the room, I sat in the robe and rubbed my fingers together while we waited. It took about five minutes for the other girl to come out of the next room, and then I was allowed to go in.

When I walked into the room, I was greeted by a man sitting behind an oval table. I stood near the door.

"How you doing?" He had creamy brown skin. His head was shaved, and he had a black teardrop tattoo under one of his eyes. He looked to be in his early thirties.

"Hi."

"I'm Percy. I cast all the films for my boy Giovanni, and you're here, so I'm assuming you want to work."

I nodded.

"First things first. So we don't waste our or your time. Are you sure you are going to be able to do this? 'Cause if you can't, that's cool. Just let a nigga know. I mean, you are a young, pretty girl. But this kind of work is not for everybody."

I swallowed hard before saying, "I want to do this."

"Okay. Take off the robe so I can see what you are working with."

With shaking hands, I undid the sash and let the robe slide open.

As soon as it did, Percy did a sharp intake of breath. He commanded, "Take the robe completely off and turn around."

I did this as well.

"Damn! I love my muthafucking job." After a few seconds, Percy said, "Okay. You can put it back on. If you want to." He winked, making me laugh.

I nodded and did, turning back around as I tied the sash.

"Giselle, right? Baby, you passed. You can go to the set," Percy said.

"That's it?"

I watched him add my name to a list of other names and write the number four next to my name.

"Yeah. You ain't at no Fortune Five Hundred company. That's it, as long as they determined you are an adult, and I know they did, because if they didn't, you would not be in here. Now, I don't mind keeping your sexy ass in here to entertain me, but that wouldn't be productive. And Giovanni is my boy, so I have to keep it professional. You're safe in our hands, baby girl. Go on in there. Now, the director I'm sending you to, Rodney, can be a little verbally abusive, but he means no harm. He has timelines and deadlines he has to get to. Giovanni be on our heads. That's my right-hand man, so I can't let no ladies on the set that are not on point, and you definitely are. Go onto the set."

I know this might sound crazy, but as much as I needed the money, I secretly hoped that they would not hire me. I didn't want to do this.

Chapter 5

This is for my brother, I silently told myself. When I made it to the main set, which had scattered tables, couches, chairs, a wardrobe, and studio equipment, two ladies beckoned me over to a chair. As soon as I sat down, one started packing makeup on my face, while the other pulled out my ponytail and started running a flatiron though my hair. There were several guys and women seated in the room. Each one had on a robe, and all the women had their hair and makeup already done. Lexi was seated with us and was as quiet as a church mouse.

Nette came into the room with a clipboard and said, "Ladies, gentlemen, listen for the room number. When I call your name and number, you will then report to that room."

Several ladies and guys rushed off as their names and room numbers were called. When some of the room numbers were called, more than one girl or guy rushed out. I remembered Lexi saying that that happened. There were still some people waiting to hear their name.

I jumped when I heard, "Giselle. Report to room four."

I stood on shaky feet and walked to the room. Once I got there, I saw that it was just like Lexi had said. I was familiar with what they were doing because I had taken a film class with Lexi our junior year of high school.

The set looked like someone's bedroom. One man was adjusting a camera. The man who shot me and that girl earlier was fiddling with a huge light, while another was positioning a huge microphone over the bed. Once he positioned the light, he started flicking on a computer monitor.

I took a deep breath as my heart started beating faster by the second.

Next, they gave me a flimsy pink negligee to put on. I was able to slip behind a divider to do so. Once I untied my robe, I heard someone say, "All right. Let's get started." I pulled the negligee over my head and walked back toward the bed.

The other two men were gone, and it was just one man behind a camera.

"Get on the bed," the camera guy ordered.

I sat down on the bed. The moment my body rested against the comforter, my hands started shaking.

"You have fifteen minutes on this bed. Then we move on to the next bitch, so you need to move your ass a little faster!"

I nodded, knowing this had to be the guy Percy had warned me about, Rodney.

"I'll tell you what to do, and you do it. And you can yell as loud as you want. The studio is soundproof."

Next thing I knew, the camera was all up in my face. After about a minute of it filming me sitting on the bed, with a fake smile planted on my face, the guy holding it ordered, "Take that shit off!" My hands were still trembling, but I managed to pull the negligee up and over my head so that I was nude on the bed.

"Action!" he shouted. "Lay down on the bed slowly. Start playing with your titties."

I did everything he requested, and then I was given a list of other orders.

"Open your legs wide. Start rubbing your clit. Faster. Slow down. Go faster! Stick a finger in your pussy hole. Open your legs wider. Moan, bitch! Bite your bottom lip. Smile, bitch!"

I did it all. Shamefully, resisting the urge to cry, but I could feel the tears burning under my lids. Therefore, I kept my eyes closed.

The lights felt hot on my skin. But I pretended that they didn't. I even pretended that this wasn't what it was. I pretended that I was somewhere else completely. That I wasn't ass buck naked in a bed, showing my birth canal in front of men I didn't know and didn't want to know. I pretended I wouldn't regret this. But I knew I would.

The bed feeling like it was being lowered and a hand caressing one of my breasts caused me to panic. When I opened my eyes, there was an equally naked man in the bed next to me.

I screamed and scooted away from him.

"What the fuck!" the director yelled. "Cut!"

The two men on the set looked at me, confused.

I looked confused as well. "I never said I was going to do a sex scene."

"What the fuck did you come here for?" the director growled.

I ignored his harshness as tears started coming out of my eyes. I hoped I hadn't ruined my chance to get the bail money. "I only wanted to do a masturbation scene," I whispered.

I heard a chuckle on the set.

The director looked baffled. "Masturbation scene? Bitch, what the fuck are you talking about? Every bitch that sits in that bed fucks!"

Before I could process what he had said, I saw someone barge onto the set and march up to the director. "Rodney, what's the holdup with this scene?"

The director pointed at me.

That was when he turned and his eyes locked with mine and I met him . . . Giovanni.

"Giovanni, this bitch is confused. She only wants to do masturbation scenes. It's enough that she don't know what the fuck she doing, and the bitch's hands keep shaking, but she ain't trying to do a fuck scene on the set."

The man the director referred to as Giovanni kept raking his eyes over my face and my body. I quickly pulled the negligee back on.

The director scoffed with disgust. "Look at her! We down to only two camera guys today, and she holding us up more!"

He said this because I was now crying on the bed.

"Escort her to my office," Giovanni ordered.

A few minutes later, I was escorted by Rodney himself. He was yanking my arm in his tight grip as he did. He stopped in front of a door, mouthing "Bitch" to me as he knocked. Then when someone said, "Come in," he walked off. I opened the door and walked inside. I paused. I watched Giovanni slip a DVD into a case before getting up and walking over to one of his brown oak cabinets. He used a set of keys to unlock the second drawer in a row of three. He placed the case with the DVD in there. As he turned the key to lock the drawer, he glanced back and looked at me. I looked away. He walked back over to his chair, sat back down, and motioned for me to sit in the chair across from him.

He then quietly studied me. Despite my situation, I couldn't help but admire how handsome he was. He had light skin, with a neatly trimmed mustache. He had a strong jawline and full lips. Everything about him was neat and immaculate, from his curly hair to his smooth eyebrows. He wasn't muscular, but was tall and lanky. But fine nonetheless.

"What is your name?" he asked.

"Giselle, sir."

"Sir." He chuckled. "The ladies we bring in here never refer to me as that, or any of the men here. Someone must have raised you well." He cleared his throat. "Makes me wonder why you are even here at all. Why are you here?"

I didn't respond. I felt so stupid. But I had made it clear to Lexi that all I was willing to do was pose for some nude pics and do a masturbation scene. She'd said it was as far as she went. I felt so stupid for believing her. Now I realized that for the amount of money she had brought home, she couldn't have possibly been able to get away with not having intercourse. I didn't know why she had to lie about it. She had put me in a compromising situation and had made money off of doing it.

He continued. "You obviously don't want to be here, either. This is a very successful and lucrative company, for myself as well as my employees. I have been doing this since nineteen ninety-seven. Young women are able to come here and make more money than they have ever made. In all years that I have owned this company, we have never had to so much as persuade, let alone beg, the women to work. So I am asking you again, why are you here?"

I took a deep breath and spilled it. "I was desperate to make money. My father passed away last year, and after his death, my mother just wasn't able to snap back. She was so depressed that she stopped going to work and got fired. Both our parents' cars were repossessed, and we are super behind on our mortgage, which meant that I couldn't start college. And on top of all that, my brother got arrested for robbing his job and my mother"—my voice cracked at the mention of my mother's death—"my mother committed suicide just a few days ago." I paused. "And now . . . now all I have is my little brother. And I'm trying to get bail money to get him out of jail and I don't know . . ."

Before I could finish my spiel, he opened a drawer in his desk and pulled out a checkbook and then a pen.

"What are you doing?"

"I'm writing you a check. What is your last name?"

"Grayson."

When he was done writing, he passed the check to me. I stared at the check. It was for six thousand dollars. Baffled, I asked, "Why are you giving this to me?"

"Because you need it."

"But—"

"Take it. I hope it helps you out, Giselle. And you don't owe me anything for it. I also don't anticipate getting it back."

I stared at the check again. It was enough for me to post bail and even put something toward the house.

"Oh my God." I stood and ran around the desk and threw myself in his arms. "Thank you so much."

He didn't hug me back. I pulled away, a little embarrassed, but still feeling relief that I could bail my brother out of jail. But as more time passed, I wondered if it really was that simple. Was this man really giving me this out of the kindness of his heart, or did he want something? Part of me couldn't help but feel that this would not be the last time I saw Giovanni, and although the money he gave me was a quick fix, it also felt like a huge debt on my shoulders. But still, I took my chances and told myself I would deal with the repercussions later. With this money, I was closer to getting my brother out of jail than ever before.

Chapter 6

I told Lexi very little about the whole experience. I even kept to myself the fact that I was paid six thousand dollars to do nothing. I felt like Lexi had lied and misled me, and I didn't really get why. She was supposed to be my best friend, but something told me that she had wanted me to go in blind. Despite feeling this way, I was too excited about the fact that I could get my brother out of jail to worry about it or even give it too much thought. Well, momentarily.

The very next day, after our visit to the mansion, I went bright and early to Aladdin Bail Bonds to post bail for my brother. They were kind enough to take me to pick him up and bring him home.

When he finally came out, I jumped into his arms. He caught me and whispered, "Giselle," and held me super tight.

It felt so good to hug my little brother and take him home. When he asked me how I got the money, I simply told him I had borrowed it from Lexi, and he accepted that.

When we got home, he went straight into the bathroom to shower, and I went into the kitchen to make his favorite meal: chicken enchiladas. When he came into the kitchen, showered and dressed, the enchiladas still had about five minutes to go, but I took them out early. I grabbed the spatula off the counter and scooped a generous portion on a plate and sat it, with a fork, in front of my brother.

"Thanks, Gissy."

He wasted no time and started shoveling the hot food into his mouth. I poured him a glass of water and sat it in front of him. He guzzled it down before returning to his plate. I sat down across from him and silently watched him eat. It felt so good to have my baby brother back home and out of that jail. Aside from the dangers posed by the inmates they had there, the place seemed so nasty and dirty. My brother didn't belong there. I prayed he had learned his lesson and would never again do anything crazy that could land him right back there. But I knew he did it to help us out.

He was eating the enchiladas so fast, he started choking.

"Brandon! Slow down." I jumped up and patted his back as he coughed.

He sipped his water and wiped his watery eyes. He smiled and went back to eating.

When his plate was empty, I asked, "You want some more?"

"Yeah."

I got up to fix him another helping.

Once I placed it in front of him, he grabbed one of my hands and kissed it. "Thanks for getting me out of there." He swallowed hard. "Even if it is just for the time being." My brother still had to go back to court for sentencing.

"I'm your sister. No thank-you needed." I sat back down across from him.

"I go back to court on Friday, you know. They say if I don't have my own attorney, they will provide me with one."

I nodded.

He started attacking the second plate of food. I smiled at him enjoying his food.

"Well, until that day comes, let's not worry about it. I just need to know you will never do something so dumb again," I said.

"I won't, Giselle. You can believe my word on that. Six days in jail was enough for me to see I don't ever want to go back to that muthafucka again."

I laughed softly. Hadn't done that in days.

He laughed as well. Then, out of nowhere, his face turned serious, and he asked, "Giselle, where's Mom?"

My face dropped. I tried to regain my composure. To do this, I took a deep breath and swallowed the lump in my throat.

My next two words had him out of the chair, on the floor, sobbing. And I was right alongside him, holding him and crying just as hard as he was.

Considering that I had spent the previous night hugging and comforting my little brother due to our mother's death, I didn't know how I was able to get through the day at work. Emotionally and physically, I was spent. However, I managed to make it through.

As the day wound down, and it was almost time for me to clock out, all I wanted to do was grab a Hawaiian Punch Slurpee from 7-Eleven and make my way home.

I had five minutes to go and was surprised as hell when Giovanni walked inside the restaurant. He looked handsome in his suit, which looked like it cost a thousand bucks. But what was he doing here?

I dropped my dishrag nervously. I swallowed hard. Was he here to collect on his money? What if he was crazy and was going to beat my ass or kill me if I didn't have it? After all, I didn't really know this man. He could be a rapist or a murderer or could even have connections to killers.

Before I could do anything, he reached down, picked up the dishrag, and placed it in my hands. "Hi," he said.

"What are you doing here?" I asked.

"I came to see you."

"Me? Why?"

"Giselle! Clock out!" my manager yelled over the counter.

I turned to him and said, "Okay, sir."

Before I could say anything else to Giovanni, he said, "I'll be outside in the black Range." He walked out.

I rushed away and went into the back room to follow my boss's orders. As I did, all I thought was that he must want his money back. After I paid to have my brother bailed out of jail, I sent the last of the money off for the mortgage.

If he did want it back, what was I going to do? Was he going to force me to work for him? Just the thought of having to be under those hot-ass lights and being screamed at and raged at by that camera guy, Rodney, while someone sexually violated me had my stomach twisted in knots. And there was no way I could do it.

I snatched up my purse, and once I made it outside the restaurant, I saw him standing near the door. He smiled at me. It was repercussion time.

I cocked my foot back and took off running out of the shopping center.

"Giselle!"

Still running, I looked back and saw him get into his truck. But I kept running. I increased my speed and ran down the street. I could see him driving, and he was honking his horn. I gave him the middle finger. There was a divider in the middle of the road, so he couldn't make a turn or ride on my side. So I knew I was okay.

But he thought smarter than me. There was an opening for the fire station, so he turned, pulled into their driveway, and stopped his car, momentarily blocking me.

When I saw him hop out of his car, I tried to run around his car, but I only got a few steps in before he grabbed me. I screamed.

"Hey. Why are you running away?"

I tried to break his hold on my arm, but he wouldn't release me. I finally turned and faced him. "I don't have the money to give you, if that's what you're here for, and I'm not working for you!"

He chuckled. "You think I'm here for money? I have far too much money to chase a young lady for chump change. Listen. All I want is to take you to dinner."

That was when two firemen came out and rushed toward us.

"Is everything okay?" one of them asked. Both of them were looking at me.

"We're fine."

I nodded, confirming what Giovanni had said.

An hour later, I found myself sitting across from Giovanni at Morton's The Steakhouse. I had been to nice restaurants before, with my parents. But being there with Giovanni—given who he was and the way that he was staring at me—made me very nervous. I devoured the succulent steak and baked potato, which was nearly the size of my head.

Giovanni ate very little. Instead, he quietly observed me while I ate.

"You like the steak?" he asked me.

"Yes," I said quietly. "It's very tender."

He smiled at that comment.

I had to admit, this whole situation still had me a little on edge, but I tried to look as normal as I could. Still, I couldn't help but ask, "How did you find me?"

"I'm resourceful when I want to be. And having money buys you all the information you need."

"But why try to find me if it's not to pay you back the money you gave me?"

He smiled, showing his straight white teeth. "For some strange reason, the moment you walked out of my office, I found myself unable to stop thinking about you. So I had to find you, and I had to see you. That's why I'm here."

I laughed at that. *Me?* "You're rich, and in your line of business you meet plenty of women willing to take their clothes off."

He chuckled. "Random women. But it's not often that in a pile of gold, you see a gem. Giselle, that's you. So I had to see you again. And I don't regret it."

I couldn't help but blush, so I pretended I was wiping food away from the corners of my mouth. I took a sip of my wine.

"You are a fucking masterpiece. I don't want to eat steak. I want to eat you."

I almost spilled the Riesling in my mouth at his comment about eating me. It took me a few seconds to recover before I said, "You're being like real flirtatious with me. How do you know I don't have a boyfriend?"

"You don't," he said assuredly.

"How do you know?" I asked.

"Because if you did, you wouldn't be here with me. He wouldn't let you out of his sight. *I* wouldn't. You're too special, and it's not worth the risk of some other man getting to you. If you were my woman, you wouldn't be able to go to the grocery store without me."

"Please stop."

"Why?"

"Because this is all too much for me."

"Baby, I'm just getting started."

I smiled and looked down at my hands, which were now resting in my lap. A series of sensations was hitting my body as he spoke to me. Those sensations were coming from between my legs. And the wine he had me sipping on was making me feel super good. No real cares, no real worries. I needed an escape like this.

I took another sip and wiped the wetness from my bottom lip.

"You're about done?" he asked.

I was, and I was so stuffed, I couldn't eat another bite. But I did swallow the last of the sweet wine. He had told me that it was a harmless wine. "Yes, I'm done."

That was when he leaned over the table and kissed me. Now, I had been kissed before, but not like this. He parted my lips with his tongue and slid it into my mouth and started gently pressing it against mine. He tasted like Riesling. I moaned softly. He chuckled against my mouth as our tongues rubbed slowly against each other. When I didn't feel his lips anymore, I opened my eyes and saw that he was paying the bill. I pulled my head back and unpuckered my lips. I didn't know if it was the alcohol or my attraction to Giovanni or maybe both, but I didn't want to leave his presence.

We left the restaurant and got on the road. As we neared the ramp to the freeway that would take me back to Carson, I noticed that he was going to pass it, and I panicked.

"Where are you going?" I cried. "You passed the freeway ramp."

"I'm not taking you home."

"Then where are you taking me?"

"To finish what I started."

Oh shit! This was a setup! He really was after the money he gave me.

"I told you—"

He signaled, got over until he was on the off-ramp, and put his emergency blinkers on.

He turned to me and said, "Giselle, you don't have to worry. I'm not going to do anything, anything at all, to hurt you. You have to trust me. I like you. I think that you are beautiful and special. And besides, I'm not a crazy man and I have a whole lot to lose and I'm not trying to lose anything."

I evaluated his words. And to be honest, I was having a good time with him and didn't want the night to end.

He went on. "Now, I would like to take you to my home, but this time you will be there under completely different circumstances. And most of all, you will be safe with me."

I didn't know this man, but something about the look in his eyes made me believe him. Also, he was rich. Why would he jeopardize his freedom by trying to harm me for six grand?

So I smiled and told him, "I would like to go."

He stared at me, smiled, and said, "All right."

He pulled back into the traffic of the freeway, and we were on our way.

Chapter 7

Next thing I knew, I was in his beautiful house, taking it all in as he gave me a tour, starting with the grounds. Although it was late, the estate was lit enough for me to see the swimming pool I had missed before, a sauna room, and the tennis and basketball courts. There was an outside deck, and it was immaculately set up like at a beach resort. When we went inside, he ushered me past the foyer, past a sitting room with velvet-looking furniture, to his living room. My eyes were busy staring at the marble floors, the expensive-looking art, the crystal lighting, and the high vaulted ceilings. The living room was the size of my house in its entirety. And our house was by no means small. It was all so beautiful. Like something out of a movie. He even had his own library. He took me down to the basement, which had a game room with a pool table, dart boards, card tables, and several huge flat-screen TVs. There was an entertainment room that was set up like a movie theater. If this wasn't enough, there was also a wine cellar.

"How many staff do you have here?" I asked.

"I have two maids, a chef, a groundsman, a gardener, and three security guards. I also have additional staff that work for the studio, but they don't set foot in my home. Except for Percy. He is the only one I would ever trust in my home. I keep my business separate from my personal life. It's almost like another world. I know that you were alarmed about what goes on in the studio. But I live a pretty normal and private life. "

Upstairs was a whole 'notha story. I mean, he had room after room, and each one had a luxurious bathroom in it. The bathrooms were the size of my bedroom at home!

"Do you have any kids?" I asked him as we visited the children's wing.

"No. but one I day I hope to. Soon, real soon."

I blushed again as he showed me another wing upstairs, which had his bedroom in it. He simply stood in front of the bedroom door, and the door automatically slid open.

The bedroom was gigantic. The flat-screen TV covered one wall completely, and the bed was so high, it was like something out of a king's or queen's palace. He obviously was living well. I secretly wished my family could live like this. Maybe if my mother and father had invested in some type of business, they could have left the oil refinery before all those chemicals they were inhaling made my father so sick that he ended up with cancer. Then my dad would still be here, and thus my mother, too. I tried to stay strong and not let myself cry. But I missed them every day.

"Don't look down," Giovanni said.

I almost screamed when I did. Pretty colored fish and a big-ass shark were swimming underneath my feet. A long strip of glass separated us.

"Don't worry. It won't break."

I smiled.

"Come here," he told me.

I walked closer to him, and he guided me out to the upper deck, which had a Jacuzzi. It also overlooked his estate, providing an incredible view of the mountains and the high-rises that stood in Westwood.

"You have a really nice home," I told him. I was staring at the view while he was standing next to me.

"Thank you."

"Now, why do you want me here?"

"I needed to see you, and now that I have, I need to feel you and I want to taste you. Will you let me do all those things to you?"

I turned around to face him. "I have never been with a man before." I had out of curiosity snuck porn films into my room and watched them. I had even played with myself, licked my fingers and got my nipples hard, and I had finger banged myself. But that was it. And the kiss Giovanni had given me earlier had me still turned on.

The mention of me being a virgin made his smile bigger. "Let me be the first. I won't hurt you. Just let me show you how good I can make your body feel."

Dear God, I wanted all of that. There was something about this man that made me want to go there with him. He made me feel like he had me and I would be safe and I would feel good. Because I already felt good. Better than I had felt in a long time.

He held his hand out to me. I took it. Before I could stop him, he picked me up like I weighed the same as Lexi's little niece Trinity.

He carried me back into his bedroom. He put me back down so I was standing, facing him. While I stood there, he took his time slowly stripping me of my clothes. I was now completely nude in front of him.

"Percy told me you were beautiful, but I didn't know you would look like this," he said, marveling. He started kissing me. I let him, and I liked it.

I moaned as his lips traveled down to my nipples. The sensations felt so good. I rubbed his curly hair as he did it.

While he suckled my breasts, one of his hands dipped lower, and he was rubbing on my pussy. I arched my back to get closer to his hand, because it felt super good.

He guided me to the bed and laid me down so I was on my back.

He went lower so his mouth was on my pussy.

"You taste good, baby."

Fire was the best word to describe what was going on between my legs with his head down there.

He licked my clit continuously, then glided his tongue up and down the opening of my pussy while fingering my clit. I moaned loudly and thrashed my head from side to side. He alternated between his fingers and his tongue. I pulled on his curls as I felt shock waves go through my body, and I felt myself go limp.

That was when he stripped down to nothing. I admired him naked. He was slim, but his body was toned. His dick was rock hard, staring back at me.

That was when he climbed up, parted my legs, and slipped between them.

"This is going to hurt for a split second."

Once he positioned his hard dick, I closed my eyes and waited for the hurt he spoke of. It was more like a pinch, and immediately after, I screamed out of pleasure. He brought his lips down on mine to silence my moans. I opened my legs wider and let him ride me. They were long and quick strokes that had me going crazy. My hands went up and down his back as he reduced the tempo, sliding all the way in and slowly pulling out.

He broke the kiss and stared down at me. "I'm going to make you mine," he told me. He gripped my thighs with his hands, and his stroking sped up to a tempo that was even faster than before, and I felt the same fire I'd felt when he went down on me. It caused me to scream yet again and my body to tighten up. Giovanni let out a loud scream as well.

The sensation hit me, and I could feel it even in my toes, and I couldn't do anything but lie there, limp.

***

I woke up in unfamiliar territory. I expected to be in my bed, but I was in someone else's instead.

"Hey."

I rubbed the sleep out of my eyes and stared at Giovanni. Then my brain was instantly flooded with memories of last night. Going to dinner with Giovanni, coming to his home, making love to him. *Damn.* How much Riesling did I drink?

Still, I knew I couldn't blame it entirely on the Riesling. I liked Giovanni, and everything he did to my body the night before had felt good. And truthfully, I wanted some more. I could feel his body resting against mine and a hand wrapped possessively around one of my breasts.

He kissed me. "Good morning," he said in a husky voice.

"Hi."

He turned my body around fully to face him.

He looked super handsome lying in bed, buck naked. Sexy.

"Thank you for last night," he told me.

I blushed and looked away. His hands were now rubbing up and down my booty.

"It never felt so good to have a woman in my bed. They are usually kicked out by now."

"What!" I exclaimed, laughing.

"I'm not by any means the type of gentleman you may think I am, Giselle. But something about you makes me want to be on my best behavior at all times."

I blushed again at that. To me, he was the epitome of a gentleman. In the past, I had been on a couple dates with guys, but Giovanni seemed completely different from them. Although they were a couple years older than me, they seemed like teens compared to Giovanni and his swag. He was a real man. I felt lucky to be in his bed. But since this was my first time having sex with a dude, I didn't know what the right protocol was. I remembered that Lexi told me that when she lost her virginity to a guy, she was fourteen and he was twenty-four. When they finished, she relaxed in the bed, reliving how it felt. The dude stood up and started getting dressed. When she didn't take a hint that that was his way of telling her to bounce, he opened his bedroom door and yelled, "What you waiting for? Get the fuck out!"

I didn't want to ever go through that, so just to play it safe, after a few uncomfortable seconds, I said, "Well, I have to—"

"No, you don't."

I screwed up my face. He didn't even know what I was going to say.

"You don't have to leave. In fact, this may sound crazy to you, but I don't ever want you to leave."

I was flattered, and yes, I believed in love at first sight. But still I told him, "You don't even know me, Giovanni."

"I know enough to know that I don't want you to ever leave my sight again, Giselle."

"My God, what are you saying?"

He had a serious expression in his eyes. "I'm saying I want you to be the one in my life. The only one. I want to take care of you, love you, spoil you. Put some pretty pieces on your fingers, wrist, and around your neck. I'm saying that I want you to be my wife."

I thought I was hearing things when he said that part. I mean, who did that? This man didn't know me from any other woman out there. What would make him want to spend the rest of his life with me? I was young, poor, inexperienced. What could I offer a man like Giovanni, who pretty much had everything and could get damn near whatever woman he wanted. And he was fine! I'm saying he had Beyoncé, Halle Berry, Serena Williams potential.

"Baby, I will treat you so good. Give you the life you deserve. Share all that I have with you. Just don't leave my side again. Not now, not ever."

His eyes looked so serious when he said that last part, "Not now. Not ever."

"But I can't promise you that. Listen, you don't understand the things my family is going through. I can't just commit to you." I licked my dry lips. "Look, in a few hours my brother's whole life could be ruined, and I might not see him for a long time. He could be facing time in prison—"

He cut me off. "The brother you bailed out?"

"Yes and—"

Before I could finish, he snatched up his cell phone off his nightstand and started calling someone. "Richard. Yeah, this is Giovanni. I'm good. Listen, I need you to go to work for me."

He put his hand to the phone and said to me, "I need your brother's name and birth date." Once I told him, he repeated it to the person he was on the phone with. "Yes, he has court today."

"Where? And what time?" Giovanni quizzed.

"Superior Court, in Los Angeles. Three o'clock," I told him.

He repeated it before saying, "Take care of that, all right?"

Then the call ended abruptly.

I stared at him, waiting for him to speak.

"My lawyer is going to represent your brother in court. He is very skilled in what he does."

"Thank you," I said gratefully. It was so nice of Giovanni to do that.

"Whatever else you need, let me know, Giselle, and I will take care of it for you."

Chapter 8

Sure enough he did.

Giovanni's lawyer was so smooth; he was able to have my brother tried as a juvenile since he just recently turned eighteen. Which meant his crime would not be on his record as an adult. He was also able to get my brother probation, so he never had to go back to jail. I was so grateful.

Giovanni paid for my brother's probation services and my mother's burial, and he stood by our side as we buried my mother. And all the debt my brother and I had, he paid it off so our parents' house didn't get foreclosed on. He said it was all on one condition: that I never leave his side. Brandon was staying there, and he was relieved that all that my parents had worked hard for was going to remain in the family. Giovanni was a godsend.

And now, just a week later—making it a month since Giovanni had come into my life—Giovanni had a surprise that rocked my entire world.

I was knocked out, asleep, in his massive, beautiful bed. It felt so good to be able to sleep with no worries.

This morning I woke up to kisses on my lips. "Wake up, baby."

My eyes fluttered open to see Giovanni staring back at me. I gasped when he suddenly, out of nowhere, sat a tiny box on the pillow my face was resting on. I sat up in the bed and grabbed it. I opened the box with shaking fingers. I was damn near out of breath when I opened the velvet box and saw a gigantic, shiny rock staring back at me.

"What is this!" I exclaimed.

"What do you think it is, baby? I told you, I don't ever want to be apart from you again. I want to make you mine." He pulled the ring out of the box and placed it on my left hand. "And if you say yes, I will make you my wife today."

"But—"

"Aye, no buts. I have never done this before, and I never thought I would want to. But you are far too special for me to let go of. And if you think the shopping sprees you have been on were a lot this past month, you are going to be in for a surprise. I'm going to make the rest of your days so good, bitches are going to hate the sight of you."

I laughed at him, but he seemed serious.

"Well?"

Sometimes I looked back. I thought about that day and what made me say yes to a man I barely knew. Was it because he had money? Because of how fine he was and the way he made love to me? Or how he catered to my every whim? All those things had a little to do with it. But the main reason I said yes was that he made me feel protected, safe. The foundation my parents had talked about and had died trying to achieve, he had it and he offered it to me. It meant my brother and I would be cared for. So I took it. I mean, who wouldn't in that moment? And in addition to this . . . I also felt like I was in love.

I looked him in his eyes and told him, "Yes, Giovanni. I will marry you."

Next thing I knew, Giovanni was making calls, and within minutes, he had people rushing into the mansion.

Then I was filled with dread. What if his family didn't like me? Who was going to give me away? What would I wear? All these questions were on the tip of my tongue.

He saw my worry. But there was something about the way he kissed my lips and said, "Don't worry. Everything will work out. Baby, I'm about to give you the wedding of twenty bitches' dreams."

That made me worry no more. So I nodded.

He gave me an air kiss and walked out of the room, still on the phone.

About ten minutes later, one of Giovanni's maids, who I now knew as Pillar, an older Filipino woman, came into the room with breakfast for me on a cart. The other one was named Nisa. She was Guatemalan. They both took care of my needs.

She smiled and said, "Morning."

"Hi."

She started placing platters and bowls on the table in the room, all the while talking. "Congratulations. I hear you are marrying Mr. Pride today."

"Yes." I went to sit at the table in the room.

She uncovered all the dishes. It was a feast. Cold crab and lobster, along with croissants and sliced fruit, scrambled eggs and bacon. There was also champagne with strawberries floating in it. After the food was all laid out, the maid turned on some soft music, and I could hear Alicia Keys's voice waft into the room.

"Go ahead and enjoy, ma'am. In about twenty minutes, someone will be here to give you a massage, a manicure, and a pedicure. Enjoy." She gave me a deep hug. Then she went and pulled the curtains back, made up the bed, and left the room.

I almost didn't want her to go. I wanted someone there with me.

I ate nervously. I sampled everything, getting an extra helping of the crab. I even sipped on some of the champagne. That was when I heard a ruckus coming from outside: the beeping sound of truck horns being honked, and people shouting.

I rushed out onto the upper deck and saw trucks driving inside the estate. Tables and chairs and a gazebo were being set up, and dozens of flowers were being placed all around the lower deck. That was when I realized that we weren't going to a justice of the peace. Giovanni was setting up a dream wedding here at his home.

I didn't have time to watch them set up. I heard a knock-knock just before two white women rushed into Giovanni's room. One of them was holding several wedding gowns. The other woman had shoes and veils.

"Good morning!" the woman with the gowns said cheerfully. "My name is Maggie, and this is my assistant, Tara. We have nine dresses for you to try on for your special day. Now, if you don't like any of these, I can have some more brought over. No worries." She displayed one dress at a time to me. "Which one do you like?"

I was speechless at all the gowns and did not have the slightest idea which one to choose. It was times like this that I really wished my mother was here with me to help me decide, but she wasn't.

Maggie saw this, my hesitation, and said, "Let's try some on."

Tara and Maggie both helped me into the first gown. It was a princess-style gown that I didn't care for. I tried on the second, which was more of a mermaid dress. They both didn't like it on me. When I tried on the third gown and looked at myself in the mirror, instantly tears poured from my eyes, and both Maggie and Tara gasped.

The moment I put it on, I knew it was the right choice. It had a sweetheart neckline, beading, and crystals. It was like it was made for me . . . the way it hugged my curves and then had a flair at the bottom, billowing out into a long train. The two ladies kept gasping and saying I was beautiful. I chose a cathedral veil with tiny diamonds on the edges of it. The shoes were a pair of strappy white heels.

I stared at myself in the mirror, still in shock. I was getting married today to this man? Me? Giselle? I pimped burgers and fries all day. I had only a high school diploma, and he wanted to marry me? I knew I was pretty. I knew I had a nice body. But there were women who were just as pretty, with bodies just as nice, who were a lot smarter, more poised, and more sophisticated than I was. This all made me feel like I was a very lucky girl. I zeroed in on all the details on my beautiful dress. Swarovski crystals were intricately beaded on the dress, which was nine thousand dollars. *Wow*. That was a lot!

"What do you think, honey?" Maggie asked.

I stared at myself again in the mirror before saying, "This is it."

These two ladies both gave me hugs and kisses, congratulating me while helping me take everything off. They hugged me again, clapped excitedly, packed their items, and left.

I went into the bathroom and took a long bath. I soaked in there for a while, feeling butterflies jumping around in my stomach. Ten minutes after I got out of the tub, dried off, and put on the robe Pillar had placed in the bathroom for me, more visitors came. The mani and pedi lady took care of my hands, my feet, and my eyebrows. A masseuse came as well. She gave me a full-body massage that put me to sleep.

A few hours later, more ladies came knocking to do my hair and makeup. They brought a pleasant surprise: my brother and Lexi!

I screamed as they came through the door.

Lexi rushed forward and hugged me. She looked very cute in her tight-fitting red dress, with her hair freshly done.

"How did you know?" I asked her.

"Brandon told me. And you know I couldn't miss my best friend getting married."

"I meant to call you and tell you everything, but it has been such a whirlwind."

"Girl, don't even trip. Where is the dress?"

I pointed to the bed. I looked at my brother, who was silent.

Lexi walked over to the gown, looked at it, and exclaimed, "Girl, this is beau-ti-ful!"

I was studying my brother, who hadn't said a word to me yet. I cleared my throat. "Aren't you going to say hello to your soon-to-be-married big sis?"

Brandon walked up to me in his suit, looking super handsome. He gave me a dry kiss on my cheek. "Congratulations, Giselle. I'll leave y'all to this." Then he exited the room.

I tried to overlook the fact that my little brother didn't look very pleased. Maybe he felt like I was making a mistake marrying Giovanni. And while I wasn't completely sure I was making the right choice, I wanted my brother to think I was and to be happy for me. But the look on his face showed that he was very displeased. He would barely make eye contact with me, and his expression was agitated. He never acted like that toward me.

"Well, girl, I got all the stuff you need. A very sexy underwear and bra. Your garter belt, for starters . . ."

Lexi continued to talk as the stylist pressed my hair. She pulled all my hair to the side with some diamond clips so a dozen curls cascaded to the side of my face. She told me that was how Giovanni wanted me to wear it.

Once my makeup and hair were done, I took a peek in the mirror. I never felt or looked more beautiful. I put on everything Lexi had given me. Something new was a toe ring; something blue was the Dolce & Gabbana Light Blue perfume that she sprayed on me. However, I had nothing old or borrowed to wear. Next, I was helped into my gown and veil, and I was ready to go.

"You look really beautiful, Giselle."

I smiled and looked at Lexi in the mirror as she stood behind me. I was startled for a second because, yeah, she was saying, "Congratulations," but for a split second, her face did not look too happy for me. It brought me back to the day that she misled me at the mansion. Made me think that you never really knew a person and you never really could trust a person. She was my best friend, so she should be happy for me. That bothered me a little bit. But then, Giovanni told me that he was going to give me a life that many women—even the nicest women on the earth—would envy.

I received more visitors. They knocked on the door, and when I told whoever it was to come in, a very pretty middle-aged woman swept through the room. She was fair skinned, with long jet-black hair. She was petite in size, and she looked very much like Giovanni. When an older man walked in behind her, an older replica of my soon-to-be husband, I knew without a doubt they were Giovanni's parents.

"You look very pretty." She sounded sincere.

"Thanks," I replied.

"You're welcome. If you're wondering who I am, I'll kill the suspense. I'm Giovanni's mother, Dana."

"Oh, I'm sorry," I gushed. I held my hand out for her to shake.

Once she did, I then turned to Giovanni's father to shake his hand. But he didn't see my gesture, because he was allowing his eyes to travel down the length of my body. But I told myself that he was just inspecting me.

"No worries. And this is Giovanni's father, Douglas."

"How are you, sweetheart?" He took both of my hands in his.

"I'm fine. And this is my friend Lexi."

His mother and father nodded at Lexi.

Lexi gave a wave.

Giovanni and his mother shared some facial features, but he looked mostly like his dad. The dress she wore was a Christian Dior that I had seen one day when Giovanni took me shopping. But Giovanni didn't let me get it, because he said it looked too old for me. The rocks in her ears, on her fingers, and on her wrists were blinding. Giovanni's father was very handsome, in an older man kind of way. He had the same build and stature as Giovanni, with salt-and-pepper gray hair and a brown complexion. His suit looked nice and expensive.

"Well, before I leave you, I just have a little something for you. Because, I tell you, I thought I'd never see the day my son would marry anyone. And I'm not going to even bother at all with asking any questions about how you met or how long you two have been seeing each other. If my son chose you as his wife, he had a good reason for it. You are getting a good catch, you know. I'm a retired teacher, and my husband is a retired engineer. We did not retire by choice. Our son forced us to, bought us a beautiful, huge home in Lakewood, and foots the bill for everything. He can be a bit bossy," she joked.

I laughed and accepted the black velvet box. I opened the box. Inside were some beautiful diamond earrings.

"Those belonged to my grandmother, and I am passing them to you. Giovanni told me that your mother passed not too long after your father. That is something hard to deal with, so I hope you can learn to accept us as your second parents and know that we are here for you if you need us."

The earrings were so pretty. My fingers passed over them. And what she was saying almost made me cry. I wanted my parents there. I had always known that my father would give me away one day and my mother would be in the room, helping me get dressed for my special day. That was how I had always envisioned it. Never the way that it was. Her sentiment gave my heart a huge tug, because it was something else that brought me back to the fact that both my parents were dead. It hurt, and I fought back tears. Giovanni's mother's words made me feel a little better; I knew I had two parental figures there for support. So I said, "I'm sure I will, ma'am. These are so pretty. Thank you."

I hugged her close. Now I had something old and borrowed! And I hoped Giovanni's parents would grow to love me. When I pulled away and started putting the earrings in my ears, I noticed Giovanni's mother watching me. And his father continued to watch me, which made me a little uncomfortable, because I felt like he was checking me out in front of his wife. But I simply ignored him.

Giovanni's mother interrupted my thoughts. "I get it. I understand. Don't know you, but I can already see . . . you are special." She had a soft smile on her face when she said this.

"I'm just a regular girl from Carson who was lucky enough to find your son."

"You're sweet." She pecked me on my cheek and turned to her husband. "Let's go."

Thirty minutes later, I was led out of the room and down the stairs to the front of the estate. I was surprised to see my brother there, waiting to give me away. Again, the feeling hit me. I wished both my parents were there. I ignored the pain from this and put a smile on my face. As the seconds went by, I could not believe my luck. This fine, sexy, and rich man wanted to marry me? That made me feel a whole lot better.

So I wasted no time walking down the aisle to become Mrs. Giovanni Pride.

Chapter 9

February 13, 2011 . . .

"Baby, you about ready?"

I smiled as my husband walked into our bedroom. I took my focus off myself in my La Perla bra and underwear and placed it on him as he came behind me and kissed me on my neck. "What's up, baby?"

"Hey."

I turned to face him and kissed him on the mouth. "You're looking nice."

His hands stroked up and down my curves. After four years of marriage, this man still gave me butterflies. In those four years Giovanni had spoiled me and had never let up. From ten-, twenty-, or thirty-stack shopping sprees to diamonds galore, to getaways. He did everything he had promised and more.

My husband's multimillion-dollar company was still thriving, and we lived well because of it. I was sure most people found the adult entertainment business seedy and degrading, but my husband's business was far from it. It was run in a very professional and legal manner. All the women my husband used were screened and had to be at least eighteen. The same for the adult males my husband used. They were all forced to get checkups every two months, and they all wore condoms. My husband was giving people work who needed work, and what they did was their choice.

He also hired black men who would normally not
have a job. Case in point, Giovanni's producer, Percy.
Giovanni told me that Percy did time for drug traffick-
ing for some drug dealer. When he got out of prison,
the offer was still on the table for him to go back to
selling drugs. Percy told his old boss he was done with
that and was ready to go legit. But that was hard for
him because he had a felony on his record and could
not find work. With a little training from Giovanni,
Percy became really good at what he did. He had been
working for Giovanni for the past seven years and was
my husband's right-hand man. Over the years Percy
had made enough money that he could have started his
own business. But Percy said he always worked better
when directed, although my husband was the same age
as Percy, thirty-eight. He had always had a fear of not
being able to make it on his own. I loved Percy, though,
and never wanted him to go. My husband and Percy
were tight as well. In fact, Percy was Giovanni's best
man at our wedding.

Although I wanted my brother to go to college, he
refused and instead decided to work for my husband.
I was disappointed at first. I got on him and told him,
"My husband is willing to pay for the whole ride, and
you are refusing to go to college?" Brandon's words
were, "Your husband is willing to pay for the whole ride
for you, too, Giselle. Did you bother to go?"

What could I say to that? So he worked as part of the
camera crew and eventually advanced to director and
was assigned to one of the filming rooms. From what
Percy told me, Brandon was doing a good job. His sala-
ry allowed him to have his own apartment, which was a
luxury one at that, in the Wilshire district, and he drove
a Hummer. Yes, my brother was showing off. We had
sold my parents' house not too long after Giovanni and

I married. My husband felt it was best. There were so many unpleasant memories there. And Brandon and I now had a firm foundation with him.

"What are you thinking about?"

I stared in his eyes. "How lucky I am to have you as my husband."

He smiled at me, with this twinkle in his light brown eyes.

"You taking me somewhere special?"

"Baby, you already know." His phone rang. He looked at the number and didn't answer.

"You smell good, too."

I chuckled.

I pulled away from him to slide into my purple Valentino dress, which fit me like a glove. I knew my husband was admiring my curves as I smoothed the dress down with my hands. Next, I slid my feet into my peep-toe Giuseppe heels. I grabbed my Dolce & Gabbana coat, along with my Gucci clutch bag.

I could hear his phone ring again. Since he ignored it, so did I. I was anxious to leave and get our special night started.

"I'm ready."

"Yes, you are. Let's go."

We went to Maestro's. Giovanni knew that was my favorite restaurant, because I couldn't get enough of their black truffle gnocchi with crab or their lobster mashed potatoes or their crab-stuffed mushrooms. Hell, I liked a whole lot of stuff at Maestro's. I could go on and on. My husband was always good for letting me stuff my pretty face with all the foods I wanted.

"Order whatever you want," he told me as he scanned his menu.

When the waiter came, I ordered half of the menu: lobster tails, filet mignon, gorgonzola macaroni and cheese, and crab-stuffed mushrooms. I loved lobster but could not do the whole lobster. I didn't like looking at the head. Of course, I knew I wasn't going to finish all of this, but the beauty of having a husband like mine was that I didn't have to just choose one thing, and I loved that. For me there never was a limit.

"Don't worry, baby. We will work it off," Giovanni added.

The thought of another lovemaking session with my husband made me shiver. My husband always put it down and had me screaming and cumming.

He ordered a porterhouse steak, with sweet potato mash and steamed spinach. He was always so health conscious. We sipped on rosé while we waited for our food. My husband wouldn't stop staring at me, and it made me feel super horny.

When his phone rang again, I asked, "Baby, who is that calling you?"

"No one important. The only reason why I haven't turned it off is that I'm expecting a call from Wingo. You know he has been a no-show all week. That's not like him."

Wingo was the security guard I first met when I came to the studio with Lexi the day I met Giovanni. I never went down to the studio. The studio wasn't a part of my life, nor were the staff who worked in the studio. I had no dealings with any of it. Matter of fact, Wingo, Nette, Rodney, and Shawn, (the guy who took my pics my first day there) were never allowed to come into the mansion. The only ones that were allowed inside were Percy and Lexi, because she was my bestie. I liked it that way. It kept my husband's business separate from his private life. I never pried in my husband's business or concerned myself with his staff. Except for Percy, because he and my hubby were super tight.

He turned off the phone and said, "It's nothing to worry about. I'll drive by his house a little later tonight. But for now, let's focus on us. How are you feeling about going into our fourth year of marriage, baby?"

"Like meeting you is the best thing that ever happened to me."

And it was. My life had been nothing but comfort and joy. I had shopped at stores I had never heard of before, been to places I probably would have always dreamed of going to: Jamaica, Aruba, Italy, France. I had a great relationship with my mother-in-law, Dana, and Giovanni's father, Douglas. I had everything I wanted. Well, except for one thing.

Giovanni broke into my thoughts. "You're looking kind of serious over there, baby."

I smiled. "No, I'm fine."

He studied me before saying, "I found a specialist, and I'm thinking that we should both go sometime this week. She's over at Cedars-Sinai."

It was like he could read my thoughts. The one thing we both wanted was a child. And in the past four years, we had not been able to conceive. While Giovanni's mother and father said that it just might take some time, Giovanni was getting impatient and wondered if I could conceive at all.

My appetizer of crab-stuffed mushrooms came, and I dug in, not knowing what to say to Giovanni. This was not the first time in the past year that he had brought up seeing a specialist. Truth was I didn't want to go, out of fear that they would tell me I couldn't have kids. How would I be able to live with that?

"Well, I just think that we need to be more patient, Giovanni. I am, after all, only twenty-three."

"Yes, and I am thirty-eight. You seem to always forget that I'm a lot older than you are," he added.

"I know. Let's just give it a few more months." I smiled wickedly and said, "In the meantime, we will just have to increase our chances by increasing our activity."

He chuckled. "I'm okay with that, baby. You know I never get tired of making love to you."

I picked up one of my mushrooms and fed it to my baby. He licked my fingers when he was done eating it.

I laughed softly. "Are you trying to get something started tonight?"

"Stop turning me on, then."

I blushed and looked away.

A few minutes later, our main course was brought. I had a little of each dish. I even made room for some of their famous butter cake, all while having a fun conversation with my husband. I was glad that we were over the whole problem-with-conceiving issue and that it didn't ruin our anniversary.

"You about done?" Giovanni asked when I set my fork down.

I laughed at my husband again. He was antsy about getting me home so we could do the nasty.

"Toast," I pouted.

Giovanni held up his glass, and I held up mine.

"To my beautiful wife. The best investment I have ever made. I love you more than life, will never hurt you or let anyone else hurt you. And I hope we can add twenty more years to our four. I'm looking to love you forever, Giselle. To our anniversary."

He made me teary eyed.

We clinked glasses. I took a sip of mine, and so did he. Then we both leaned over the table for a deep kiss.

I pulled away to dab my eyes and felt this incredible feeling in my chest.

"You okay, baby?"

I nodded. "These are happy tears."

He stared at me before saying, "You know I love you, right?"

"Yes. I do."

"And that I want to fuck your brains out tonight?"

I hit him on the hand playfully and looked around, making sure no one heard.

"You about ready to go?" he asked.

I nodded.

They wrapped up all the food I'd ordered. Giovanni had nothing left.

The wine had made me sleepy, and I hoped I didn't fall asleep before we made it home. In the past I had, and Giovanni never woke me, just carried me in the house and put me to bed. I wanted to stay up for our anniversary and get in a session of lovemaking. *Who knows?* I thought as we made it to our car. *Maybe I will get pregnant tonight.*

My husband opened my side of his black Range Rover and closed the door once I was settled safely inside the car. He then walked around to the front and pulled out a cigarette to take a quick smoke. He usually did this, so that I didn't have to smell the smoke.

Just then my cell phone rang. I pulled it out of my bag and answered it. "Hello?"

"Giselle. This is Percy."

"Hi, Percy—"

"I hate to do this to you, but it's time the truth comes out. Whether he wants to hide it from you or not. Where's Giovanni?"

I looked at my husband as he ground his cigarette into the concrete and walked toward the car. "He's coming. Hold—"

"No! Giselle, put the phone on speaker. I want you and him to hear this."

My husband opened his side of the car, sat down, and closed the door.

"Okay, Percy." I looked at my husband, confused by the look of alarm on his face at the mention of Percy's name. I pressed the speaker button, and Percy's voice flooded out of the phone.

"Since you don't want to answer my calls, I had to find a way to get at you, and that was through Giselle! I just wanted to let you know that I'm done with you and your shit. You sick, twisted muthafucka! And you got some go—"

Before I could hear the rest, the back of my husband's truck was hit. The glass in the back window shattered.

I screamed and ducked down, dropping the phone. In the side-view mirror, I saw a man standing with a bat and two more men with bats creeping up to the front of the car.

"Giselle, keep your head down!" Giovanni yelled.

I heard more glass shatter, and I knew that they had busted the front window as well.

"Giovanni!" I screamed as two of the men yanked him out of the driver's window of the car. They dropped him to the ground and started beating him with their bats. I started crying, and my heart was thudding in my chest.

The other guy then climbed on the front hood of the car. When he reached for me, I screamed and un-snapped my seat belt so I could escape to the back of the car.

"Come here!"

With only seconds to make an escape, I leaped into the backseat, terrified, as I felt him grab one of my heels. I kicked, landing a blow to his face.

"Bitch!"

"Giovanni!" I screamed, helpless. I was super terrified.

The guy came through the window, yanked me viciously by my arm, and pulled me out of the car through the busted front window. My body slid down the hood of the truck to the ground. Before I could move, he snatched me back up. "Keep your fucking hands to yourself!" he growled. He slapped the hell out of my face in a way I had never been slapped before. It was done in a way that made the side of my face numb.

As if the physical pain wasn't enough, I had to witness my husband lying helpless on the ground, with blood oozing from his head. Yet they continued to assault him. I watched as they beat him to the extent that I wondered if he was dead or not.

I started crying really hard at that moment. And as I cried, the three dudes grabbed me and put me into a black Magnum.

I stared out the windows at my husband and screamed hysterically. I was in the middle of the backseat with two of the men on either side of me, with the other dude driving.

The one driving said, "You screaming now, bitch. Your pain is just getting started, and life, as you know it, is over."

I literally pissed in my pants at his comment.

One of them tied a blindfold over my eyes. After what felt like twenty minutes of driving, the car stopped. I heard the car turn off, seat belts being unsnapped, and car doors being opened. I was dragged by my hair with the blindfold on me, so I had no idea where I was.

"Don't be easy on that bitch. Fuck her," one of the guys said.

One of my shoes was gone, so it was a little difficult to walk, much less walk fast. When I couldn't keep up with them, the guy dragging me tightened his grip on my hair. I moaned from the pain.

"Shut the fuck up, ho! 'Fore I make it worse."

I nodded fearfully and hurried to keep up with them, which was also hard because I couldn't see anything in the darkness. At one point, I lose my balance and fell. The guy didn't bother helping me up. Then I heard keys jingle and a door being opened. I was roughly tossed on a floor.

I was scared out of my fucking mind. What if Giovanni was dead, and what if they killed me? I was also curious as to why I was even here. I had done no one wrong in my life. Neither had my husband.

"Aye, yo. Set up that shit on the phone," one of the guys yelled.

I wanted to take off the blindfold so I could see where I was, but I didn't want to make them angry.

That was when I felt someone standing over me.

The blindfold was snatched off my face.

I blinked and looked around. It was an empty house. I stared fearfully at the two guys hovering over me, while the other guy fiddled with a cell phone.

The guy with the cell said, "Take her fucking clothes off."

"No!" I screamed. I hoped they were not going to rape me. And I wondered who the hell they were and what they wanted.

They ignored me. I tried to crawl away, but a foot easily landed on my back, knocking me flat on the floor. My pretty dress was ripped to shreds, and my other shoe was flung off. My bra and panties were next.

"Damn, that bitch thick!" one of them said.

I was left naked and shivering. *Please don't let them rape me,* I prayed.

"JB, you got the shit on there?" one of them asked.

"Yeah, Ponce."

The two dudes snatched me up, while the guy named JB held up the phone to my face. JB talked while the other two dudes held me.

"Listen, Giovanni. You dirty, grimy-ass muthafucka. As you can see, we got your bitch! And if you think this shit is about a fucking ransom, you're wrong. You done fucked with the wrong one. See my boss, Bryce, knows all about your sick, twisted ass, and you made the worst mistake of your life when you decided to fuck around with his little sister. So he looks at it like this. An eye for an eye."

What was he talking about? Who was Bryce, and who was his little sister?

The dude named Ponce, who was holding me, snatched one of my nipples and squeezed it. I felt so violated, but I kept quiet.

JB went on. "Everything you did to the boss's sister, we going to do to this bitch! And when we done passing her around to all the homies, we're going to send this bitch back to you in a box!"

I freaked out at what he had just said. So they did plan on forcing themselves on me. They were going to rape me to get revenge on my husband. "You must have the wrong person," I wanted to yell. And they were going to make the mistake of raping me. I panicked when one of the dudes holding me, Ponce, released me momentarily to unzip his pants. Before I could even blink, he placed his dick in my face.

My heart was beating a mile a minute, and my body was shaking.

"You got her, E?"

E laughed. "Yep."

I closed my eyes as the warm liquid hit my face, and I resisted the urge to heave right there. Having a complete stranger pee directly in my face was a very humiliating experience.

"Yeah, you see that shit, nigga?" JB said. "Your bitch just got a golden shower, and before the night is over, she is going to suck all our dicks and take these dicks any way we want her to."

At the part "any way we want her to," the guy that had just pissed on me started slapping me in the face with his dick. I moaned in my throat in disgust. Fear started rising in me again at their threats.

JB was fiddling with the phone now. "Hold her so I can send that nigga this one."

A few minutes later JB said, "All right. Let's send another one. Torture this nigga. Stick your dick in her mouth."

No way was I going to give this stranger, who probably had AIDS, head. "If you stick that in my mouth, I can't be responsible for what I do," I warned.

"Shut up, bitch." E attacked me with a blow to my face.

I shook off the pain that rushed to my head. But the blow made me light-headed, made me want to pass out. Why were they doing this? And was my husband alive? I wondered if I would live past this night, after they inflicted their so-called revenge on me. Then I wondered if they would realize they had the wrong people. Because I knew my husband was innocent of whatever they were accusing him of. He probably didn't know of any Bryce, just like I didn't know of any Bryce.

I started crying.

Ponce said, "Yeah, bitch, I wish you would even think of injuring my dick. If you do, I will injure you for life."

JB positioned the camera. "Go ahead, P."

The thought of him stuffing himself inside of me was sickening, and I would take my odds. So as soon as he shoved it inside my mouth, I clamped down real hard.

Ponce screamed for his life. It was a shriek I would never forget. The phone fell to the floor, and JB was on me, gripping my hair in his hands, trying to get me to loosen my hold. He couldn't. But then E started strangling me as I continued to bite down. The pressure tightened around my neck to the extent that I could not breathe, so I had to let Ponce go.

As soon as I did, he held his dick with one hand, and with the other, he came down hard on my head. I collapsed back into E's arms. That was when Ponce went crazy.

"You stupid bitch! You done fucked up and got my shit throbbing." He started pounding me. Left hook, right hook, a few kicks to my stomach, but when he pulled my head back by my hair and gave me a punch in the face, I was literally out for the count. Literally. . . .

Chapter 10

I woke up to someone prodding me. In a spot I am ashamed to even mention. But it was my insides.

"Good morning, bitch. Your husband called."

So my husband was alive. I was relieved at that, but I was so afraid to open my eyes to the reality of what they were doing to me now and were about to do. I opened my eyes to find the phone once again aimed at me by the dude Ponce. E was also there, but the other guy, JB, was gone.

It was Ponce who had just spoken.

E sat back, with a huge smirk on his face, as some chick I didn't even know, had never seen before, continued to stick her fingers inside of me.

"Yo, dawg, this shit is turning me on!" E exclaimed.

I tried to inch away from her. But E positioned his gun on me, leaving me helpless and hella scared.

"Yeah, rich nigga, you see this shit. We getting your bitch turned out by a dyke, dawg. So stop calling, muthafucka, and enjoy the fucking show!" said Ponce.

I looked at the girl, who had a shaved head and piercings all over her face. She was buck naked.

"Could you please stop?" I whispered.

She simply winked at me. Her two fingers snaked in and out.

"Now, what else you got in your little bag of toys, Mama?" E asked her. He was seated across from where we were on the floor, in a plastic chair. He had a big purse on his lap. He rummaged through the purse while the girl giggled at me, not shy at all about the fact that she was violating me much like I was violated the night before.

When she made a move to slip her head between my legs, I tried to close my legs.

Ponce smacked the shit out of me and shouted, "You fucking up the shot! Bitch, open them legs!"

My shoulders shook with sobs, as I had no choice but to open my legs and let her slip between them and proceed to go down on me. It felt like my face was on fire from the smacks.

E started rubbing his dick in his pants. "Goddamn!"

"How that shit taste, Leslie?" Ponce asked.

"Sweet."

She started thrashing her head from side to side and licking up and down my pussy like my husband would do to me. But instead of it making me feel good, she was making me really sick. I wanted to throw up, and I felt violated beyond description. I felt the way a rape victim would feel, because that was what she was doing to me. She was performing oral sex on me against my will. I couldn't understand how she was getting pleasure out of this. Out of seeing me get assaulted and crying. She was just as sick as they were.

E tossed something toward her. "Here, I got something for you."

She pulled her face away from my pussy and picked it up. It was a gigantic dildo. Without waiting, she started slapping it against my pussy. "Look how wet I'm making you," she purred. I was dry. She had to see that.

She then got on her knees, so her ass was facing E. Ponce still had the cell phone on me and was filming this. She took the dildo and shoved it in my pussy. "Moan for me, baby," she said.

At that point I knew if I begged her to stop, she wouldn't. So I shook my head and closed my eyes, and she slammed it harshly inside of me.

After five strokes, I heard E say, "I can't take this shit no more, man." He stood and yanked down his pants.

"Come on, Daddy. I like dick, too."

He pulled his pants and boxers down to his ankles and slid behind the girl. I watched, horrified, as he fucked her. All while the dildo was inside of me. With each thrust he gave her pussy, she would match it, sticking the dildo into me just as hard.

When E's eyes met mine and he gave me a lustful look as he continued to pound into her and she started moaning loudly, I looked away from him, because it was almost like he was saying, "You're next, bitch."

"I'm cumming! Shit, I'm cumming!" E yelled.

Ponce laughed. "I wish I could see that nigga's face after I send this one."

"I'm cumming, too. You cumming, Mama?" she asked me.

I just kept my eyes closed and waited for it to be over and prayed that the guys didn't force themselves on me.

Finally, E started yelling at the top of his lungs, and the girl, Leslie, matched his pitch. E then pulled out and rushed closer to me. He then allowed his cum to splash on my face and hair. This was also something my husband had never done to me. I heard his mocking laugh when he was done.

"Cut!" Ponce said. "Ain't that what they say when they make those fuck movies?"

I wiped the cum from my face as best I could.

"You gonna get some of this?" E asked, referring to the girl who had gone down on me.

"No. I want to fuck that prissy bitch right there, and as soon as I send this video to her husband, I'm going to hit that," Ponce replied.

"Let me rinse off my dick." E slipped into another room. I figured it was the bathroom.

Survival tactics kicked in. I wondered if the bathroom had a window that I could escape out of.

Leslie stood and said, "Shit, I can go for another round."

"Ease back, bitch," Ponce told her.

She giggled, unaffected, and said, "Can I watch?"

"I don't care." Ponce started stripping out of his clothes.

I started crying again. There was no way I wanted any of those bastards inside of me. If they forced themselves on me, they might as well kill me, because I couldn't go back to my husband. I would never feel the same. I would be too ashamed of this day.

Ponce came toward me with a sinister look in his eyes. "Come here, bitch." He kneeled down some and grabbed one of my legs, pulling me closer to him.

"No, please!" I begged him. "Don't!"

He ignored me and straddled my body with his. He started squeezing my breasts roughly with one hand, while using his other hand to go inside me.

E came out of the bathroom, took one look at us both, and said, "Like that?"

"Yeah. I'm going to fuck this bitch."

"Well, shit, me too!"

"Grab the phone and film this," Ponce told him.

"Okay."

I started fighting, in hopes that I could free myself. I tried to slide from underneath him, all the while using my fist to hit him. It had no effect whatsoever. He was going to take what he wanted. The look in his eyes was too determined as he reached down and started licking my nipples. I managed to scratch his face, and he yelled out in pain. Then he slapped the shit out of me. The hits made me cry out loudly.

"Don't scratch me." He then spit in my face.

Once the spit hit my face, I sobbed and closed my eyes. That was when someone's phone rang.

"Turn over, bitch. I don't wanna see your face. In fact, I'm going to fuck you in your ass." He flipped me on my stomach and started sticking his fingers in my asshole.

I could hear E talking. "What's up, Bryce? Yo, man, we . . . Yeah, that bitch is here. She a bad bitch. E about to get some of that." He paused. "Why? Naw, I'm not questioning you."

I could feel his dick pressing against my asshole, trying to gain entry. I struggled against him. What if he had something like an STD or AIDS? He was trying to go inside me with no protection. He could ruin my marriage and my whole life! I tried to drag myself away, but he took one hand and gripped my hair so tight, I thought he was going to pull a huge plug out. I didn't want to go back to my husband after another man had forced himself on me. I had to get away, so I continued to struggle against him, despite the pain he was inflicting on me. When I wouldn't stop moving, he gripped the back of my head and slammed it down on the floor. I screamed and felt dizzy. I blinked and tried to regain my focus.

Then, suddenly, E said, "Ponce, stop!"

Instantly, Ponce moved his penis away from my butt. I took a deep breath of relief.

"Fuck! What? Why?"

"Bryce said not to rape her."

Ponce groaned deep in his throat and shoved me away roughly. "Bitch!"

I hid my face in my forearms and continued to cry. But I couldn't help but feel relieved. Whoever Bryce was, he had just saved me.

"You come here."

I peeked from under my forearms at the girl, Leslie. She crawled over to Ponce, still naked.

"Don't worry, Daddy. I'll take care of you."

I closed my eyes tight as I heard slurping sounds coming from her and him moaning deeply.

A few minutes later I heard, "Yeah, swallow all my nut. The nut I wanted that bitch to swallow. Now, get it hard again."

"No problem."

Next, I heard the sound of bodies slapping against each other. When I heard three people moaning, I was horrified to see E on his back, the girl on top of him, and Ponce behind her. She was having sex with both of them at the same time. I was going to try to get away.

They were so into it that they didn't see me walk toward the room that E had come out of earlier. As I eased toward the door—with about three more steps, I would have been there—I heard, "Where the fuck you going?"

I didn't turn back to see if E or Ponce had said it. I just said quickly, "To the bathroom. I have to use it."

"She naked. She can't go nowhere, Ponce," said E.

Silence. I peeked and saw they were back into their threesome and didn't care.

I took a deep breath and closed the space between me and the bathroom. Once inside, I locked the door and rushed over to the window. I was so relieved to see that it was a sliding window with no bars. I opened it slowly. There was a screen, so I pushed it out the window. Then I stood on the toilet and climbed onto the windowsill. I looked outside. It was nighttime, but I could see a small backyard. The window wasn't very high up. Luckily, there were no dogs back there. I climbed out the window and leaped.

I landed on my side, and although I felt a stinging on my legs, I stood to my feet quickly and took off running down the street. I didn't know where I was or what to do, so I ran to one house and knocked on the door. When they didn't answer immediately, I ran off, scared that the two guys would see me. I knew I needed to get as far away from that street as possible. That was the best bet.

Being naked didn't make the situation any better.

As I ran farther up the street, I saw a car driving slowly down the street. I flagged it down and screamed, "Wait! Help!"

Thank God the car stopped.

I rushed up to it and snatched open the passenger-side door and hopped inside. "Please just drive!" I yelled, fearfully looking behind me for the two men.

"Is everything okay? Where are your clothes?"

"I will tell you if you please just drive away!"

He busted a U-turn and sped off.

"Thank you! My husband and I were at dinner, and these guys beat him up." I took a deep breath, because I was crying again at the mention of what they did to my husband. "They kidnapped me and beat me up and forced themselves on me!"

His speed increased. The car was dark inside, because it was nighttime, and I could barely make out the face of the man who asked me that.

"I don't know why they did this to me and my husband."

"Because your husband fucked up!"

I gasped. *Oh no.* My heart started pounding wildly in my chest. He must be a part of this. I reached for the door handle, but his hand was on mine.

"Please let me go."

"Listen, Giselle. You look real sweet, but the fact of the matter is Ponce and E and JB, they work for Bryce. I work for him, too. In fact, that's my big bro. You should have picked another car. Now, I'm not going to hurt you, but you not going home or nowhere near it. You are officially the property of Bryce."

I continued to cry silently. I thought that I had found an escape, someone who would help me. Now I wished that I had just tried my luck at one of the other homes I had passed. But now it was too late to change anything. They had me. I shuddered at the thought of what they would do with me now.

Twenty minutes later the car came to a stop. The guy had held one of my arms the whole ride there and did not release me until he got out on his side. I hopped out on my side and tried to make a run for it. He caught me easily, and tossed me over his shoulder like I weighed ten pounds. Like I wasn't still naked. I wanted him to let me go. I wasn't a baby and didn't want to be carried. But at least he wasn't dragging me by my hair or being rough or brutal like those other guys were.

He walked toward a house, knocked, then shoved the door open. He carried me through it. I shoved my hair out of my face so I could look around the large living room.

He paused and asked, "Bryce, where you at?"

"In here, Angel."

He carried me down a hallway to a half-opened door. He pushed the door open and walked inside. "I got her right here. And they fucked baby girl up."

I was then unceremoniously dumped at someone's feet.

I met the gaze of another man I did not know. He was seated behind a desk.

I scanned his face to see if there was anything familiar about him. Thought maybe he was a past employer of Giovanni and had it in for him. He was a big, buff guy, I could tell, and although he was seated, I could see he was also tall. He had dark brown skin and well-sculpted features. A broad, firm nose, full lips. Light brown eyes. His hair was cut so that he had just a little bit on his head. It was in waves. He reminded me of the new fiancé of Lil Wayne's ex-wife, Toya. He wore a white T-shirt, and up and down his arms were various tattoos. I studied them. There were several tribal bands, some writing in Chinese, and a sun. I was also surprised to see a hog tattooed on him. *Who does that?*

Looking from him to the guy that brought me here, I observed that they looked a lot alike, except the guy who brought me here seemed much slimmer and shorter that the guy called Bryce.

"I was just on the phone with those fools. I can't believe that they are dumb enough to let a female get away."

"They need to be fired after what they did to her."

I felt Bryce's eyes on me again. He was scanning me from head to feet. His eyes traveled all over my naked body. I tried to cover my private parts with my hands.

"Yeah, it looks like they fucked her up good."

"Yeah, baby girl looks bad."

"But it could be worse. They could have done to her what her husband did to our little sister. You were always fucking softhearted. Don't forget about what they did to our little sister, Angel."

Angel tried to harden his soft-looking face when he looked at me again. "Right."

I looked down and bit my lip to keep from defending my husband against their lies.

Bryce said, "And it's a damn shame that I have to stop what the fuck I'm doing to babysit because their dumb asses couldn't keep up with her. They are always fucking shit up. Man, this is the last straw. They gone."

His brother was silent.

"So the operation is shut down at this spot. I can't afford for her to get away again. So I'm going to need you to hold shit down while I deal with this situation."

"Don't worry. You know I got you, bro, anything you need."

"You need me, you know where you can find me." Bryce's eyes were on me again. "Now the question is, what am I going to do with her?"

After Angel left, he just stared at me for a while. I tried to keep myself covered but couldn't. With the condition that I was in—all bruised up, with dried blood and semen on my face—I knew I couldn't look or smell too appealing.

He stood and walked toward the door. "Get up," he told me coldly.

I stood to my feet.

"Walk."

My legs were cramped, which caused me to miss a step as I attempted to walk.

"Walk!" He towered above me.

I ignored the pain in my joints and walked out of the room. When we got to a staircase, I paused and asked, "Where are you taking me?"

Instead of answering, he snatched me up and tossed me over his shoulder and carried me down the hall. "You taking too fucking long," he growled.

I screamed loudly for help. "Please let me go!" I was a grown woman, capable of walking on my own. I was tired of being carried from place to place like I was a child.

He swatted me on my ass so hard that when I tried to scream, no sound came out. He stopped in front of a room. He opened the door and walked toward a big bed. He tossed me on it.

I fell back on the bed. I did not move for a good minute. I was too scared. I prayed that he didn't try and finish me off. Rape me, like the other guys tried to do. Or worse. Because this man had the eyes of a killer.

"Don't get off that bed, if you know what's good for you," he warned.

He stepped through another door in the room, which, I assumed, belonged to the bathroom. I scooted over to a corner of the bed. I looked around the room for the nearest window. But in a flash, he was back with some alcohol and some cotton balls.

He sat next to me on the bed. He poured some of the alcohol on a cotton ball and tried to dab it on my face. He was the reason for the bruises in the first place, so the shit was insulting to me. I slapped his hand away from me and scooted away from him.

He snatched one of my hands and roughly yanked me back toward him. He acted like he detested me. I cried out from the pain. *Why does this man hate me so much?* I wondered. I should be hating him, since he had those guys kidnap me and hurt me, and he was probably the one that put them up to attacking my husband.

When he tried to wipe my face again, I defiantly spit in his.

"Bitch!" His head snapped back in outrage. He shoved me away so hard, I fell on the floor. I scooted away and curled my body into a ball.

He stood to his feet and walked toward the door. Once there, it seemed that something made him stop. I peeked from under my forearms as he turned back around to face me.

"Look, bitch. I can barely stand the sight of you. But the fact of the matter is this. Until I get what I want from your husband, you ain't leaving. So if you think you going to escape, you dead fucking wrong."

What was he talking about? I was brave enough to say, "Get what? Who are you, and why did you kidnap me and hurt my husband?"

"Look, it's best you don't ask me any questions. Seeing that you married that piece of shit, you should be well aware of the fucked-up, sick shit that he does and why anyone would want to kidnap you."

Again, I was confused about what he was talking about. My husband wasn't a bad man, and I knew he would never lower himself to deal with anyone like Bryce and his crazy goons. So I had no problem defending my husband to him, and I did it with confidence. Because Bryce didn't know what the fuck he was talking about. He had the wrong damn person. "You are mistaken. My husband didn't do anything. I'm telling you, you have the wrong person. So it is in your best interest to take me back home to my—"

He cut me off. "Oh, I got the right mufucka. He's been blowing up my phone to get you back. Which I highly doubt will happen. And since you wanted to run your ass off, your ass will be here with me. Which is costing me time and money. That frustrates the hell out of me. And trust me, all my anger and frustrationwill be taken out on you. Trust and believe you ain't going to escape from here. Matter of fact, get comfortable in this room, 'cause you ain't leaving it."

So he wasn't going to let me go. After all I had been put through on account of him, and he was going to continue on with this? I yelled angrily, "Fuck you!"

He flinched at that, took a step toward me. But then he stopped himself. "I'm going to say as little to you as possible. Because, bitch, you going to make me kill you if you don't shut the fuck up." With that, he walked out of the room, locking the door behind him.

As soon as he did, I stood to see if I could get one of the windows in the room open. There were two, and I tried both of them. They had bolts on them, as if this shit was already set up for me to come here. I rushed to the bathroom. I swore when I got there and discovered that there was no window in the bathroom. Now, how was I going to escape? The seconds flying by while I thought of an escape sent me into panic mode, because truthfully, I didn't know how I was going to get out of that room.

When I started yelling at the top of my lungs for someone to help me, Bryce came back to the room. He rushed toward me and said, "I'm telling you now to shut the fuck up."

I continued yelling.

Next thing I knew, he started throwing the comforter off the bed. He grabbed one of the sheets and walked toward me. I tried to run, but he grabbed me quickly and dragged me to the bed. I started screaming again, but it didn't stop him from tying each one of my limbs to the bedposts with the sheet, which he ripped up. Then he tore off another piece of the sheet, stuffed it in my mouth, and then secured it by tying another piece around my head.

Tears streamed from my eyes. I stared at him hatefully. Being tied up and not being able to defend myself against whatever they had planned for me had me terrified.

He took in my tears. "Now, I didn't want to do this. But you won't stop making all that goddamn noise. You decide to shut the fuck up, and maybe I will come back and untie you."

With that he left the room.

Chapter 11

It was not until the next day that he came back. By the time he did, waiting on him, I ended up peeing on myself. I was given no food. It made me hate his ass even more. You didn't treat a dog that way. How could a person let another person sleep in human waste and go without any food?

I was relieved when he came into the room with a bag, a drink in his hand, and a dress. He sat them down on the dresser. He walked up to me and just stood there for a moment. He was so tall, towering over me. His appearance was nothing like my husband's. My husband wore thousand dollar slacks and thousand dollar shirts and expensive shoes. This man had on a long white T-shirt, some jeans, and a pair of tennis shoes. *How juvenile.* I gave him a hateful look as he kneeled down in front of me.

"Listen. It's very obvious to me that you need to be humbled, and I have no problem humbling you some more if you choose not to act right. I have some food for you, something to drink, and even something to wear. It is in your best interest to shut the fuck up and get cleaned and fed. Do you understand?"

I nodded, because I was starving, but my eyes displayed the hate I already had for him.

Slowly, he removed the tie around my head, and I pushed the piece of sheet in my mouth out with my tongue. My mouth felt so dry. He let me sip on the soda first. It felt so good sliding down my throat. Then he started pulling french fries out of the bag and started feeding them to me one by one. I chewed each one quickly, my eyes looking at the wall.

He allowed me to sip on the soda some more before he unwrapped the burger. He fed me this as well. A couple of times he sniffed and looked around. I knew he smelled the pee on me and on the bed from the night before. It embarrassed me. But what could I do? He had me tied to the bed. He continued to feed me in silence. I also felt uncomfortable with this man I didn't even know feeding me like I was a baby. But it seemed that this was what he wanted. To humble me. But for me it was more like humiliation.

When I was done eating, he put all the trash in the bag and said, "I'm going to let you go in here to use the bathroom, and after that you can shower and get that piss off of you. Don't do anything crazy," he warned.

I nodded. I was going to play along.

He untied me. I stood to my feet, still nude, and walked into the bathroom. And sure enough, he stood in the doorway as I used the bathroom. Since there was no window in there and no way for me to escape, I wondered what the purpose of not letting me close the door and watching me pee was. Probably to humiliate me more than he already had. I was already embarrassed by the fact that I smelled like pee and I was naked in front of a stranger who would, under normal circumstances, never be in my world. It outraged me that he was able to see parts of me that were off-limits to everyone but my husband and doctor.

He turned on the shower. I wiped myself with tissue, flushed the toilet, and stood to my feet.

He turned around, looked at me, and flicked his head toward the shower. "Get in."

I complied. There was a washrag inside the shower and some shower gel. I started soaping myself up, all the while thinking that I needed to find a way to escape.

"Hurry up," he ordered.

I rinsed off in a fast manner. This might be my only opportunity to try to get away again, so, thinking quickly, I poured some of the shower gel on one of my hands and let that hand hang like my other one, loosely at my side.

He opened the shower door. I stepped out quickly. My heart was pounding. If I was unable to escape after I did this, I knew I would have to feel his wrath, whatever it was. But I needed to try to get away.

When he bent over and pulled out a towel from one of the cabinets, I knew that was my chance. As soon as he turned back toward me, I took my hand that had some of the shower gel on it and smeared the gel directly in his eyes.

"Fuck!"

He was blinded temporarily, and I took that as an opportunity to run out the bathroom. I rushed toward the door and tried to open it. I screamed in frustration when I could not get the knob to turn. I started pounding on the door and yelling over and over again, "Help me please! He kidnapped me!"

"I warned you about that shit!"

I turned around fearfully. Bryce was now standing in the bedroom, with a look of fury on his face. His legs were shoulder-width apart, and his fists clenched. He was ready to do battle . . . with me. My heart was beating so fast. I had pissed him off. What was he going to do to me now?

As he came toward me, I tried to run to a corner. He stormed up to me, blocking me in.

"I tried to be nice to you, bitch. But you always manage to fuck it up." His eyes were red. He dragged me by my hair back to the bed. He tossed me on it. He straddled me as I struggled against him and tried to fight him. I managed to slap his face with all my might. I knew it had to sting, because I slapped the shit out of him. I then pressed my fingers into his eye sockets, digging my fingernails in. He growled and grabbed both my arms, twisting them, and flipped me over, so I was now on my stomach, with my arms pressed up against my back. I screamed in pain, but I knew my screams were muffled because my face was pressed into the bed. There was pain shooting up and down my arms from his tight grip. I thought he was going to break my arms. In addition to this, I could feel his erection poking me in my butt.

After a few seconds of me crying out in pain, he asked, "You done?"

"Yes!" I said to get him to release me.

"Good." He held my arms there for a few more seconds before he released the tight grip on them and flipped me over onto my back.

Tears shot from my eyes from the pain I was still feeling in my arms. I wished I could kill that bastard. Giovanni had never put his hands on me.

When I saw him get the sheets again, I begged, "No! Please don't tie me up again." I started fighting him again. But it was like a rabbit going up against a bear. He flexed my rigid body on the bed and tied me up. All the punches and kicks I gave him must have felt like those of a toddler attacking him. He secured my limbs to the bedposts.

"I'm going to be nice and not put on the gag. But if you so much as sneeze, I will be in here to put it back on you."

I glared at him hatefully as his eyes lustfully traveled down my naked body. "I fucking hate you."

"I hate you, too, bitch."

"Then what the fuck are you looking at?" I looked pointedly at his erection poking through his jeans. It was so big that there was no way for me not to have noticed it. And felt it. "If you even think about raping—"

Suddenly a gun was pressed into my face. "What?" he demanded.

I grew silent. The sight of the gun and the feel of its cold steel scared me. My heart pounded fiercely in my chest.

"If I so much as rape you, what? What the fuck you going to do about it?"

I remained silent, and I was sure my eyes were as big as golf balls.

That was when he took the gun, trailed it down my face, down my neck, to my chest, and started playing with my nipples with the tip of it. They hardened against my will. As he did this, he said, "But something tells me . . ." The gun slid down my stomach before positioning itself at my pussy. "I won't have to rape you at all." The tip of the gun gently rubbed against my clit.

And . . . before I could stop myself, I moaned. What the fuck was wrong with me!

He heard it. Next thing I knew, he moved like a predator on me. I could feel his upper body on mine, and he had his head against one of my breasts and was teasing one of my nipples with his tongue, while the gun continued to rub against my clit.

I closed my eyes in shame as my body felt a way my mind knew I had no business feeling. I wanted to die inside. Why did it feel good? Why was *he* making my body feel this way? Why was it betraying me? I didn't know this man, and the little I did know about him, I disliked. The way he spoke to me, calling me a bitch. Being rough with me. Yes, still, my body continued to betray me as it responded to his touch.

I moaned again.

That was when he pulled away. And as shameful as it sounded, I didn't want him to.

He simply locked his arrogant eyes on me and smiled, showing his white, perfectly straight teeth, and said, "Rape, huh?"

"Fuck you!" I yelled.

He simply slipped the gun back in his pants and walked out of the room, locking it behind him.

Lockdown. Incarceration. That became my routine. And since I knew that if I started making noise, he would gag me again, I didn't bother with any more screaming. But that didn't stop me from trying to get the sheet ties off my wrists and ankles. But all the struggling did nothing for me. I couldn't break the tight knots he had made with the sheets.

He would always come, bring me food, feed me, and let me shower. He remained as hateful as ever, and so did I. I had nothing to do but collect my thoughts. And day in and day out, my circumstances really drove me crazy. When I was home, in my normal life, my mornings were usually filled with breakfast with my mother-in-law and my father-in-law or with Lexi or my brother. I would take shopping trips and blow ten or twenty stacks if I wanted to. Or my husband and I would steal away for lunch or for a random excursion to Vegas, to a random amusement park, or to a winery. Or we were attending fancy charity events with rich folks like us. My life prior to getting kidnapped was happy.

Now it was utter misery. I had tried to find any way I could to get away, from trying to attack Bryce when he untied me to hiding in a spot in the room the moment he turned his back. None of it ever worked. It just made him continue to treat me like shit. I wondered what it would take to get him to let me go. I knew my husband would get to the bottom of this and come get me. And for Bryce's sake, they better pray, because my husband would probably show them no mercy for kidnapping and hurting me.

Finally, after about a week of captivity, Bryce came into the room with some folded-up clothes, linens, and fresh towels.

I said nothing. But inhaled the fragrant smell coming from the bags of food he had brought into the room.

He sat the stuff down and stood with his back against the dresser, staring at me. "You ready to come up out them ropes?"

I nodded.

"All right. You start that craziness again, you will be right back in them, and I'm sincere when I say that."

I nodded.

As soon as he untied me, I rubbed my wrists and then my ankles, super relieved. He allowed me to shower, and I didn't bother to plan an escape from him again. What for? He had the key to the door. The only way to get out would be to get the key. How would I be able to do that? I just had to trust in my husband. That he would come up with a way to get me out of here.

When I tried to close the sliding door to the shower, he gripped it with his hands so it stayed open. Yes, he was in the shower with me again. As I showered, I noticed him snap several pictures of me.

"Why are you doing that?" I snapped angrily.

"To send to your husband. He wanted to know if you were still alive."

"Can I please talk to my husband?"

"No," He took one last shot. "Rinse off," he ordered.

I did so furiously. Once I was done, I turned the water off and stepped out of the shower.

I dried off with the towel he gave me. Once I was dry, I stood there tapping my foot and waiting for him to hand me the dress. He gave me an arrogant look before tossing it to me. I pulled it on quickly.

He gestured for me to leave the bathroom and go back into the room. I walked to the bed and sat down. My stomach started grumbling. Bryce placed a closed foam container in front of me. It was fried fish, hush puppies, and french fries.

I ate in silence, and he sat there and watched me. I knew I must have looked like a wild animal. All ashy, with my hair uncombed. The bruises his friends had left on me were just about cleared up, but still. I hated the fact that he had me in this position, and because of what? Something he was falsely blaming on my husband? I would love to see the proof.

"I'm not going to tie you up or put a gag on you, but if you try something else crazy, they go back on."

I nodded, relieved. I had exhausted all ways to get out of the room, anyway. At this point it would be a waste of time to try again. I would just have to have hope that my husband would come for me. And at least I knew he was alive. I didn't really know Bryce, so I had no idea how much manpower he had, but I knew my husband had a whole lot of it. I felt sorry for Bryce when my husband got to him.

Bryce took me out of my thoughts. "You are married to a piece of shit. He fucks with young girls that are underage. Some refuse, and he forces them to do it anyway. We are talking about young girls. My sister was one of the girls he made the mistake of *molesting*. And I believe that he still has her."

After I got over the initial shock of what he said, I almost laughed. The fact that he was accusing my husband of not only rape but also of having an affair didn't faze me one bit. I knew my husband. He would never do either of the two. And with little girls? *Please.*

I swallowed the piece of fish in my mouth and said, "I don't want to hear any of your lies. My husband does not have to force women or girls to do anything. Nor would he. He takes his vows seriously, and most of all, he is not a child molester!"

"Either you are a really good fucking liar or you are a fucking dingbat. To not see what's going on in your own household—"

"You know what? You seem to have so much hate toward my husband, and you put him down so much. What do *you* do?"

"I sell dope. That's what the fuck I do."

"And you think you are better or more of a man than he is? You kill people. Let me tell you about my husband. He is a hardworking, God-fearing man. He built his whole empire by himself. He gives women who *choose* to work, work. He gives young men steady work. He gave my brother a job. He provides for his whole family. We have a charity organization that helps youth and the community. While you kill your own people. You are the reason why fathers and mothers are in jail or walking dead on their feet, unable to raise their kids because of their drug addiction, which you heavily feed! Because what? You don't want to get a job like the average person? You are beneath us."

"Is that right, you stuck-up bitch?"

I gritted my teeth at him calling me a bitch. "Why all this waiting, then? If you hate my husband so much, then let's get this over with! Rape me! Kill me! Get it over with!"

"Because I want him to suffer. I want that ho-ass nigga to spend sleepless nights worrying who is in his wife's pussy."

"You are fucking disgusting. Trash! That's what you are, a piece of trash."

He went on, as if he wasn't insulted by what I had just said. "And when I'm done torturing that mufucka, I'm going to kill his ass."

I jumped at that comment and at the look in his eyes. The thought of someone harming my husband in any way instantly brought tears to my eyes. I loved my husband so much, and I couldn't imagine a life without him. Especially for some nonsense that Giovanni had nothing to do with. Good, innocent men lost their lives all the time, so I knew that it could happen. But what would I do if it did? I'd want to die right alongside him. He was my world, and my life would never be the same without him. I sobbed on the bed and prayed that God would protect my husband.

With that Bryce left the room, of course, locking the door behind him.

Chapter 12

"Bitch! Wake the fuck up!"

My eyes shot open to find a woman leaning over me who I had never seen before in my life. Then, before I could blink, one of her fists came down and punched me directly in my forehead. I ignored the pain and rolled off the bed so that I was on my feet, facing her.

"Bitch, you in one of my muthafucking man's spots, asleep? Oh, hell no!"

"No! You have it wrong. He kid—"

"Ho, shut the fuck up!"

"No, wait, please!"

She swung at me again, connecting with my nose, busting it. Blood spurted out.

That was it for me. I recovered from her blow quickly and threw a punch at her, landing just underneath her right eye. She rushed toward me and tried to get another blow in, but she couldn't, because I moved my face over an inch and threw two more her way. Those hits knocked the wind out of her, and she flew back from the impact.

Before she could get up again, I rushed forward, knocking her completely off her feet, and straddled her with my body. I was damned if someone else was going to attack me again. While I couldn't handle men, I knew for sure I could handle her. She was the same height and weight as me, so I used my lower body to keep her down. That was when I started punching her repeatedly. She started screaming. But I didn't stop. I gripped her neck with one of my hands and punched her in the face with my other hand. Her head flew with each hit.

That was when Bryce rushed into the room, wrapped in a towel. When Bryce saw me on top of the crazy girl, who was claiming that he was her man, he quickly pulled me off her and held me, since he thought I was going to go for her again. I could feel Bryce's naked chest against me. He was still wet from his shower.

Angel walked in the room next.

I snatched myself away from Bryce.

The girl stood up and tried to rush toward me again with a bloodied face. "Bitch!"

Bryce caught her in time, and as he held her, his towel fell down, exposing his nakedness in full view.

Her eyes went to me as he used one of his hands to fix the towel. "The fuck you looking at?" she snarled.

I looked away, embarrassed.

"Get her!" Bryce told Angel.

Angel grabbed her and said, "Brandy, what the fuck are you doing? Always snooping and shit!"

"Mind your business, Angel! He got women's clothes and towels stacked up, and I wanted to know who the fuck they were for!"

"Look. She's business, and that business is none of yours. Stay in your fucking lane! You know better than to be snooping in my shit," Bryce said angrily.

She was silent and looked furious. That was when I studied her. She was a pretty brown-skinned girl. Her look was similar to mine. Same type of frame, complexion. Except her hair was in a curly weave.

"Are you fucking her?" she finally asked.

Bryce ignored her.

"Well, why is she here?"

"Let's go!" Angel commanded, pushing her toward the door.

I took this opportunity to plead my case to her. Maybe she could help me. "No, listen to me! Call the police please. Your man kid—"

Before I could finish, Bryce placed his hands over my mouth. I struggled against him and tried to pull his hands away.

The girl's eyes widened. And she didn't fight Angel now.

"Get her out of here." Bryce's tone was icy.

"I'm sorry, baby! I didn't mean to mess nothing up. You know I'm still dealing with my insecurities!" she yelled as she walked out of the room with Angel.

Once she was gone, Bryce released me. I slapped him with all my might. He just stood there and looked at me. It made me so angry, I lunged at him. "I'm sick of this shit. Let me the fuck out of here!" I started attacking him. I was able to get a few licks in before he grabbed both my arms. His towel dropped again. He didn't reach to pick it up. Instead, he started kissing me. I struggled against him and against his mouth and said, "Get the fuck off of me!" I started beating his back with my fists.

But he was relentless, and he wouldn't stop rubbing his lips against mine and sliding his tongue in my mouth. He massaged my butt until the pounding of my fists on his back grew less and less. He was rubbing all over my body with his hands, and I, for some dumb and weak reason, was returning the fire of his kiss! His hands cupped my breasts, and he started playing with my nipples.

I could feel his hard dick pressing against my thigh. He continued to tease my lips with his, making me moan. Then, when I felt my knees get a little weak, he pulled away, breaking our kiss. Bryce turned off the lights before he exited, leaving me completely alone.

I lay down on the bed. I didn't know why I couldn't get the image of Bryce naked out of my head, and the things he did to me. And the fact that I couldn't get those images out of my head made me feel like crap. I mean, he was my abductor. He had hurt me, called me out of my name. Had not only accused my husband of things, but had also threatened to kill him. Still, I knew there was some type of attraction. I told myself that that was all it was. Bryce was a handsome man. At the end of the day, I still loved and believed in my husband.

A vision of Bryce's naked body flashed before me again. Before I knew it, I turned over on my back. I pulled the dress up to my neck and started playing with my nipples with both my hands. I moaned deeply, then licked my fingertips before rubbing them across my now hard-as-rubies nipples. I allowed one hand to rotate across them both and let my other hand rub my thighs before resting between my legs. I rubbed my fingers against my clit. It felt so good, I rubbed it with a faster motion, grinding my body into the bed, trying to create the illusion for myself that I was having sex.

I raised my legs higher, stuck two fingers inside myself, and drilled extra hard. I continued to moan and tasted myself with one hand before adding a third finger inside myself. I was so wet, and I felt the familiar sensation of cumming. I stroked faster, and the feeling continued to creep up toward my insides. When the euphoric feeling finally hit me, I tossed my head back and moaned. I had come so hard and good, I knocked myself right out, falling into a slumber.

***

The next morning Bryce came to my room bright and early. I didn't know what time it was and I was still half asleep when he walked in and laid fresh linens, clothes, and towels on the dresser. There was also some food and drinks.

Thoughts of last night flashed in my head. I saw Bryce naked again. The muscles in his chest and arms. Droplets of water running down his body. The way he had kissed me and how wet I felt when I started playing with myself. It was the craziest thing in the world for me, because I didn't even like Bryce. But I guess there was sexual tension. I wondered how he felt. The funny thing to me was the fact that he acted like he hated me just as much as I hated him, yet he felt the need to kiss and touch me.

When he caught me staring, I looked away quickly.

"Go shower," he ordered.

He tossed a towel to me, and I went into the bathroom to do what he said. When I came out about ten minutes later, with the towel wrapped around me, I held my hand out for the clothing he'd brought for me.

He hesitated before handing me the clothes and said, "I saw you last night."

I gasped, my eyes wide. He must have a camera installed in the room.

"You were definitely getting it in, baby. I only have one question for you. When you were stroking your pussy, were you thinking of your husband or were you thinking of me?"

"You son of a bitch!" I rushed up to him in anger and started attacking him. I was throwing blows like I had done to him and his crazy girlfriend last night. "I was thinking about my husband!" I tried to slap his face. He caught both my hands easily in his.

"Oh yeah?"

I found myself for the umpteenth time being pulled over to the bed, because I would not go on my own free will. I was sick of that shit. I wasn't a damn rag doll. Bryce sat down on the bed while still holding me. I struggled against him.

"Let me go!"

He held both of my wrists in one of his hands and took his free hand and yanked the towel off me. Now I was naked in front of him. He lay back on the bed, and before I could slip away, he grabbed me by my waist, lifted me in the air, and before I could stop him, sat me on top of his face.

I struggled at first and continued to yell for him to let me go. But when I felt his tongue flickered inside of me, all I could do was toss my head back and moan loudly.

He suckled on my clit and mashed his face all into my pussy.

"Oh God!" I moaned.

He eased back and started sticking his fingers into me. "You were thinking about your husband, huh?"

I didn't respond, just kept moaning as he teased me.

"You thinking about your husband now?" he asked before flickering his tongue over my clit again.

The pleasure was so intense that I grabbed his head and kept it on my pussy. He continued to suckle and then lick the opening of my vagina. I felt my legs grow weak, but his strong arms held me there.

He continued to feed off of me. And when I came, I came hard and flooded his mouth with all my wetness.

I was too weak to pull myself off him, so he tossed me aside on the bed and stood to his feet.

And all I could feel was shame and embarrassment that I had allowed him to make me feel that way, when no one except my husband had ever done that to me before. If they did ever release me and I made it back to my husband, how would I be able to face him?

I started crying and asked him, "Why are you doing this to me? I love my husband! So if you think that going down on me or lying on him is going to make me stop loving him, you are wrong!"

"So you really do believe—"

"I know for a fact that you have the wrong man. Tell me this. When and where did my husband do this? This supposed rape."

"In your home. Six days before you were kidnapped."

I laughed and waved a hand at him.

He ignored me and continued, "She went there with two other girls. My sister ran with an older crowd. One was her friend from the neighborhood, Dreka. She's fourteen, and her older sister, Yonique, is eighteen. The eighteen-year-old had done work for your husband before, and that night she was going to do more. Her film name is Butta. She let them tag along with her that night. I spoke to both of them myself. When Yonique told them she was going to make some money at a big mansion and she went on to describe the pad to them, they went crazy and begged to tag along.

"Yonique said that Wingo made a call and that your husband came over to the studio, saw my little sister, and invited her to go swimming. She left with him. They never saw her again. Yonique and her little sister were both kicked off the premises without my little sister. The security guard told them that my little sister had already left. Well, why didn't she come home, then?"

I swallowed hard and ignored his question. What he was saying didn't make a bit of sense, so it had to be untrue. I remembered the first time I came to the mansion. Wingo checked my ID before I was even let inside the studio. Why would it be any different now? It was not, I told myself.

"We don't let underage girls into the studio. We have security. He has been working for my husband for years. Trust me, he would not let them in."

"Then why were she and her friend let in?"

"Listen to me! My husband is a businessman. Legit. He makes millions of dollars off the films he makes. Why would he jeopardize that by letting young girls into the studio and hurting them? Secondly, our marriage is rock solid. He keeps no secrets from me, and he does not cheat! Not with women and not with little girls!" Over the years I had seen how committed my husband was to our charity organization, how respectful he was around the kids, and Bryce was implying that my husband was pretty much a pedophile. And he was the most trustworthy man I had known since my father.

Bryce simply stared at me and listened.

"I mean, you sound foolish. You sound like someone who is jealous of my husband's success and you want to ruin it for him."

"You know what? I'm going to let you see the shit for yourself."

Ten minutes later Angel had set up a television and a DVD player in front of me.

"Hey, what's up?" he said to me.

"Hi," I said dryly.

Bryce slipped a DVD in.

I focused in on the screen. There was a very beautiful girl on the screen. Yes, she looked young, but that didn't mean anything. I could easily pass for someone in my teens. The video was silent, but I could see her opening her mouth as if she was screaming. She rushed around the room, much like I had done when Bryce locked me in his room. She yanked on the door but was unable to get it open.

"You know I can't watch this shit," Angel said before leaving the room.

"Does that place look familiar, Giselle?" Bryce asked. I ignored him.

Yes, judging from the set, the footage was filmed in my house, so what did that mean? It proved nothing. So I continued to watch her sobbing on the bed. This was also something that did not surprise me. Then I saw my husband in the film. That did not surprise me, either. I experienced something similar when I couldn't go through with it the day I met Giovanni. In fact, to this very day there were times when Giovanni would walk on the set if the filming was delayed to find out what the holdup was. That was how we had met. It never bothered me, because my husband was trying not to waste time or money. But he was usually edited out of the film or the camera was stopped. This had to be an unedited version. But I wondered how Bryce got his hands on it. Still, there was nothing to support what Bryce was saying.

I stood and went to the bed, saying, "I don't need to see this. You just wasted your time trying to slander my husband! You look so stu—"

I glanced back at the TV as I walked away, and what I saw on the screen next made me freeze and made the hairs on my neck stand. My hand went to my mouth as I watched. Not because of the fact that he was in the film, since it could be the unedited version, and like I said, if there was a delay in shooting, my husband would want to know why and would do what he could on the set to move things along. It was because of what my husband was doing in the film: stripping off the girl's clothes while she cried and tried to fight him. But she was a very petite girl, and my husband overpowered her, so finally she was completely naked. Then he stripped down. What I saw next made me tremble. He started slapping the girl around the room. Then what I saw after this made me cry. He started touching the young girl all over. Rubbing on her breasts, her pussy, sticking his fingers in her. Then what I saw next made me sob. He was forcing himself on her. In her mouth, in her pussy, then her ass. She was sobbing as hard as I was, and although I couldn't hear the sound, I knew as he sodomized her, she was screaming at the top of her lungs. And so was I.

My knees felt weak, and I sank to the floor.

Then, as if that wasn't enough, Bryce walked up to me and showed me the school ID of the girl in the film. The ID said that the girl was only twelve.

I covered my face with my hands and bawled like a baby. Who was I married to?

The next morning Bryce came to the room with breakfast. I declined to eat. My throat was super dry from all the crying I did the night before, so I sipped the orange juice he passed to me. My husband was not the man that I thought he was. And I felt like an idiot, because I hated what he had done. It was sick. Inhumane. But, on the other hand, he was still my husband, the man I loved and with whom I had vowed to spend the rest of my life. I didn't know what to do, and I didn't know how to feel. One thing was for sure. I understood now why Bryce hated my husband and why he hated me. He thought I knew my husband was raping young girls, when in reality I had no idea. None. And I wondered how many other young girls my husband had raped during our marriage. Giovanni was a sick, sick man, and I was an idiot for marrying him.

I changed out of my clothes into the fresh clothes Bryce passed to me, which included a dress, a bra, and a pair of underwear. I was surprised when he tossed a pair of flip-flops to me, and after I placed them on my feet, he stood and said, "Come on."

A few minutes later Bryce pulled into a parking lot at Mayfair Park in Lakewood. Since it was early, the park was pretty much empty.

He put the car in park and said, "Now I'm going to give you the opportunity to stretch your legs and get some air. For your own sake, don't embarrass yourself. I know nobody at this park got what I got in my waistband. So you need to behave, little girl."

I nodded.

I was able to get out of the car. Just twenty-four hours before, this would have been a perfect opportunity to make a run for it. But now I was so confused about what to do. I felt I was in just as bad hands with my husband as I was with Bryce. On top of this, the house my parents had owned, I'd let Giovanni talk me into selling it about a year into our marriage. Now where was I going to go? I was so lost and didn't know what to do. And since Bryce had already advised me not to try anything stupid, I obeyed. I needed to figure out what I was going to do, anyway. Why piss Bryce off and try to run away, when now I didn't know where to run away to? For the time being, he wasn't doing anything to hurt me. And all the times I tried to escape before, I didn't get anywhere, and any attempt to flee now would probably end the same way.

I was forced to walk close to Bryce, and he had a gun in the small of my back. He wasn't playing.

After a few seconds of awkward silence, I said, "I'm sorry about the things I said." My voice started trembling.

"Oh. So now you believe me? I'm not a piece of shit, dope dealer to you?" he threw back at me.

"Don't get me wrong. I still don't like your ass. That won't change. But what my husband—"

Before I could finish, I was drowned out by loud music coming from a car as it sped into the parking lot. Normally, I would have paid it no mind. But I knew the car and the driver, who hopped out quickly and came walking toward us. It was Percy.

"Percy!" I tried to rush toward him, but Bryce held me back and shoved the gun into my back, silently reminding me of what he had already told me.

Percy came up to us, and before he even spoke to me, he gave Bryce a hug.

I was in shock. They knew each other.

"Any word yet?" Bryce asked him.

Percy shook his head. Then he finally looked at me. "I'm sorry you had to be swept up in this bullshit, Giselle."

"You two know each other?" I asked.

"You remember my story, how I did a stint in the pen and how I used to traffic in dope?" Percy aimed a finger at Bryce. "I moved weight for Bryce."

I was stunned at the revelation.

"When I found out what Giovanni was doing to young girls, I had to bounce, Giselle. I flat-out didn't agree. The first time I found out about it was a few months after y'all wedding."

My heart sped up when he said that—a few months after our wedding. I was getting confirmation after confirmation that my fairy-tale life really was a lie. My life with Giovanni. My happy, wholesome, solid marriage was bullshit. I swallowed, trying to get the lump out of my throat, and closed my eyes briefly. More and more, the revelations were hurting me so bad.

"When y'all came back from y'all honeymoon, he asked me to find him a young girl. When he said *young,* I was thinking, 'How much younger can he get than you?' But the sick muthafucka said, 'Eleven'! I kind of laughed it off, and he did, too." Percy took a deep breath. "I wish that I hadn't. Then maybe we would not be here now. I also wish I hadn't taken off early that night, either. Anyway, he has help on the inside. People to supply him with his fetish. Wingo."

I gasped. *Is that why he was missing?*

Then Percy said, "That's all me. So would your husband have been. But Bryce wanted Giovanni for himself. He's going to play this game with him."

My eyes shot to Percy. I was in shock. He had killed Wingo.

"Anyway, when I came back to work, I'm getting ready to erase the surveillance of the night before like I normally do. But I saw a young girl that looked very familiar. That's 'cause she is the baby sister of one of my closest friends. I watched that girl growing up. And she still ain't fully grown up. Then I see your husband on the surveillance with her. He must have forgotten to turn off the camera."

So that was how Bryce got the video. Percy. There was a hidden camera in every room so that Giovanni could watch what was going on in the rooms from his office.

"I was so shaken up. I left. It was the only sane thing I could do. Being that Wingo had worked for Giovanni for some years, and I felt that I could trust him with the information, I stopped by his crib. Never in a million years would I have thought it would be Wingo supplying him. Wingo has four little girls himself. The oldest being ten, the youngest being four. When I got there, his little girls were playing that Wii game in the living room, while him and his wife were cooking in the kitchen. I even remember what they were cooking. Spaghetti, like they were these wholesome parents." He gave a dry laugh.

"When Wingo saw how shaken up I was, he tossed me a bottle of Henny. I tossed some back and blabbered out that I had seen the young girl and Giovanni on the surveillance. Wingo took one look at my face and busted out laughing. Then Wingo told me that he got that girl for Giovanni. He said she came in with two other girls. One of them was a chick named Butta that works for us and her little sister. We had waited for Butta that night, but she ended up being so late that the camera crew went home. When they got there, Wingo called Giovanni upstairs and told him he had one that was fourteen and the other was twelve. He came down and got the twelve-year-old.

"But that wasn't the worst of what he said. He told me that several times a month he hand delivers young girls to Giovanni. He said it was like a second job for him, and for every girl he gets, Giovanni gives him four hundred dollars. He said that Giovanni always waits until the studio closes, sets the camera up, and films himself having sex with the young girls. Then he keeps the DVDs locked up in his office, and watches them."

I gasped and thought back to the day I was in Giovanni's office and he put a DVD in an oak cabinet. Percy wasn't lying.

Percy chuckled bitterly. "But you know what's worse than all of this?"

"What?" I asked.

"Wingo. This is a man with four little girls, and you can do this fucked-up shit to somebody else's little girls? And what was worse than this was the fact that his wife was standing in the same room as us, hearing the whole conversation, and she was okay with it, too. But I wasn't. And that's why I put a bullet in his head, so he can't trick off someone else's little girl."

I blinked and rubbed my face in between my hands. "But why is my—"

Percy grabbed me by my shoulders and shook me. "Giselle! Your husband is sick, plain and simple. A fucking pedophile that needs to be murked. As much as I appreciated all the good Giovanni did for me, I had to bounce. Bryce is like a brother to me. What Giovanni is doing is sick. I can't have any more part of it. We kill niggas like him in the pen. So I walked away. Now my only priority is to find out what happened to Bryce's sister." He released me.

"Ain't heard nothing?" Bryce asked.

"Naw. But I tell you, Bryce, I can't help but feel that Brianna is scared you going to kick her ass for sneaking off, and she is scared to come home."

That is her name? Brianna? I thought.

"I'm thinking the same, P," Bryce said. "But did you talk to the sisters?"

"They pretty much told me the same thing they told you. Wingo told her Brianna had left already."

Bryce nodded, studying Percy.

"But I'm on it, so don't worry. If we have to comb every city in Cali, we will. Hog is on it, too."

"Thanks, man," Bryce said.

"Don't trip. We are going to find her."

I looked away, not knowing what to say.

"Well, I have to get going," Percy announced. He and Bryce bumped fists before hugging.

When he turned to go, I said, "Wait, Percy! What about me? Bryce kidnapped me."

"How you think Bryce figured out where to nab you?" Percy replied.

I gasped. Percy had set Giovanni and me up. That hurt a little bit. I understood how Percy felt about my husband, but what about me? I was innocent in this. I had always looked at Percy as an older brother who loved me.

"I can't be on your side, Giselle. Bryce is my boy for life. I can't do nothing for you, baby. Charge that shit to the game."

"But he is holding me against my will. I did nothing wrong, Percy! Do something."

"I can't do shit!" Percy asserted. "Let the shit play out how it's going to play out. And you're safer with my boy than you are with that twisted muthafucka you married." He turned and walked away.

"Wait!" I screamed. "Percy, don't leave me here!" I continued to scream his name.

Percy ignored me and walked toward his car. When I saw him get in his car and speed away, I sobbed and threw myself on the ground in defeat. This was all too crazy for me. Percy had killed Wingo. Wingo was slime, just like my husband was. And I was left with Bryce, to be used as a pawn against my husband, whom I now hated. *Then suppose they find Brianna,* I thought. *What will happen to me? Do I go back to my husband and continue to live a lie, which I now know my life with him is?*

I felt so dumb. I had married a child molester. I had gone into this marriage blindsided. He seemed like the kindest, sweetest person in the world, one who would never hurt a child, and he was destroying their whole world. And there I was, like a dumb ass, standing proudly right beside him. Flying all across the world and shopping while he was doing this crazy shit in our house! Why in the fuck didn't I know about something happening right under my nose? My marriage was over; my magical life was as well. And no one cared about what was going to happen to me. I guessed I was going to pay for my husband's sins.

I refused to eat when we got back to my cage. Bryce didn't give a shit. He let me throw myself on my bed and cry my eyes out.

I felt so lost, and I didn't know what to do about my situation. If Giovanni still had Bryce's little sister and if he gave her back, I would be expected to go back to Giovanni. I couldn't. I had to divorce him. But that meant I faced yet another dilemma. Where would I live? How would I live? What about my brother? Since Giovanni was clearly not the man I had thought he was, he was a stranger to me. Judging by the DVD that I saw, he was a dangerous and violent man that I would not, for any reason, want in my life. My mother and father were probably both rolling over in their graves at the mere thought of me being married to someone like him. I again wondered if, when Bryce got his sister back, he would send me back to my husband. And if I told Giovanni that I had no further desire to be married to him, would he let me divorce him? It was too much to think about. So I slept the day away.

Later on that night I was surprised when Bryce came to my room. He usually did not come back until the next day. He cleared his throat and stood in doorway. Now when I look at him, I couldn't help but feel bad about what he was going through with his sister being missing—and about her violent rape at the hands of my husband. I could only imagine the hurt he felt and the dread of not knowing where she was. I mean, I had

a little brother, and as an older sibling, you felt it was
your responsibility to protect them. I knew that was
how I felt about my brother, and Bryce probably felt
the same. Judging from what I had learned about him
in this short time, it seemed that he was the protective
type.

It would also kill me if I didn't know where my
brother was. I didn't even think I would be able to
function. It brought me back to when my brother was
in jail. I was so stressed, I couldn't eat or sleep until
he was back home, safe with me. Despite all the hate I
initially felt for Bryce, my empathy for him warmed my
icy heart a little bit and it made me not see him as such
a bad guy. I still didn't like his ass though. And the attraction was just that. He was an attractive man. That
was all. Someone more handsome than my husband.

"Giselle, I got some business that can't wait. I will be
gone for about four days. I'm leaving you here with my
brother. Don't try no stupid shit, or I will be on your ass
when I come back," he threatened.

I ignored him and crawled under my covers.

He walked over to the bed and sat down on it. I wondered why but ignored him. When he wouldn't leave,
after a few seconds I asked, "Don't you have a crazy
girlfriend to go bother?" I wanted to kick myself in the
ass for saying that shit. I was showing what I felt—jealous about another woman saying he belonged to her.
Why the fuck did I even care?

"She was never my woman. Just some chick I fucked
with from time to time, when I wanted to hit on something. But after what she did, I had to let her ass go. She
was bad for business. Why you care?"

Yes, Giselle. Why do you care? I asked myself silently.

"You trying to be my girl, Giselle? Fulfill all my needs
and shit?"

"Fuck no!"

That made him laugh. During all these weeks, I had never heard him laugh before. It softened up his face some, seemed to relax his body. He looked even more handsome. There was alcohol on his breath. So I guessed he was being nice because he was drunk.

Next thing I knew, his lips were on mine and he was kissing me. I was kissing him back. Our tongues battled with each other. I could now taste the liquor on his tongue. His fingers started playing with my nipples. I moaned against his mouth as they hardened. What the fuck was I doing, and what was I allowing him to do to me? *Something that felt good,* was the only reply I could give to myself. He stuck two fingers into my pussy and started finger banging the shit out of me. I moaned loudly as his mouth started licking my nipples. The rush of his mouth on my breasts and his fingers plunging in and out of my wetness were all too much for me to handle. Then I felt shock waves pulse through my feet and on up to my legs, until I felt myself convulsing.

That was how he left me. With more confusion and dread. I liked what Bryce was doing to me, even before I knew about my husband, and although I didn't want to admit it, I liked Bryce, too.

The four days that Bryce left me were not too bad, because of Angel. He didn't just bring my food to me. He played cards with me and even brought a TV, a DVD player, and DVDs for me to watch. He even brought a Wii for us to play. He was so sweet, it was hard for me to hate him. Actually, he reminded me of my little brother. He was only two years older than him. But the thing I couldn't understand was why Bryce had his brother selling drugs for him. So I got the courage up to ask him.

"Angel, you seem really smart, and you have a nice personality. You don't have to work for your brother. So why do you?"

He chuckled. "Okay. How can I explain this? Have you ever seen the movie *American Gangster* with Denzel Washington?"

I thought back and remembered seeing it. "Yeah. I saw it."

"Do you remember T.I.'s part? He was a baseball player. His uncle had enough pull that he could have gone to the leagues and played. But in the end he decided against it because he wanted to be just like his uncle."

"But I'm sure any older brother who knows where selling drugs will lead you would be against their younger sibling selling it as well, so—"

"Plain and simple. If I didn't do it for my brother, I would do it for someone else, whether my brother approved or not. So why not have me do it for you and give you the opportunity to mentor and monitor me in the game?"

"I guess. I never thought about it like that." It made sense, though.

"To be honest, my brother doesn't know. I didn't want to tell him and he get his hopes all up and then I don't follow through. But I recently applied to go to school for aviation. I don't know. . . . I have always been interested in that. Being able to fly airplanes and shit. Imagine me, your boy from the hood, flying across the country. That would be some way-out shit."

I laughed. "I think that would be a good field for you to get into."

"Yeah?"

"Yes!" I slapped him on the arm gently. "Why question it?"

"I'm not. I'm just questioning myself. I tell you what. If I can get through the first month, I'll let Bryce know. I'm sure it will make him happy. He doesn't want me working for him or anyone else in the dope game, anyway. My mother"—he swatted his hand like there were flies present—"she don't care. But I'm sure my sister will be happy." His face looked a little sad when he mentioned his sister.

"I hope you find her."

He offered a smile. "I hope so, too. Sometimes I wonder if we had just ignored her wants and forced her to stay with one of us, would she be gone?"

"What do you mean?"

"My little sister was staying with our mother, and, well, all she cares about is getting high. So that gave my sister the opportunity to get caught up with the wrong crowd. And thus with your husband. But she is so attached to our mama and was always feeling like she had to stay around her to take care of her. But I guess that's a typical kid. When I was that age, I felt that I had to protect my mother, too. But while I was protecting her, all she kept doing was letting me down, and eventually I gave up. My brother and I always made sure Bri had everything she needed. I can't help but feel that I should have forced her to come stay with me. I could have kept a better eye on her."

"Kids disappear all the time. No matter how good or bad the parents are, there is always that risk. From the hood to the suburbs. You know that. So please don't beat yourself up for that. It wasn't your fault. When a kid wants to do something, they are going to find a way to, and parents, grandparents, and yes, big brothers can't do anything to stop them." I hoped what I was saying was helping. He had to stop blaming himself, and if he didn't want to stop doing that, he needed to forgive himself.

He gave me a soft smile. "Thanks, Giselle. For having a fucked-up hubby, you are not half bad."

I laughed. "Anyhow, I hope to be on a plane you fly one of these days."

"Really, you would put your life in my hands?"

"Yeah. Why not?"

He chuckled. "Yeah. I'm going to start. For some strange reason, you gave me all the motivation I need."

"When is school?"

"Two weeks."

"You better go."

He chuckled and said, "Let's get into this Wii."

I laughed with him and stood as he switched the game on.

The day that Bryce was supposed to come back, Angel got an urgent call. He didn't tell me what it was about but said that he needed to hit a corner. He called up his homeboy named Bear and asked him to stay in the house until Bryce came back.

I understood why Bear was called that. He was big, black, hairy, and sweaty. But since he was Angel's friend, I figured I'd be okay. And if I wasn't? What could I do about it? I had no phones to call anyone. I was still their prisoner, or maybe a casualty of war.

Bear was also a little strange. What made me uncomfortable about him was the fact that he would not leave the room right away. He brought me food and water, and he would linger for a minute, watching me. And I didn't like the way he looked at me. When he stopped in to bring me dinner, he stood near the door, watching me while I ate. But it was more like he was watching my body parts. Why would Angel leave me with someone like him?

I rolled my eyes and concentrated on the club sandwich I was eating. The sandwich dropped out of my hands when he turned around and I saw he had his dick out.

I jumped off the bed as if I had been burnt and backed into the wall, away from him. "What are you doing?"

He came walking toward me, blocking me into a corner. Then, out of nowhere, he slapped the shit out of me. I screamed as heat rushed to my face. He started tearing off my dress, and before long I was nude in front of him.

My heart started speeding up, because I knew he was going to rape me. With Bryce being gone, he was going to be successful. Images of being in that house with that crazy girl, Ponce, E, and JB flashed before me. I was going to get violated again. Although I was scared of this man, I knew I had to try to do something about it.

I tried to fight him off but was unsuccessful. I closed my eyes as he rubbed his hands all over my naked body.

"If you tell him, bitch, I will kill you! You ain't shit. Just a fucking prisoner. Angel told me all about you." He shoved me down to the floor and straddled me with his big body.

I thought quickly. I had to find some way of distracting him. "Wait, Bear. Slow down. Don't you want your dick sucked?"

He froze and smiled. "Yeah."

With a shaky voice I said, "Well, get up so I can do it already. Do it to you good."

He got off me, walked to the edge of the bed, and sat on it. I followed him and dropped on my knees in front of him.

"Just close your eyes and relax," I said, trying not to sound nervous with each word. But I was. I was scared shitless. I didn't really know Angel or Bryce, and I definitely didn't know Bear. So I was even more fearful of what he would do to me.

I rubbed my hand along his dick. I checked to make sure his eyes were closed before I stood quickly, pulled one of my legs back, and kneed him in his balls with all my strength.

He howled in pain and rolled onto the floor.

I stood to my feet and ran into the bathroom.

"You bitch! I'm going to kill you!"

I locked the door and frantically looked around for a weapon. But there was none. I jumped when he started kicking on the door over and over again, until the wood cracked. I stood nervously as the door gave way and he rushed inside.

"Bitch!" He slapped me again, and before I could recover from the blow, he threw me into the shower door with all his might.

The glass exploded, and I fell into the tub, landing on pieces of broken glass. I winced from the pain as a few pieces pierced my flesh. I slid my fingers along the tub, feeling for a wide, sharp piece. Once I felt one, I curled my fingers around it.

"I'm getting that pussy. And if you tell anybody, I will come back and fucking kill you!"

He kicked the remaining glass out of the shower door. Then he pulled me by my hair out of the tub to the floor. More pieces of the broken glass cut into my skin. I ignored the pain and the blood.

He straddled me again and forced my legs open.

As I continued to fight him with one hand, while I had the piece of glass hidden in the other, I begged, "Please don't do this. Please let me go."

It was like he snapped. "Bitch, you think you're too good for me?" He started strangling me. I struggled underneath him, but he used all his man power to choke me. And he wouldn't stop. The pressure on my neck was so tight, he was cutting off my windpipe. He repeated, "Bitch, you think you too good for me! I'm sick of bitches like you turning me down."

When he refused to release his hold and I felt myself getting weak, I took the glass and plunged it into his neck with all my might.

His skin broke easily, and the glass went right in. He froze. I pulled it out and stabbed him again with it. I stabbed him over and over again. Blood started coming out of the gash and out of his mouth. But I kept on stabbing him relentlessly. His body collapsed. His entire weight fell on me, and he went limp.

I screamed and kept stabbing him. That was when I saw someone rush into the bathroom. It was Bryce, with a gun drawn and pointed at me.

He took one look at my naked body, then at Bear, and gasped. There was blood all over me, and I knew Bear was dead.

Chapter 13

Bryce rushed forward and yanked the piece of glass out of my hand. He then pulled me up and away from Bear.

The sight of Bryce caused my heart to beat at a more normal pace.

"He tried to rape me," I whispered. I sobbed, my head buried in his shoulder.

I had just killed someone. I closed my eyes as tears slid down my face. The realization of what I had just done would change me forever. I knew I would never be the same. I wondered what would happen to me now. Would I go to prison for this? I knew how police were to rape victims, based on stuff I had seen on TV. They treated rape victims like they were the criminals. How much better would they treat a woman who was trying to stop a man from raping her and ended up killing him—even though she was never raped? And look how many times I stabbed him to make sure he was dead. Would they feel that I should have stabbed him only once or twice so that I could get away or that I didn't have to end his life? *Damn*. They would lock me up.

These thoughts that were flying through my head were torture. Thoughts of whether they would or would not lock me up, and whether I got away with this without anyone knowing? How would I be able to live with myself, knowing that I had killed someone? I had always been pure, gentle, calm, sweet, and pliant. Now I was a murderer. But I had to remind myself that I didn't know Bear at all, and if I hadn't killed Bear, he would have killed me. Still, I couldn't get the image of me stabbing him in his neck out of my head.

Bryce carried me to the bed. He sat me on it gently, pulled out his cell, and started dialing someone's number. "Where the fuck you at? I told you not to fucking leave!" He paused. "Look. I got a situation I need you to attend to. Call Hog!" He sat the phone on top of the dresser.

All I saw was the image of Bear's face as death took over. I covered my face with my hands and felt the wetness of Bear's blood. I felt even more sick.

Fifteen minutes later someone was banging on the door downstairs. Bryce left the bedroom, and I could hear him running down the steps. A minute later I could hear voices and running up the stairs.

One of them was Angel, with a guilty look on his face, and there was some other guy I had never seen before. But I assumed he was Hog. I guessed that Bryce had really fired the three guys that he had had kidnap me.

"Where is he?" Angel asked. He passed a look my way, then turned his attention back to his brother.

"In the bathroom," Bryce told him.

They rushed past us. Bryce stood to his feet and carried me out of the room.

Bear's voice came back into my head. *You think you too good for me!* I saw Bear's face again as he choked me. I closed my eyes and started crying again.

Bryce held me tighter to his chest. The feel of his chest against mine comforted me. I wrapped my arms around him. "Please don't leave me again. Please," I begged.

"I'm not."

I took a breath and continued to cry as more flashbacks came.

He carried me to another bedroom, walked inside, and laid me on the bed. I didn't mind now. I saw him stand and go through another doorway in the bedroom. When I heard water running, I assumed it was the bathroom.

I nodded and buried my head in the pillow, the tears still falling. When I closed my eyes, I saw Bear's face again.

Bryce came back into the room. He lifted me again in his arms and carried me to the bathroom. For some reason, when he was near, I felt a lot safer. Once there, he sat me down and turned the running water off. He helped me out of my clothes, tested the water with his hand, and told me, "Get in."

I obeyed.

Bryce kneeled near the tub, took a washcloth, and started washing me with it. I allowed him to bathe me. I knew that I was just too shaken up to do it myself, to get the blood off of me. I kept my eyes closed as the cloth was pressed against my face to clean off the blood that had leaked from Bear's body. I was so scared about what would happen to me now. And who was his family? Despite the fact that he had tried to hurt me, I couldn't help but wonder how his loved ones would feel about him being dead.

Bryce took a deep breath and said, "Giselle, his body is gone. That's over and done with. The best thing to do is to try to put this behind you. Angel was not supposed to leave. And dude, he saw an opportunity and he took it. Angel left to bail my mom out of jail."

I nodded my head. He was right about that part. The guy saw an opportunity and tried to overpower me and take it. But inside I didn't think that I would be able to put it behind me. I had killed a man. All these things that had happened to me just seemed a little too difficult to just put behind me. Bear had terrified me so much that I had murdered him. What should I have done? Although the murder was going to affect me for a long time, I knew I had made the right decision. I hadn't tried to kill him. I was fighting for my own life. I was protecting myself.

"You can stay in my room with me tonight."

That was a relief. I didn't want to go back to the room where it had happened. It would be like reliving it all over again.

After a few more minutes, Bryce rinsed the soap off of me. He helped me stand and held out a towel for me to step into. He wrapped it around me, and I followed him into the bedroom. I let him dry me off and help me into a long, crisp white T-shirt. For once, I cared less about the fact that I was naked in front of Bryce. I didn't want him to leave me alone at all. He made me feel safe and comforted. I didn't want that feeling to go away, even if it had to do with a man I had once hated. Once he was done, he pulled back the covers on the bed and allowed me to slip underneath them.

He went into the bathroom again and came back with a paper cup filled with water and a pill. He sat down next to me. "Take this. It will help you sleep."

Bryce didn't seem like the bad person that I initially thought he was, and right now he was being so gentle and caring toward me. So I had no reason to think the pill was anything other than what he said it was. Easily, I accepted the pill, tossing it down my throat and swallowing the water in the paper cup before giving it back to him.

When Bryce stood, panic rose in me. I did not want to be left alone. So I protested, "No! Please don't leave."

"I'm not." He put the cup down on a nearby nightstand. Then he lay down next to me on the bed.

I knew that a part of me hated Bryce for kidnapping
me, but another part of me hated him for exposing
the truth about my husband, a truth that had caused
me to question our whole marriage and realize that
it was one big-ass lie. For a brief moment after Bryce
showed me the DVD and I talked to Percy at the park,
I had wished that I didn't know anything. I had wished
that the facade of my life hadn't been torn down and I
wasn't aware of the truth. I mean, back then life was so
perfect. I guessed I'd been lost in all the materialistic
things and all the stuff my husband told me and did for
me. I had thought I would live out the rest of my life in
bliss, with my husband and his money. And now . . . my
future was in question. Everything was just a mess in
my life.

But just as I had to admit that my husband was horrible, I also had to admit that Bryce wasn't as bad as I
thought he was. He was showing me that he wasn't a
monster; he had a heart. From the start he had stopped
his goons from raping me. Then, when he got me, he
could have done everything from torturing me to raping me or beating me. But he did none of that. And now
he was taking care of me, and I was someone that he
hated, despised. Although I had plenty of reasons to
feel differently about him, he had no real reasons not
to still despise me. And I still didn't know what Bryce
had in store for me. But in that moment I welcomed his
arms wrapped around me. By Bryce being there and
not leaving my side, I felt I was safe from anyone else
trying to violate or hurt me. At least I hoped. I didn't
know what other surprises were in store for me.

The next morning I kicked the covers off me and
rolled over onto my back. I blinked a couple times before finally noticing Bryce standing over the bed.

"Morning," he said in a husky voice.

He had never said "Morning" to me before. *He must be warming up to me a little bit,* I thought.

"Hi. How long have I been asleep?"

"Almost two days."

"Wow. Doesn't seem like it."

"There are clothes for you on the nightstand. Get dressed, and I will get you out of this house."

I nodded and stood to my feet. "Where are you taking me? Is something going on?"

Memories of what had happened with Bear flooded my thoughts. I definitely didn't feel as paranoid as I was before, but it was still in the back of my head. I shook my head and tried to focus on something else.

"I was thinking you may want to get some air. And I figured that now you would probably act like you got some sense and would not try to get away."

The thought of getting fresh air sounded good, so I agreed.

The drive was superlong and seemed never ending. But it was a relief to be out of the house. He exited the 5 on Lake Hughes Road, stopped at McDonald's, and grabbed us some food. Then we ended up at Castaic Lake. Bryce allowed me to get out of the car and sit on a nearby bench with him.

"You ever been out this way before?" he asked me after stuffing his last french fry in his mouth. I was surprised. This was the first time he had tried to engage in a conversation with me since he had kidnapped me.

I took a sip of my Coke before saying, "Yeah. My father took my brother and me here once when we were smaller."

"Did y'all do a lot of things together?"

"Not too much." I took another sip of my soda. "My parents were workaholics. They always had this notion of building a foundation. They worked their asses off to provide my brother and me. It just sucks how things panned out."

"Why do you say that?"

"My life is supposed to be different. I'm supposed to be a college graduate by now. My brother should be one as well. It's the way it was supposed to be. That is what my parents always wanted. They sacrificed their whole life for that. But when things went bad and my father passed and my mother just couldn't hold it together. My brother and I were really stuck. Then my mother killed herself."

He looked surprised when I said that.

"But with my husband, things were different. I always felt he represented that security blanket. His foundation was vast. My future and my brother's future were set the day I became his wife. My worries were over. I had more money than I could ever imagine needing and wanting. Up until meeting you and discovering what I discovered, I never felt a need to question the life I had with my husband. Or the way he acquired his wealth. I never felt a reason to be concerned. And you're right about what you said about me. How you felt that I was a stuck-up bitch. You were right. I had no right to look down on you, Bryce. After what my husband did to your sister, I'm surprised you haven't done that to me by now."

"I may be a lot of things, but I'm not a rapist or even a woman beater. I'm not a violent man at all, unless I have to be. But sometimes in life, circumstances cause you to act out of character."

He was right about that. It took me back to murdering Bear. I never would have known that I had it in me to do something like that. I didn't want to discuss it, though, or think about it. So I said, "But what about your life? What made you follow the path you followed?"

"Look, just so we're clear, the shit I do, I don't like it. In fact I hate it. And there is some truth to you saying that I'm committing genocide. But in my defense, this is the only life I have ever known. Imagine your father getting arrested, and you, at the age of ten, have to bag up a brick of cocaine, put it in your backpack, and ride it over to your father's homeboy's house. That was the only life I knew. To take care of my brother and my little sister while my father was locked down, I had to take over the business. I was doing something I didn't want to do but had to do.

"What made the situation worse, hell on earth, was when my mother succumbed to the same thing I was pushing for my father. So then I realized that I was the only person in our household strong enough to hold us down. I stopped going to school and sold drugs to support my family and to support my mother's addiction, so she didn't have to be out there selling her body. I couldn't bear to see that." He took a deep breath. "So if there's anybody more ashamed about what I'm doing, believe me when I say it's me. I don't glorify shit about the dope game."

So he had a conscience. He wasn't one of those big-time drug dealers doing it for the money, hoes, clothes, or the lifestyle. It made me respect him more. I also understood how he felt about having to be the backbone of his family. That was what I became when my father died.

"So we relate on something," I observed.

"What's that?"

"We were the source and support for both our families. The one everybody else depended on."

"You could say that." He nodded.

"Is your father still alive?"

"No. He died in prison. He was killed in a riot."

I gasped, in shock. "What about your mother?"

"She is a fully functioning drug addict. Meaning she can't function without it. Matter of fact, Brianna was born addicted to crack. We don't know who her father is. But somehow, she turned out okay."

Damn. We had more in common than I thought. He had lost his father as well. But it seemed that I really had mine and he never fully had his. It gave me a little peace with my father's death. Because all this time I had felt unsettled about it. I had felt he went too soon and that his death led to my mother's death, which had devastated me further. Bryce never really had his father. And while his mother was alive, she really wasn't, because of her addiction. Don't get me wrong. I still felt like I had two chunks of my heart missing. But nonetheless, his story made me feel a little better. Because I connected with him. He shared my pain.

"You know what, Bryce? You're an orphan, just like me."

He chuckled. "I never thought about it like that. But I guess I am. A twenty-nine-year-old orphan."

"You know what I think our problem is?"

"What?"

"My husband offered me stability. For years, I was afraid of not having something my parents gave me. But it's that same stability you found in drugs. And to be without it, probably even to this day—"

"Scares the shit out of me."

"Right."

Our eyes locked for a few seconds before he said, "Come on. Let's walk and talk further."

"Okay."

   We had more in common than I ever imagined. I felt like such a bitch for judging him and for how I'd looked down on him, like he was beneath me. Really he wasn't. In fact my husband was beneath him. Money didn't make my husband a better man than Bryce, and if I stripped the money away, what good could I possibly find in my husband given what I now knew? God would probably be more forgiving to Bryce than he would be to my husband.

   I hoped Bryce would stay with me again tonight, because I had not completely healed from the Bear situation. I needed Bryce by my side.

Chapter 14

For the next few days, Bryce was kind enough to let me out of his house, and take me out somewhere. Most of the places were remote, but nonetheless I appreciated it. A couple of times, he took me along with him when he went to visit his little brother, whom I had grown to like so much.

Right after the incident with Bear, Angel came over with lobster tails, which he threw on the portable George Foreman Grill he had in the kitchen. He apologized to me over and over about the incident.

"You didn't know he was going to do what he did, right?" I asked him.

"Right. I swear."

"Well, then it is okay. Yeah, it still bothers me, but I will be able to push past it eventually. And whatever is left of it, hey, I will just find a way to deal with it. 'Cause from the way my future looks and the things that I have discovered, there is going to be a lot more stuff coming my way that I am going to have to deal with."

"I like the way you think, Giselle," he said, flipping over the lobster tails. "Damn, I wish things were different and you—"

"Boy, don't even try it!"

"I was going to say you and my brother could have hooked up." He changed his tone so he sounded nerdy. "Damn. What kind of a guy do you think I am?"

I laughed. "Your brother and I are from two different worlds. Our meeting is simply by circumstance."

"Yeah, but you two connect on some shit. He told me. And I'm over here enough to see the way he looks at you, and you be looking at him back on the low. I'm good at reading body language."

I laughed it off. But I was thinking about how Bryce had talked to Angel about what we discussed. Made me feel like I was on Bryce's mind. But not in a bad way.

"Look at you blushing."

I laughed again. I really liked Angel. It sucked that he, his brother, and his sister were born into the predicament that they were born into. And I really hoped he did what he said he was going to do, go to aviation school.

"Giselle, go look in the bottom cabinet," he whispered.

"Okay." I pulled the cabinet door open and saw a birthday cake. I peered closer at it and saw Bryce's name on it. "Today is his birthday?"

"Yeah. And that's why if you try to do something dumb, like escape, you going to ruin what I got planned."

I laughed at that.

I knew that no matter how cool Angel was, I would not be able to get away from him, so I didn't bother. I was trying to make the best of my situation. And Bryce had already told me that if I did anything stupid, I would be tied to the bed again, with a gag in my mouth. He was cool, but he was still sticking to his plan. He didn't talk too much about it to me, but I knew he was still using me as a ploy to get his sister back. I understood and respected it. I didn't want to test the waters. And I was happy to get out of the room, so why not? That did not mean I was happy with still being held here. I didn't want to be a prisoner of anyone, and that included my husband. But I had no say in this ordeal. I just prayed that Brianna would be found and Bryce would let me go, so I could make my own decision about where I would go. I knew it wouldn't be back to my husband.

Angel went on. "What you think the lobster tails are for? That nigga loves them. He don't like celebrating it, though. Our little sister, Bri, would always make him a cake and sing 'Happy Birthday' to him, whether he wanted her to or not. She started making them out of her Easy-Bake Oven. Then she learned how to cook them in a real oven." He chuckled. "That girl loved to cook. She started watching the Food Network and trying to make shit off of there. That Paula Deen and that couple that cooks together. She said she wanted to open up her own bakery when she finished up school."

His lips twitched for a second before he added, "So, anyway, year after year she would always make my brother and me a birthday cake. She said we had to have one every year." He chuckled sadly. "So I couldn't stop her tradition, even if I had to bring a store-bought one. Even if it meant she wouldn't be here."

"When is this stuff going to be done?" Bryce asked, walking into the kitchen, interrupting the conversation.

I closed the door to the cabinet quickly.

"Giselle, how that potato salad looking?" Angel asked.

I had made the sides, potato salad and corn on the cob. I didn't mind doing it. I checked the corn, which was boiling in the pot. "Let me pull the corn out, and we're good."

Bryce looked surprised to see me so at peace with what I was doing. But I liked Angel. Really I did. He took my mind off current things. Things my mind needed to be off of.

I pulled the corn out of the pot and placed it on a plate, while Angel put the lobster tails on the table. I handed him the corn and then pulled the potato salad out of the fridge, like I was at home.

"I didn't think you could boil water, as pampered as you seem to be," Bryce told me.

"I haven't been rich all my life. When I lived with my parents, I did most of the cooking," I replied. I locked eyes with Bryce and saw his approval.

"As far as I'm concerned, that shit's unheard of. All the broads I run into want to be taken out and get an attitude if I ask their ass so much as to make a sandwich, man. So Giselle got a plus from me," Angel said.

Bryce didn't respond to his brother. He just continued to stare at me.

When we sat down to eat, I laughed at Angel. He and I could not get enough of the lobster tails, and we both went through six of them on our own.

I was surprised to see Bryce sample the potato salad and corn.

"How is it?" I asked him.

"Good, bab—" Bryce cleared his throat before he got the full word out. "Pretty good," he said, correcting himself.

I looked down at my lap. It sounded good to hear him call me that, even if only halfway. It was funny how at first I was every bitch in the book. Now he had to stop himself from calling me "baby." Like he couldn't let on that his view of me, as well as his feelings, were changing. But I knew they had, because mine had.

When I looked at Angel, he looked surprised, too. He glanced from me to Bryce, with an amused look on his face.

"Well, I'm glad you like everything," I said.

"Thank you," Bryce said gruffly.

Once we were all stuffed, Angel got up and pulled the cake out of the cabinet. As he did, he said, "Aye, I ain't got no candles, dawg, but you can blow the fire out from the pilot on the stove."

Bryce chuckled. But the moment Angel put the cake in front of Bryce, his eyes got watery. And before Angel and I could even sing "Happy Birthday," Bryce pushed his chair back and left the kitchen.

When Angel was going to take me back to my room and lock me in, I asked him if he would allow me to go to Bryce's room. He looked like he was against the idea, but I told him, "Come on. I'm not going to try to get away. You can walk me there if you don't trust me."

A few seconds later we stood in front of Bryce's door. Angel gave a couple knocks on the door and then barged inside. I followed behind him. Bryce was playing Lil Wayne. I saw that Bryce was seated on his bed, with a huge notepad in his hand and what looked like a piece of black chalk. He was wearing the jeans he had on earlier with a black wife beater.

He looked up at Angel; then his eyes went to me. They lingered on me for a moment before he turned to his brother and asked, "What's up?"

"She asked me to bring her up here." Angel left the room, leaving Bryce and me alone.

Bryce looked surprised. He leaned over and picked up a Heineken off the floor, then took a swig of it and put it back down.

"Uh, what are you doing with that?" I asked him.

"Just messing around, doing some sketches. It's just something I mess around with from time to time. I been doing it since I was a kid."

I walked farther into the room. I sat down on the bed next to him. "Can I see them?"

He handed me the notepad. I went through all the pages, which had various sketches. There was a sketch of a hand, a sketch of a baby, and there was one sketch of Bryce's brother. The one that impressed me the most was the sketch of this high-rise with a beautiful sunset in the background.

"Wow. These are really nice, Bryce."

"Yeah. My mother used to sketch. She is a lot more talented than I am."

How sad, I thought. Because judging from the sketches, if she was better than he was, she was a pure waste of talent. Because Bryce was good.

"You need to share this with the world!"

He chuckled at my enthusiasm.

"You're laughing, but I'm serious."

"When I was younger, I thought about going to college and one day owning my own art studio. But it never really materialized, because I dropped out of school. I never really gave it any more thought after that."

I didn't want to preach to him about how he shouldn't give up on his goals, because truthfully, I gave up mine when the opportunity presented itself for me to accomplish them. And besides, he probably wouldn't listen to me. So instead I asked him, at the risk of him shooting the idea down, "Could you sketch me? Just my face."

He didn't respond, just flipped to a blank page and grabbed another piece of black chalk out of the box sitting on his bed. I positioned myself so that I was facing him. He stared at me intently and then looked at the page as he sketched. His stares caused me to fidget on the bed. "Stop moving," he told me.

"Sorry." I tried to stay still.

A couple minutes later, he put down the chalk and turned the notepad my way.

Wow. I had a drawing of myself done for Giovanni. It was done by a so-called professional artist, who drew for a living and charged thousands of dollars. But Bryce's sketch was just as good as that one. And I didn't have on all the makeup I usually wore or the fancy clothes and jewelry. It was just me, and he was still able to capture just as much beauty.

"This is really pretty."

"Ain't hard to make it pretty."

"What do you mean?"

"Come on. You know you're fine. I'm sure you have heard that before. All I did was capture you. Draw what I saw. Beauty."

I had. My husband had always told me I was, and he was always getting praised by his friends for having such a "beautiful wife." But I blushed upon hearing that from Bryce. To have approval for something felt good, coming from Bryce.

"Would it be okay if I kept it?"

"Yeah." He tore the page out and handed it to me.

I took it out of his hands looked at it again and folded it in half.

He downed the last of his beer and studied me. I watched his eyes scan my whole body before coming back to my face. "You are not what I thought you were."

My eyes narrowed. "What do you mean?"

"These past couple months I have come to understand you to be something different than what I assumed at first. You ain't that person. What I mean is, I see why your husband fell in love with you. It don't seem like it's hard. I'm not saying I'm in love with you, so don't think that," he said quickly. "You sweet, without a doubt. You seem pure. You have a heart. And I think you are honest. You seem like an overall good woman who chose the wrong man to share her life with. That's the only spot you seemed to go wrong in."

I was shocked that Bryce saw all those things in me. I was glad that he did. Because if anything, I wanted him to believe me when I said I had no idea what my husband was doing. And he was right. My husband was where I went wrong in my life.

"I'm glad you feel I'm trustworthy, Bryce. Because I want you to know that I swear I would never be with a man who would do something like that to an innocent child. I swear to you I would . . ." My voice cracked and I had gotten teary-eyed, so I stopped talking. At first, I was confused by my sudden emotion. Then I realized my emotion came from the fact that I now knew Bryce and Angel and I liked them both, and what they were going through was hard. To not know where their little sister was? To see her treated so inhumanely? Rethinking it made me cry. I felt bad before, but now it was at a different level, because I now cared for both of them. It was like their pain was mine, like she was my family.

Bryce saw it. He looked like he wanted to touch me for comfort. But he fought it and simply looked away.

I wiped the tears in the corners of my eyes.

"I think I said too much." He stood and stretched. "Come on. I'm going to take you to your room."

I stood and walked after him out of his room. Once we got to mine, Bryce hesitated in the doorway. He had his arms stretched out and was holding on to the top of the door frame, flexing his muscles in his arms.

I placed the drawing on the nightstand and sat on the bed, watching him.

"I may take you out tomorrow. To get some air, if you act right."

"Okay. Thank you." I pulled the covers back and slipped underneath them.

Bryce was still standing in the doorway.

I closed my eyes, and it seemed like five minutes passed before he flicked off the lights, closed and locked the door.

The next day, Bryce decided to take me to one of his small houses in Chino so I could go swimming. When we got to the pool, Bryce walked over to a table and dialed a number on his cell phone.

I asked him, "How am I supposed to swim without a bathing suit?"

"Improvise, little girl," was what he said before going back to his call.

"Improvise with what?"

He put his hand over the phone. "I don't have time to go back and forth with you. Either you are going to get in that shit or you not."

I sucked my teeth and pulled my dress over my head. I jumped in the pool in my underwear and bra. I swam around the pool while Bryce continued with his phone call. A few minutes later, he ended his call, turned his attention to me, put his phone on the table, and walked toward the pool. He kneeled down and dipped his hand in the water a few inches from me.

"How is it this pool is supposed to be heated?" he mumbled.

Quickly, I grabbed him by his collar and pulled him, and he lost his footing and fell forward.

"Shit!"

I laughed as he took the plunge into the pool, getting soaking wet.

"You play too fucking much."

I swam away quickly as he came after me. When he caught me, he dunked my head under the water. I managed to escape, bobbing my body in and out of the water, laughing. When I tried to evade him again, he caught me and hemmed me up against the wall of the pool. He put his lips to mine and started kissing me.

It was a long, passionate kiss, too. When he invaded my insides with his tongue and I liked it. I was really getting into it and was playing with his tongue with my tongue.

Bryce broke the kiss by pulling away and asked, "What are we doing?"

I shrugged. I was attracted to and felt this connection to the man who had abducted me. I knew deep down he had a conscience. I knew deep down he cared when others were hurt. He wasn't the bad guy. My husband was. To me, the bad Bryce did was based on necessity and circumstance. No matter how mean he was to me at first, the good in him showed through. And I liked him more than I cared to admit at first. The "like" was getting deeper day by day. And I found myself antsy late at night, when he locked me in my room, and I got up extra early, waiting for him to return.

"This is not supposed to be like this," he said.

"Like what?" I asked breathlessly.

"You are the wife of the man I want to kill. I'm supposed to hate you, hurt you any way that I can." He kissed my lips again and lowered his voice so it was husky. Giving me a stirring down below. "But all I want to do is make you feel good. I want to do this" He kissed me on my neck. "And this." His lips trailed down to my breasts. He then whispered in my ear, "I want to lick you here." He placed a hand over my pussy.

I moaned, wanting him to touch me underneath my panties.

I felt the same way he felt. All he wanted to do, I wanted him to do to me. I knew Bryce was the man that tore away the facade of my life. But had he never done that, I would still be living that facade, not knowing it was a facade, and I would still be happy with my husband. I would probably be shopping for clothes, jewelry, and lingerie, waiting for my husband to spend his quality time with me, totally oblivious to the fact that he was a monster. Never in my marriage did I have the urge or desire to lie with another man. But I wanted Bryce. I wanted him to touch me in all the spots he wanted to. The reality of that made me feel a mixture of emotions I didn't quite know how to handle. Bryce made me feel so good. But I knew, despite the situation my husband was in, that it was wrong. I was married for the time being. But that didn't stop me from letting Bryce put his lips on mine again for another kiss.

It was a kiss that was so deep, it seemed like our tongues were battling with each other to see who could explore the other's mouth better.

"I know how you feel. Bryce, it's not supposed to be this way. And those things you want to do to me, I swear to God I want you to."

Then I felt Bryce pull my panties down, spread my legs open to play with my pussy. I moaned deeply as he rubbed my clit.

His voice was husky in my ear. "I like you, Giselle."

I could no longer talk. I closed my eyes as the pleasure pulsated throughout my whole body.

Then his phone rang, putting a halt to all of that. *Damn.*

He pulled away from me and leaped out of the pool. I took a deep breath and pulled my underwear back up. Bryce snatched up his phone off the table and answered.

"What's up, Percy?" He paused and then said, "Give me an hour, and I will be there."

He turned back to the pool, looked at me, and said, "Let's go now."

"Now, I don't want to do this, but I need to make sure you stay put, and there is only one way to make sure of that. Yeah, you been cool lately, and I like you and think about you a whole lot more than I care to admit. But my obligation is to my sister first. So I gotta do this."

I frowned but nodded my head as he put the torn sheets around my wrists and ankles and tied them to the posts of his bed. I understood his position. He needed to get his sister back, and he had to be sure I didn't run off.

Still, I didn't want to be tied up again, so I tried to give him a pitiful look, but it didn't make a difference.

"I'll be back." Then he walked toward the door. I figured it had something to do with his sister. I hoped he found her safe and alive. I ignored the question that popped in my head. *Then what will happen to me?*

As he reached for the doorknob, I called his name. "Bryce?"

He turned around. "Yeah?"

"Ever since you told me, I have been praying for your sister's safe return. I hope you find her. I really do."

He smiled and said, "I hope so, too." Then he slipped out of the room.

Later that night, I heard the key turn in the door and someone come into the room. When the light was flicked on, I saw it was Bryce.

I blinked a few times before saying, "Bryce, did you find out where your sister . . ." My voice trailed off when I caught sight of the murderous look on his face. "What's wrong?"

Another man followed behind Bryce, fiddling with a phone. It was Angel. They both stood in front of the bed. I was surprised when Angel didn't say hi to me.

Coldly, Bryce spat, "Your husband murdered my sister."

I gasped. "What?" I instantly felt so bad for Bryce and his brother. I didn't know the sister, but my eyes started to get watery.

"Untie her!" Bryce shouted.

Angel quickly rushed forward and removed the torn sheets from my wrists and ankles. I lay there, confused, as Bryce pulled his shirt over his head and came toward me.

"Bryce?"

He yanked off his shoes and pants next.

Now knowing what he was going to do, I panicked and leaped off the bed. Bryce blocked me from moving and slapped me so hard, I screamed and flew back on the bed.

"Is it ready?" he asked his brother.

"Bryce, come on. Don't do this, man."

"Get it ready!" Bryce barked.

That was when I got it. He was going to rape me on video. The way his sister was raped. That was his revenge to my husband.

And the thought of it . . . It looked like Angel couldn't even stomach it. He looked away. Neither could I.

I tried to fight Bryce with my fists, beating them into his chest, but to no avail. He was able to open my legs and straddle me. "Bryce, stop!"

"Shut the fuck up! Aim it now, Angel!"

His brother pointed the phone at us.

"Angel, stop him. Bryce, please don't."

But he ignored me and rammed his dick into my pussy.

I screamed.

"Bryce, the battery is dying. It won't record. Man, let's just forge—"

"Get the fuck out, Angel!"

Angel left the room quickly.

I screamed at how rough it was, giving me no pleasure at all. He was unable to look me in my eyes. After a few strokes, he flipped me over onto my stomach. The worst fear crept up into me. He was going to rape me anally. I had never had anal sex before.

I begged him with my eyes and words. But it fell on deaf ears and cold eyes.

He plunged his dick into my butt with so much force, my head hit the headboard. I screamed and cried all at the same time from the tremendous pain. Bryce yanked my hair and rode my buttocks savagely. I sobbed into my arm and bit my lip from the pain.

After a few more thrusts, Bryce came inside of me. He then shoved me away and got off the bed.

I peeked out from under my forearms at Bryce's face.

He glared at me hatefully, despite the fear on my face, my shoulders racking with sobs, and the hot tears sliding from my eyes. He continued to glare at me like he hated me. And it hurt. All the gentleness he had been showing me was long gone. I was filled with shame over what he had done to me. He had brutally raped me.

Bryce walked to the door. He turned and gave me one more murderous look before exiting the room, leaving me there sobbing.

I remembered his words. *I may be a lot of things, but I'm not a rapist or even a woman beater. I'm not a violent man at all, unless I have to be. But sometimes in life, circumstances cause you to act out of character.*

And that was exactly what he had done.

Chapter 15

Bryce stayed away from me for several days after he raped me. Although I was sore during those days, I was able to heal. My feelings didn't, though. Not initially. I was hurt, embarrassed, and I felt ashamed. I had never experienced something like that from a man before, and I never wanted to again.

Bryce hired an older black woman to care for me during this time. And during this time Bryce was pretty much a ghost. If I were to make some sense of the situation, and if I were to be honest with myself, I would have to say that I understood Bryce's anger. Why he was so upset, even why he treated me as badly as he did. The reality that my husband was responsible for his sister's murder . . . Every time I thought about it, it made me sick to my stomach. I felt so stupid for marrying Giovanni. I hated Giovanni to no end.

It all made sense. This was why she never came back. She was killed. I wondered how she was killed. What she endured that night, aside from the rape Giovanni committed. I wondered why. Then I shuddered to know. I could only imagine his pain, Angel's, and hers. What would I do if someone killed my brother? I would probably want to die, too, but not before killing the person responsible for my brother's death. I also wanted to be there for Bryce. I didn't want him facing this alone. No one should be alone in a circumstance like this.

Which was why, as soon as the maid opened the door and said, "This will be my last day here with you . . ." I pushed past her before she could finish and ran out of the room—despite her yelling for me to stop—and straight into Bryce's room.

The door was slightly ajar. I barged inside without knocking.

I scanned the room for him. He was seated in the corner, on the floor, drinking from a Hennessy bottle. He was wearing a wife beater and a pair of jeans.

He looked up when he saw me and said nothing. I walked over and kneeled in front of him. He wouldn't look at me.

"Bryce."

"Get out of here," he growled in a low tone. I didn't let it affect me. I knew he was upset over his sister's death.

"I understand." I stepped closer.

He shoved me away.

I lost my balance and fell back. I regained my balance and repeated, "I understand."

"Get the fuck out!"

But I wouldn't. I knew why he was angry. And he was hurting. That was why he was lashing out. But I wasn't going to bend.

I tried to hug him. He pulled back, as if I had burnt him. But that didn't stop me. I pulled the bottle out of his hands, set it aside with tears in my eyes. I hugged him. His body felt rigid at first; then slowly it softened, and he let me embrace him.

"I'm sorry, Giselle," he said in a low tone. "I didn't mean to hurt you, baby—"

"It's okay. I understand, Bryce. I'm not mad. I understand!" My voice was shaky. The rape was his way of dealing with the pain of losing his sister. He was trying to inflict on me what had been inflicted on his sister, despite not wanting to. I knew deep down he didn't want to do me that way.

He held on to me and kept repeating, "I'm sorry, baby," and then he sobbed on my shoulder. I rocked him like he was my baby. I provided him with comforting words and kept rubbing his back until his sobbing stopped.

I pulled away and wiped the tears off his face. Then I kissed him on the lips with a sense of urgency and a need to feel his mouth on mine. He kissed me back, matching the intensity. He grabbed both of my breasts in his hands and squeezed them until my nipples hardened. I moaned against his mouth. He started licking them through my dress. I threw my head back in pleasure.

When I tried to lift my dress over my head, Bryce stopped me. "No, not after what I did to you."

I took my dress off anyway, and slid out of my underwear. "I want to give myself to you."

"But I hurt you."

"It's okay. I forgive you."

He gripped my thighs with his hands while I was sitting on his lap, then leaned down and started eating my pussy. I moaned loudly; and his tongue lapped up all my juices; and he kept slipping multiple fingers in and out of me, then rubbing against my clit.

When I was screaming in agony and couldn't take any more, he yanked down his pants and lifted me right on his big dick. I felt him inch by inch slide into me.

"Ahhh!" I moaned. The shit felt so good.

He gripped my hips with his hands and shoved me up and down on him all the way. His tongue bathed my breasts with his saliva. Then his lips met mine again.

I ground my thighs into his lap and continued to ride him, feeling incredible sensations brought on by his dick entering and exiting my pussy.

He pulled out shortly to eat my pussy again, and it drove me insane. "Fuck me again please!" I yelled.

He lifted me back into his lap, entered me again, and slowed the motions down. His eyes locked with mine. I couldn't look away. His face had a hooded expression, and he would not look away, either. I bit my bottom lip from the pleasure, and he gripped my waist and one of my breasts possessively, all the while continuing to look in my eyes.

"You gonna cum for me, baby?" He jerked in and out of me with a quick motion.

"Yes."

"Yes what?"

"Yes, Bryce," I said weakly.

"I'm gonna cum with you, baby." He speeded up the rhythm. I wanted to ride it out with him, so I wrapped my hands around his neck and held on as he jabbed me in quick spurts, so quick you could hear our thighs slapping against each other.

When I felt myself cumming, I let out a loud scream, and he bit down on one of my nipples, telling me that he was on the verge of cumming as well.

When I did come, it was a feeling unlike any other. It seemed that Bryce felt the same way.

Bryce collapsed on me, and we both fell to the floor. He held on to me, telling me silently that this was much more than what it was supposed to be.

I silently wiped away tears, because I knew my future was filled with so much fucking uncertainty. But for some reason, being a part of Bryce's world made the uncertainty worth it. There was no way I would ever go back to my husband, and I had no desire to leave Bryce's side, either.

***

I woke up to find myself in Bryce's bed. I moaned instantly when I felt someone licking me. I moaned even before I could get my eyes open. When I did open them, I saw the top of Bryce's head and his shoulders, as he was in the crook of my thighs, tasting me.

"Ooh. Shit." I gripped his head with my hands as he went to town. Didn't know what it was, but he was adding an extra something I had never had before.

He started prodding the inside of my pussy with his long, thick fingers. He leaned up and watched the ecstasy take over my face before he reached up and mounted me. I spread my thighs as wide as I could. He reached for my breasts and massaged them, as if he was trying to tease me by not touching my nipples. He dabbed his fingers with my tongue, then rubbed them along my nipples so they were as hard as rubies. He worked his dick inside me in a certain rhythm, where with each stroke I would get less, then more, driving me insane. I thrashed my head from side to side, feeling heat rush through my body.

"You cumming for Daddy?" he whispered.

"Yes."

He stuck his dick in to the hilt.

When we heard strange noises in the house, Bryce pulled out of me, stood to his feet, and quickly stepped into a pair of boxers. He snatched his gun out of the drawer.

I sat up in the bed nervously.

"Stay here."

He rushed out of the room.

I wondered who the intruders were and wondered if it could be my husband. I feared what he had in store for Bryce. I now did not want him to get hurt.

I waited a few seconds, got up, and yanked on one of Bryce's shirts. Then I snuck out of the room. I tiptoed toward the staircase and hid in a corner.

Bryce was on the middle step, with his gun pointed. I recognized his brother walking through the living room.

"Angel, what the fuck are you doing, popping up without calling? I could have shot you!" Bryce lowered the gun.

"I tried to call, but you not picking up your phone."

Bryce lowered the gun. "What is it?"

Angle paused near the bottom of the stairs. "I'm being followed."

My breath caught in my throat.

"By who?"

"I'm thinking her husband is finally on to us. I dumped my car and rode out here in another one, just in case they are still following me. But, Bryce, that ain't the worst part of it."

I took a deep breath and waited to hear what his brother was going to say.

"When I went to Mom's, she was gone. But her purse was there and her keys."

Someone knocked on the door. I jumped at the sound.

Bryce aimed his gun at the door.

"It's okay. That's probably my boy Pooh. He was waiting outside." Angel walked to the door.

Bryce lowered his gun again.

Before Angel could open the door, someone kicked it in, knocking Angel into the wall. I gasped as two men rushed inside the house with guns pointed and started firing rounds into the living room.

I ducked down, screaming.

Bryce looked back at me, then at his brother. "Angel! Get down!" Before returning fire.

But it was too late. Several bullets pierced his brother's chest. Angel flew back from the impact.

I watched, horrified, as Angel went down. I prayed he wasn't dead. But something about the force of those bullets told me that he was.

"Angel!" Bryce started busting shots at both the men as they scattered around the living room, trying to hide from his bullets.

Bullets were going everywhere. Busting out windows, knocking pictures off the walls. I covered my ears and tried to stay as low as I could. The gun smoke was making me choke.

One of the gunmen was hit by Bryce's bullets as he fired fiercely. He fell to the floor. The other one continued to shoot from behind a couch. I watched one bullet pierce the love seat that matched the couch and then fly toward the staircase, causing one of the wooden balusters in the staircase to explode.

Bryce backed up the steps, still firing. When he reached me, he pulled me up. "Come on!" We ran back toward Bryce's room. Bullets were still coming.

Once inside, still holding on to me, he rushed to one of his drawers and pulled out another gun. He then hid in the corner of the door. "Get behind me," he whispered. The door was slightly ajar.

Shots continued to be fired; then, suddenly, they stopped. Then we heard nothing. Then footsteps.

When he heard the footsteps, Bryce aimed his gun at the door and fired again. The shooter fired shots into the bedroom, hitting walls and busting out windows.

I kept my hand over my mouth and clutched Bryce's back in fear. I watched Bryce use the mirror on his dresser to see the position of the shooter. He was trying to hide outside the door. He was close, so close to both of us, and it scared me.

Bryce waited and allowed dude to fire more shots.

As soon as he poked his head in the door, Bryce aimed the gun at the door hinge and fired, hitting him directly in his skull. He fired four synchronized shots. The gunman froze. His head split open like a watermelon. And brains splattered everywhere. I looked away quickly. Bryce ran outside the room and rushed up to him. He fired several more shots into his chest.

He ran down the stairs. I followed him. He rushed up to his brother's body. I watched him hold his brother's dead body in his arms and saw his shoulders rack with sobs.

I thought quickly and rushed back up the stairs. I put on my dress and flip-flops, grabbed Bryce's clothes, shoes, keys, and wallet. I had to get him out of the house before more gunmen or maybe even the cops came.

"Bryce, come on!" I yelled. He didn't budge. I walked up to him and used my free hand to pull at him with all my strength, until he finally released his brother.

I helped him into his clothes and out of the house. But it was a struggle.

Chapter 16

We drove to San Diego and got a hotel room there.

Over and over again I replayed what had happened. Angel was now dead. *Like really?* All Bryce did was stare into space and say how this was all his fault. What made matters worse was the fact that my husband had sent a video to Bryce's phone with Bryce's mother on it.

It sickened me. And most of all, it showed me that my husband and Bryce were both at war. It made me hate my husband more than I already did, and hope that he died because of how dirty he was. No doubt about it. Despite all the riches and years of happiness my husband had provided me, I wanted no part of him. None at all. Easily and carelessly, he had taken two lives.

All I could do was try to provide comfort to Bryce and tell him that I wasn't going to leave his side. I meant it. While Bryce slept, I cried for Angel. Not only did I empathize with Bryce—because what would I do if my brother was killed?—I also had cared for Angel. He was so sweet, and he didn't deserve to lose his life. He just didn't. Now more than ever I was so confused and worried about this situation. And worried about what Bryce planned on doing about it.

After four days of staying in the hotel room, Bryce finally turned to me and told me, "Giselle, we need to talk."

"Okay."

He was silent for a moment. So I took the opportunity to ask him something I had been wanting to ask him since he found out his sister was dead.

"Bryce?"

"Yeah?"

"How did you find out that your sister was dead?"

"When I first found out my sister was missing, I made my mother fill out a missing person's report. I didn't think it would do shit, because there are so many missing people that are never found. And when they are found, they are found dead. I didn't want to face that. But it was the best thing to do. I couldn't *not* have my mother file the report, because I would have a hard time dealing with the outcome. I mean, we needed to know. We needed to exhaust all avenues. They bullshitted, though. Took their time. In the meantime, Percy was on it.

"Anyway, they called my mother and told her that they may have the body of my sister. The day I took you swimming, I went to see Percy and dropped by my mother's crib just to visit her. Imagine that shit. Then she told me the police had called her. Funny thing was, they had called her weeks ago to come and identify the body. But she was so high out of her mind that her only focus that day was getting another blast. Imagine that. Your own child could be dead, and getting high is more important to you than finding out. So during those weeks that passed, they performed an autopsy. That day when I went over there and my mother told me, I forced her to go with me to identify the body, praying it wasn't my little sister."

He took a deep breath. "It turns out it was her. She was beaten to death. Struck in the head so hard, she ended up having a seizure. . . . And, well, you saw the video. She was raped and sodomized. They gave her no medical attention. They found my sister's body in a fucking Dumpster at a park in Westwood. The mutha-fucka was so cocky about his shit, he didn't even bother to dump her body farther out. Like he knew no one would care and he wouldn't get caught." He shook his head. "They just threw her away. Like she was a piece of garbage." Tears slid down his cheeks. "I guess I should have known that I'm not powerful enough to battle your husband. And now they have my mother and my brother is dead." He covered his face with his hands.

"Bryce, you know what I was thinking? My husband is friends with the police chief, Hank Chisym. He has been over to our home so many times. We can go talk to him. Bryce, I know he will listen to me. We can take that DVD and have Hank search Giovanni's office for others." I thought back to that day I first met Giovanni, when I was in his office, and how he had locked his cabinet up. I just had to find a way to get his keys and find out what was in there. Percy had said that that was where he kept the other films. "After he sees what we saw, I know he won't hesitate to do something about it. Giovanni will spend the rest of his life locked up!"

He chuckled and shook his head. "Don't you think if I was going to go to the cops, I would have done that long ago? Giselle, I'm a street dude. I don't handle shit by going to the cops. And I don't know a real nigga that do."

I shook my head, confused. Giovanni had raped and murdered his sister, and I knew he was behind his brother's death, and he didn't want to go to the police? They had all the power Bryce needed to get the ulti-mate revenge on Giovanni. I tried to talk him into it. "Bryce—"

"Giselle, I'm not going to the police. I'm gonna han-dle this shit on my own."

"So you do plan on going after my husband alone?"

He refused to answer that question. "That's not what I need to talk to you about. And saying this shit is a lot harder than I thought it was going to be. But shit has gone too far."

I closed my eyes at his next words.

"Giselle, you have to go back."

I gasped. I couldn't go back to Giovanni. I didn't want to go back was because of what I knew now about my husband. How sick he was. I wanted no part of that lie anymore. Some other chick could have it. And it wasn't just that.

"I don't want to, Bryce."

"Why, Giselle?"

Did he really not know? What woman in her right mind would go back to someone like Giovanni, knowing what he had done? She would have to be as sick as he was to want to. Like Wingo's wife.

I swallowed. "With what I know he has done, I can't willingly be his wife. I don't want any parts of that man anymore. He is disgusting to me. And . . ."

"And what?"

I was scared to say what was on my heart. What if Bryce didn't feel the same way? What if he shot me down? I ignored those voices in my head and went for it. "I also don't want to be with him, because I . . . I want to be with you."

Bryce's eyes got wide, and he gave me a soft smile at my revelation. Then it was back to the severity of what we were going through.

"Bryce, don't send me back."

"That shit sound so good coming from your lips. Makes this harder, though. I don't want to send you back, baby. But I have to. This shit has to end. My brother is dead because of me. I can't have anyone else I care about on my conscience."

"But—"

"Listen. Your husband wants you back, and he ain't willing to stop the bloodshed until you are back with him."

I got choked up. Tears slid down my face.

"I understand why, Giselle. You make me actually want to do right. Other women I was with before I met you applauded me in my wrong and worshipped me for being this bad guy. The money, cars, and shit had them thinking I was the man, while inside I knew it was blood off others' backs. Made me feel like I wasn't shit. And I'm pretty sure that if you had truly known what your husband was doing, you would have had no part of him." He chuckled. "Here, I planned on doing whatever I could to you to hurt him through you, and I ended up falling for you."

He stroked my face and looked so sad. "And that kills me, because I want to see where this can go. I want to spend more time with you. Be your man. The way you used to speak on your husband with so much respect, love, and loyalty, I want to make you speak on me that way, Giselle, and really feel it. If the way we had met was different, we could have done all of that without a problem. But it wasn't. I have to send you back to him."

"Bryce, no! We can go away somewhere, both of us, and not ever come back here!"

"I can't leave my mother with him, Giselle. Baby, you gotta go."

"Well, I'm not going back!" I got up from the bed and tried to run away from him, but he caught me and pulled me into his arms.

He kissed my forehead and said, "Now, you are going to have to be strong. Here is the time. You can't be weak here, baby. Believe me when I say I don't want to do this. But your husband promised me a peace treaty.

He said that if he got you back, all the killing would stop."

I wiped my tears away and said, "When? When are you taking me back?"

He grabbed his phone and, without answering me, dialed a number, placing the call on speaker.

"Hello?" I instantly recognized Giovanni's voice.

"When you wanna do this?" Bryce asked.

"Let me speak to my wife!"

"No."

I placed a hand on one of Bryce's, letting him know it was okay. He passed me the phone.

"Hello?"

"Baby! Are you okay?"

"Yes, Giovanni, I'm okay. Bryce is going to bring me back to you. He agrees with your arrangement." I took a deep breath before continuing. "But I need you to make me a promise."

"Anything for you, baby. What is it?"

"Giovanni. I don't want any more bloodshed. No more people dead. You have to promise me that you won't try to kill Bryce when he brings me back to you. And don't hurt his mother, either."

"Awww, baby. All I want is to have you back home safe. If that happens and that is your wish, I promise you, Giselle, this will be over. He has my word. You have my word, baby. I love you."

I knew my husband was waiting for me to say "I love you" back. So I did. "I love you, too."

Bryce looked away.

"Baby, put him back on the phone," Giovanni said.

Bryce took the phone from me and said, "Meet me behind the Game. It's a bar on Manchester. Meet me there at four A.M. Don't bring no people, and I won't bring no people. Just bring my mother, and I will bring Giselle."

"Yeah, all right. You better have my wife or—"

"Or what?" Bryce countered.

There was a pause before I heard, "You just better have her."

I couldn't count the times I had made love to Bryce that night. It was too many to count. And it didn't make a difference, because he still woke me up at two o'clock in the morning for our trip back to Los Angeles to meet my husband. The car ride was super silent. Neither of us spoke. I wished so badly that he would just turn the car around. But I understood why he didn't and why he continued on. Giovanni had his mother. And Giovanni was unpredictable.

When Bryce made a left, I saw the bar he was speaking of, but instead of pulling into the parking structure near it, he drove farther down, where there was nothing but dirt and gravel, past two open gates. It was an abandoned space.

We sat in the car and waited.

"You okay?" Bryce asked me.

I nodded, trying my best to hold back my tears. I was not okay.

A few minutes later I saw my husband's Range Rover turn down the street. Bryce flicked the lights on his car. My husband paused in the street, then drove in our direction. He parked his car on the opposite side of us.

Bryce turned to me. I knew he wanted to kiss me. But I shook my head and kept back my tears.

"What do I do?" I asked him.

"Nothing. Just follow my lead."

Bryce slipped out of the car and walked over to my side. He opened my door and let me step out. He slipped something into my bra. Then he guided me by my arm to the front side of his car.

The headlights from both vehicles shone. Giovanni followed his lead. He clutched onto a woman, who I knew was Bryce's mother. She favored Bryce and his brother but also looked like a drug addict. There were bruises on her face, which I knew came from my husband. Jesus Christ, how could he put his hands on an older woman and inflict bruises? Then I felt stupid for even asking myself that. My husband was garbage—that was how he was able to do it.

The wind was blowing our clothes and hair. I watched Bryce nod to Giovanni. At the same time Giovanni released Bryce's mother, Bryce released me. I was expected to walk to Giovanni, and Bryce's mom was expected to walk to Bryce. His mother ran past me, sobbing. I turned back and watched her throw herself into Bryce's arms. I wished I could do the same and leave with him. It was so crazy, because two months ago this was a moment that I had begged and prayed God for, reuniting with my husband. And it was here, and now I didn't want it at all.

Once I reached my husband, he grabbed me in his arms. That was when I heard Bryce yell, "You know, losing my mom . . . it's almost worth it. To rid the world of a twisted mufucka like you."

My husband simply said, "You know one day real soon you will be seeing me again, young 'un." He then walked me to the passenger side of the car.

"I can't wait," was Bryce's reply.

I knew this was far from being over.

My husband closed the door on my side and got in on his side of the car.

Then we drove away. I couldn't stop the tears that rolled down my cheeks as I watched Bryce in the side-view mirror. He got smaller and smaller, and then . . . he was gone.

Chapter 17

"Listen, baby, I don't know what happened while you were gone. All I do know is that it haunted my thoughts day and night. And if you feel comfortable talking about it . . ."

I closed my eyes as I sat in the bathtub while my husband scrubbed my back. He wanted to discuss the stuff that had transpired. I did not. I didn't want to discuss anything with him.

He rubbed the washcloth in a circular motion around my back. It made my skin crawl to no end. "I understand if it is hard, but, baby, I have to know. They sent me videos. The first two I couldn't see, but I was able to see the one of a woman going down on you. Did he or anyone else?"

"No. I wasn't raped, if that's what you want to know," I lied.

I could feel some of the tension leave my husband's body as his hand relaxed on my back. He also took a deep breath.

"Did anyone touch you in any way?"

"No. I wasn't touched in the way you are speaking of. Only what you saw on the video." I tried to keep my voice steady as to not let on the truth. I had definitely been touched, and I had encouraged a lot of the touching Bryce had done, because I wanted it just as much as he wanted it.

A few minutes later, after Giovanni rinsed the soap off of me, he asked, "You about ready to get out?"

I nodded.

He held up a towel for me, and I stood and stepped out of the tub and into it.

My husband would not let up. He followed me like a puppy dog. As I dried off, from the corner of my eye, I saw him strip down to his boxers. I was standing nude in front of him, and was about to pull something to wear out of my drawer, when he said, "Come here, Giselle."

As I walked toward him, he was grabbing himself between his legs. "See how much he missed you?"

I gave a tight smile.

I knew he was going to want to have sex, but not this soon. As soon as I made it to the bed, he was all over me, when honestly all I wanted was to see my little brother and Lexi and sneak away to call Bryce. I had hid his number in the bottom of my underwear drawer while Giovanni ran my bathwater. The last thing that I wanted was this sick bastard's hands touching me. All I could think about was what I saw on the DVD and him killing Bryce's sister and little brother.

My husband started touching me all over; nothing about it felt good. Not like it used to. His kiss left me distracted, and when he licked my nipples, I felt repulsed. And I prayed he didn't try to go down on me, but he did.

"You like it, baby?"

I lied. "Yes." But inside I was squirming.

I moaned, though, and told him how good it felt. I even pretended to cum, just so we could get this over with. He mounted me, and I felt even more disgusted.

"I missed you so much," he said as he stroked in and out of me.

More lies. "I missed you, too." There was no sensation coming from my pussy, nothing. Only dryness, tightness. A soreness from what he was doing. No secretion at all. I wondered if he noticed. All I saw was his dick shoved in the girl's mouth. And the look of pain on her face as he sodomized her.

When he leaned down to kiss me, I tried to act the part. Like I was enjoying it. And he obviously couldn't tell, because he came.

A few moments later, after he went into our bathroom and cleaned himself, he came back, got into the bed, and spooned me.

"I thought I was going to go crazy. Honestly, Giselle, I didn't think I was going to get you back alive. I felt like a piece of myself was missing while you were gone. And your brother was going crazy."

I smiled at the mention of my little brother. "Where is he?"

"He should be here tomorrow."

"Okay." *But I would rather see him than you,* I thought.

"I told him to give us a little time. He respected that."

"And Lexi?"

"She knows," was his quick response. "I never told my parents you were kidnapped. I didn't want them to worry. I told them you wanted to do some traveling in Italy, and that is where you have been for the past two months." He turned my whole body around and said, "Tell me exactly what they did to you, baby."

I closed my eyes briefly and said, "Nothing. I'm fine. I mean . . . you saw what they did on that video. Look, Giovanni, I just want to put that behind me."

"Okay, baby. It's just every time I think about what they did . . ." He tightened his arms around me in an aggressive manner. All the anger and aggression came back to his face. "Those sick ba—"

"I just want to sleep, husband."

He smiled, and his hold loosened. "Go ahead, baby. Get some rest. You're home now, so you know you're safe."

After what seemed like an hour of him holding me, I managed to drift off to sleep. But in that hour I never once felt safe. In fact, I felt like I was sleeping with the enemy. *Wow*. What a change from how it used to be.

The next morning, knocking on the door was what woke me out of my sleep. I looked around for my husband. He was gone. I rose from the bed and slid into a robe.

Expecting it to be either my brother or Lexi, I instantly had a smile on my face when I opened the door. It was Lexi. But the moment I saw the frown on her face, as opposed to hearing a shriek of joy and getting a hug, my smile vanished.

"What are you doing here?" she quizzed.

My head snapped back. I was confused. What did she mean?

"You didn't hear what the fuck I said? Why are you here, bitch?"

"Lexi, you are supposed to be my best friend. Why are you saying that to me?" I replied in a harsh tone.

"I'm not your fucking friend. Let's get that shit straight right fucking now! And just to let you know, I was your husband's source of comfort while you were gone. And that means that I have been in your bed, and I have been fucking your man!"

"Bitch!" a male voice yelled. I watched my brother come out of nowhere and rush up to Lexi. "What the fuck are you trying to upset my sister for?" he growled. "She didn't do anything to you!"

"Shut the fuck up, Brandon! I say what I want!" Lexi said angrily. "She thinks she is just going to come back, and then I'm not shit—"

"Don't say another fucking word! You're not going to humiliate my sister in front of me!" Brandon bellowed, threatening her.

"Fuck you, Brandon! I have been fucking Giovanni, and you know . . .'"

Her voice trailed off when Brandon snatched her up and slammed her against the wall with so much force, her head hit the wall. "Get the fuck out of here, Lexi!"

I had never seen my brother so aggressive. I didn't know what to make of it. He had never put his hands on a woman before. Had he changed while I was gone? But I just told myself that the anger came from her disrespecting me.

Lexi snatched herself away from my brother, cast me one hateful look, and sauntered off. And as she walked away, I swallowed a huge lump in my throat. I mean, she was my best friend, and she was telling me that she was fucking my husband. I could care less who my husband was fucking, but I did care who my best friend was fucking. That betrayal hurt.

I did not know how to respond to the situation. I just stood there, staring blankly at her as she turned down the hallway and left.

"Welcome back home, sister."

I turned my attention back to my brother. I gave a shriek and reached up and hugged him close to me. The moment we embraced, I could feel him sobbing against my shoulder.

It made me cry as well. I had missed my brother. I was still thinking about Lexi betraying me. And, damn, what the fuck was I going to do about my fucked-up situation?

I pulled away from my brother just as he said, "Don't worry about that bitch. You know that she is trash, and she has always been jealous of you."

"But she has always been my best friend. It hurts that she would say those things, truth or not. And it hurts that she would do them. And to be honest, I think it is the truth. The man I married is not the man I thought he was."

"What do you mean?"

I wanted to tell my brother, but what would it do? I didn't want my brother raging at Giovanni because his shady dealings had gotten me kidnapped. Not when I still had not figured out what I was going to do. And whatever that was, my brother was coming with me. *Only where?* Without my husband, I didn't have a pot to piss in. I again regretted letting Giovanni sell my parents' house. It was probably all a part of his plan, so my brother and I were completely dependent on him.

"All men cheat is what I mean."

Brandon laughed. "Put some clothes on, and we can go get something to eat, Giselle. I'll meet you downstairs," he said before turning and walking away.

"Okay." I went back into the bedroom, showered, and threw a pair of jeans on and a top. After I dressed, I took out Bryce's number and called him from the cordless we had in our bedroom. I had to hear his voice.

"Hello?"

I paused and licked my dry lips, not knowing what to say.

"It's good to hear your voice, Giselle."

At that, I burst out crying.

"Don't cry, baby."

"I want to see you."

"No. It's too soon. Let some time pass between us."

"Okay. But I miss you. I miss you so much, Bryce. I don't know what you did to me."

He chuckled. "Damn, baby. That shit is good to hear."

When I heard our bedroom door open, my heart sped up. "I have to go. Bye." I hung up the phone quickly and spun around just in time to see my husband enter the room.

He stood in front of me. "Hey, babe."

"Hey."

He looked at me, all dressed, and asked, "Are you going somewhere?"

"Brandon wants to take me out to get something to eat."

"Oh. I was hoping we could spend some time together."

I thought back to the past, about how he would get jealous if I spent time away from him with Lexi or my brother. I had thought it was cute and that he just couldn't get enough of his wife. Now I just thought it was his way of trying to control me.

"I just want to catch up with my brother. I won't be gone long." I hoped I didn't look guilty for just calling another man. I looked away, because my husband continued to study my face, and said, "Anyway, we won't be gone long."

"Why don't you take one of the guards with you?"

"I'm fine. I don't need a security guard to follow me around!" I walked up to him and distractedly gave him a dull kiss on his lips. "Where is my purse?" I hadn't had it since the day I was kidnapped.

He opened a drawer, pulled it out, and handed it to me.

When I looked inside, I noticed my iPhone was there but not my keys. Oh well, I could get them later. My phone battery was dead. Since my brother had an iPhone, too, I figured I could charge mine in his car.

Giovanni said nothing. But as I walked out of the room and into the hallway, I turned and saw that he had stepped out of the room and was watching me. My husband had never watched me so much before. I hoped he couldn't read what my heart told me and how I felt now. That I really didn't love him or want him anymore.

Lunch with my brother was so much fun. It gave me a chance to take my mind off the state of things, even though I had to dodge several questions about Bryce. Brandon was relentless. "Who took you?" "Where did they keep you?" "Did they rape you?" I assured my brother the best I could that I was never hurt. I also lied and said I didn't know the names of those who had kidnapped me. He seemed convinced and left it alone.

We went to Roscoe's in Long Beach. It kinda reminded me of when we were teens, with not too many cares in the world, other than the trials and tribulations of being teens, dealing with homework, finals, peer pressure, what clothes to wear, and staying in style. This was a different time now. And the fear I had been experiencing since I found out the truth about Giovanni made me feel how I felt after my father passed. That everything would be on my shoulders. Because I knew that eventually, I would have to leave Giovanni. I just didn't know when, or how we were going to survive when I did.

"I'm just glad you are home safe. I'm not going to rehash the shit over and over with you. I don't want you to get PTSD. You're home. And, man, I'm just glad you are home and you are unharmed. And I'm sure my boy Giovanni is going to be on them fools."

I hoped not. I didn't want Bryce to get hurt. So I prayed Giovanni really would do what he promised and drop this shit.

The waitress brought our food to us.

While Brandon dug into his, I smiled and watched him eat. He stuffed pieces of waffle in his mouth and poured damn near half the bottle of hot sauce on his chicken. When he saw me watching him, he busted up laughing.

I started laughing, too, which made him laugh harder. Then he started coughing like he was choking on his food. I panicked, stood from my seat, and rushed over to him. I patted him on his back until his coughing subsided.

"Boy, slow down!"

His eyes were watery. He took a sip of his water.

"You okay now?" I asked.

"Well, you made me laugh."

"Sorry. It just feels good to see you again. For a little while I didn't think I was going to."

"I didn't, either, Giselle. To tell the truth, I wasn't eating right, and all I did was stress about you being gone. You don't know how happy I was to find out that Giovanni found my sister. I wish I could kill that motherfucker who took you!"

I swiftly changed the subject. "Brandon, I think it's time you reevaluate working for Giovanni."

He munched on a chicken wing. "Why?"

"Well, because you are far too smart to continue to work for my husband. You are putting all your talents and smarts to no use."

"Yeah. But I'm okay with what I do. I make a lot of money, interact with beautiful women all day. I drive a fly-ass ride and got a nice crib. Giselle, life can't get better for me than this."

I aimed a finger at him. "See, that's where I have to stop you with that bullshit, Brandon. Why do you want to be lazy and not apply your damn self? Shit!"

He looked at me and took in my sharp tone with surprise. "Where did all that come from?"

I took a deep breath and buried my face in my hands. "Nothing. I'm sorry. I am proud of how hard you have worked over the years. Let's . . . let's just leave it at that, little brother."

"Okay, big sister." He broke into an affectionate smile and said, "My Gissy."

Then, before I could stop him, he walked over to my side of the table and put his big ole self in my lap, making me crack up laughing. I loved, loved, loved my little brother.

Chapter 18

My brother dropped me off and had the nerve to tell me, "Hurry. I got a date."

"What?" I said as I hopped out of the car. "I thought we were hanging."

He smiled, reminding me once again how handsome he was. And still so very naive. "Giovanni texted me on the way there and said I couldn't keep you out too late, and plus, some girl is on me, so I think I'll go ahead and give her the time of day."

Did Giovanni think he was going to control me? Track all my whereabouts? The shit was cool before, when I was his little, docile, submissive wife who looked up to her husband like he was a king, but I was no longer that type of wife.

"I told him I would have you back by twelve. And you know I can't turn down cookie, big sister."

I laughed. "Boy, shut up talking like you one of these freaks out here."

"I *am* one of these freaks out here."

I laughed harder at my brother.

"Call me later, Gissy."

"All right."

I watched his Hummer speed to the gate and then out of the estate. Once it vanished, I took a deep breath and headed up the steps.

Our maid, Nisa, opened the door for me. "Mrs. Pride, welcome back. Would you like something to eat or drink?"

"No thank you."

She stepped back so I could walk inside.

Once inside, I went straight past the sitting room and the living room, which had always felt like home to me. I had always admired all the beauty and the immaculacy of it. Now I couldn't give a shit. I went straight toward the spiral staircase. I walked up the winding steps, and my mind wandered to Bryce. I wondered how he was holding up, if he was thinking of me, missed me. I again couldn't believe what I did. I had fallen in love with my captor. In my eyes, he was a far greater man than my husband was. Sometimes the gods could be so cruel. I wished that I could have met him before I ever laid eyes on my husband. Things would have been so different for me.

As I walked down the hallway, I could hear voices. I walked closer and recognized one of them as belonging to my husband; the other was a woman's voice. I continued to walk slowly, so as to not let on that I was eavesdropping. I tiptoed toward the edge of the hallway and turned like I normally would but stayed close to the back wall. I walked farther and could see that our bedroom door was not closed completely. I stayed pressed against the wall and looked through the crack in the door. My husband and Lexi were arguing.

"What the fuck are you doing in here?" I heard him yell. I could see a naked body lying in our bed. He stood with his back to me, facing her.

"The fuck you think? I want some dick."

"Bitch, get the fuck out of here! Giselle will be back soon, and I don't want—"

"Oh, you don't want what? Her seeing the truth? You know damn well that when they took her, you were so devastated that you lost your precious Giselle that you threw yourself all over me!"

"How the fuck could I not, bitch? You were supposed to be her closest and only friend, and you deliberately set out to seduce me, because you knew how fucked up I was about my wife being gone."

"So where the fuck does that leave me now?"

"My wife is back, so whatever we were doing is over. You are lucky you still have a job here. You got what you wanted for the moment. You really didn't think that I would choose you over my wife, did you?"

She leaped off the bed, still nude, and stood in front of him. "*What?* You just used me like I'm not shit?"

"You ain't shit. You never were."

"Guess I'm too old for you." She spit on him.

I gasped. Lexi knew? I wondered who else knew besides her, Percy, and Wingo.

He stayed calm, shook his head, and said, "You stupid bitch." Before she could stop him, he punched her in her face so hard, she flew into the wall. Then, before she could get up, he rushed forward and lifted her off her feet by her neck. Her feet were dangling in the air.

I watched as he strangled her, and Lexi looked so scared. So scared, I almost felt bad for her, for being so pathetic.

Snot flew from her nose she clasped her hands over his, and it still did not stop him from strangling her.

"Listen up and listen well. I want you to cash out for your last movie, leave, and stay the fuck away from my house, or I will kill you. Understand?" he snarled.

When she didn't answer, he took one of his hands and punched her in her mouth. Her mouth opened, but no sound came out. A light stream of blood leaked from her lip.

He dropped her on the floor and said, "Now, get the fuck out."

When she hesitated, he kicked her in her back. She stood to her feet, clutched her neck, and rushed from the room. I stood back from the corner of the door so she could see me.

She looked surprised, with sweat, tears, and blood on her face.

I was silent. But she wasn't.

"You!" she raged. "Always fuckin' *you! Why* didn't he want me?"

Giovanni came out of the bedroom in a flash, but he paused in surprise when he saw me.

I pierced him with a glare before placing my eyes back on Lexi.

She sobbed, stomped her feet, and yelled, "Four years ago why did he pick you to be his wife? Why you?"

I didn't respond. But I was going to play this situation, what I had just discovered, to my advantage.

I cried tears, and I knew Giovanni saw them. Not for him. Who fucking cared? But I had lost my best friend; that was enough sentiment for tears. I was glad about that, because I needed Giovanni to feel like shit so I could have an excuse to hit a corner. Go see Bryce.

She stood there and bawled, mumbling, "Sweet Giselle. Everybody loves you. No one loves me. Not even my own mama."

Giovanni took a step toward her, making her cower and run to get away from him. She ran down the hallway, crying all the way. I did feel bad for her. Even after she was gone, I could still hear her bawling. She wanted this life, and she couldn't understand why I had gotten it over her. Why I had been the chosen one that Giovanni married. But what she didn't understand was that she was better off since he had not chosen her. Look what I had gone through. Look at where I was now.

Despite the fact that she had betrayed me, I felt bad about her pain, the pain he had caused her by stringing her along. Lord knows for how long. I swallowed a lump in my throat for her. Only for her. And also I felt pain because she had hurt me. At the end of the day she had still betrayed me by sleeping with my husband. I was supposed to be her best friend, and I had never done her wrong.

I rummaged for my keys in my purse. They weren't there. They should have been. This purse was used the night I got kidnapped, and my keys were in there then. Then I remembered they weren't there when I went to lunch with Brandon.

Before Giovanni could even get my name out, I said, "I noticed that the keys to my Range are gone."

"Giselle—"

"For better or worse? I guess you forgot your vows. My kidnapping was for the worse, I suppose. But still. You were supposed to remember your vows. To love and honor, remember? Forsaking all others till death do us part. You were supposed to be strong and stay faithful to me!" I had him convinced with my melodrama.

He took a deep breath before saying, "Baby, let me—"

"You love me, right, Giovanni?"

"Yes. With all my heart."

"Really? Does your heart hurt to know that you hurt mine?"

His eyes were watery. "Yes, baby."

"Then give me my fucking keys," I hissed.

He looked surprised. I had never cursed at him before.

He went into the bedroom, and a few seconds later, he came back with my keys. He cleared his voice and said, "Baby we can talk about this. You don't have to leave."

"I just found out that the man I love, my husband, slept with another woman, who happens to be my best friend! Do you think I'm going to sleep in that room, in that bed?"

I turned to leave and heard him say, "Giselle, I'll leave if you want. Baby, I'm sorry."

I started walking away, never turning back around. "No! I will." As I said this, there was a smile on my face. I did better than I thought. I had convinced him enough for him to let me escape from there and see the man I wished I were with.

As soon as I drove out of the estate, I punched in Bryce's number on my iPhone.

"Hello?"

"I don't care what you say. I need to see you, and I will. Meet me at the L'Ermitage Hotel in an hour."

I hung up before he could respond.

I drove like a bat out of hell on the freeway. Once I hit the freeway exit, I drove to Neiman Marcus. I got myself a pair of Christian Louboutin leopard, red bottom stilettos. I bought a matching La Perla thong and bra to go with them. Once I had all my goodies, I headed over to the hotel. I had butterflies and couldn't wait to be in his arms.

I went straight over to the desk and requested a suite for Bryce and me. When I felt someone come stand behind me and rub a hand across my behind, I smiled, knowing it was Bryce.

I handed the woman working behind the desk my black card, but Bryce shoved it away and tossed three hundred dollar bills on the counter.

The woman handed us our room card. "You will be in room thirty-four. It is on the fifth floor."

"Thanks," I said.

"What you got in the bag?" Bryce asked.

"A surprise."

"Surprise, huh?"

I had my hand in his as we walked to the elevator. Since there were other people in the elevator, we kept it cool and simply held on to one another's hands. But as soon as we made it to the room and the door closed, I threw myself into Bryce's arms and hugged him close.

"I missed you," he said in a husky voice.

"I missed you, too, Bryce."

His lips found mine, and he kissed me.

The kissing alone had me anticipating what was to come.

I broke the kiss and said, "Let me change." I handed him my iPhone. "Put on some music, and light some candles. There should be an iPod dock in here."

He chuckled. "Yeah, okay."

I grabbed my bag and my purse and went into the bathroom. I took a quick shower and rubbed my body down with some strawberry-scented lotion I had in my purse before slipping into the sexy bra and panties. Then I slid my feet into the heels. I brushed my hair so it hung around my shoulders and cascaded down my back.

The room was dimmed. I could see the flicker of the candles and could hear Usher playing from my iPhone. The song "Okay" was playing. Bryce was sitting in a chair near the bed. I walked over to him slowly to the beat of the song as Usher crooned, "I can't believe my eyes. Looking at your sexy-ass body."

I stood between his legs and let him get a glimpse at *my* body.

As the music played, I twisted my body slowly. Bryce just sat back in the chair while I did the work. I ran my hands up and down my curves, singing, "You probably saying that's a damn shame. I don't even know your name."

I dropped my body all the way to the floor, gripped Bryce's thighs, and rose enough so that I could turn my back to him and grind my ass in his lap. I then bent over a little and let him rub my round ass. I stood, turned around, teasing him, then ran my fingers through my hair and licked my lips while turning around in a circle. I came closer to him and sat in his lap. I moved seductively, while whispering in his ear, "Are you enjoying my dance?"

"Yes. Damn, baby, you getting thick."

His hands started rubbing my curves as I straddled one of his thighs, with my back to him, and ground my pussy into his crotch. In a quick, smooth motion, I removed myself from his lap, turned around, and bent over so that my head was in his crotch, then slowly rose. I lowered my body all the way to the floor in front of Bryce so that I was lying flat and my legs were spread in front of him. He put his fist in his hand and bit it. I laughed and continued this way for a few moments.

I then stood to my feet. As Usher said, "Drop it to the floor real slow," I dropped down and then twisted my body up again in a slow, sensual motion. I increased the speed, until my booty was bouncing up and down.

The song changed to Tank's "Sex Music." I turned, undid my bra, and sat on his lap. The moment I did, Bryce gripped both my breasts and started suckling my nipples. I moaned and tossed my head back. He pushed aside my thong and eased two fingers inside of me. His lips found mine in that moment and drowned out my moan.

He gripped my waist and whispered, "You like that, baby?"

"Oh yes," I moaned.

He started sliding his fingers in and out of me in a quick motion, making me so wet. I continued to kiss him, sliding my tongue in and out of his mouth.

He broke the kiss and asked, while still easing his fingers in and out of me, "Can I rip these panties off of you?"

I continued to enjoy the sensation he was giving me. "Go ahead."

"All right. We gonna keep those heels on, though."

I felt the thong rip, and then Bryce positioned me over his dick. I eased down on his dick slowly, all the while looking in his eyes. I saw all the desire for me hovering there in his expression. The look alone had me on the verge of coming. I started riding him.

He rose to meet each thrust and then increased the speed, saying, "Damn, baby."

My moans got louder, and I was to the point where I was bouncing on his dick.

He stood while keeping his dick inside of me. He carried me a few steps toward the bed, laid me on in, slapped me on my ass, and said "Get on your knees."

I did so quickly, anticipating feeling his hardness inside of me again. Once it was back in me, my hands gripped the sheets from the intense, rough pleasure.

"This my pussy now," he said.

I pushed my body backward against his dick, and each time I did, I heard a loud slap. I didn't know how much longer I was going to be able to hold on. I felt my pussy pulsating around his dick and felt the twitches in it.

Bryce reached around and grabbed my breasts as he continued to fuck me from behind. His dick fit perfectly into my nest, and I was so wet, I could feel it leaking out of my pussy every time he slid out of me.

He then flipped me over onto my back, and his dick dived right back into me. The motions were hard and fast.

When the sensation of cumming hit me, I dug my nails into Bryce's back, telling him silently that I was cumming. Seconds later, so did he.

Chapter 19

My mission from that point forward was to find different ways to get away to see Bryce.

I never said too much to my husband. All meals were eaten in silence. The little trinkets he gave me to make up for having sex with Lexi didn't mean shit to me, because my husband didn't mean shit to me. I kept it cool, though, for the sake of my brother and for my own sake.

It had been a total of two weeks since I had seen Bryce, and I was dying to be with him again. But I knew I had to be careful.

I woke up one morning to find my husband getting dressed. I didn't bother asking him where he was going, because I didn't give a shit.

He sat down next to me on the bed. "Giselle?"

"What?" I snapped. I didn't bother disguising my disgust for him any longer.

"I'm going to go handle some business today. So I'm going to be gone for a while. But that's not what I wanted to talk to you about."

"What is it?" I asked tersely, sitting up in the bed.

"For the past two weeks, I have been feeling so bad about what I did. I almost feel like I have lost your love forever. You don't even look at me the same way anymore. You move away from me in bed, and you won't talk to me at the dinner table. Giselle, nothing means more to me than you—"

"I didn't matter too much when you were fucking my friend!"

"Baby, that didn't mean anything. I was hurt over you being gone, and she threw herself at me. I'm a man. Prior to that piece of shit, I had never slept with another woman since we got married."

"No. You just slept with kids," I wanted to say. "What if I told you some shit like that? What if you found out that I had had sex with another man? Could you handle it, Giovanni?"

"With all you have been through and the hurt I caused you by giving in to temptation, baby, I would just have to accept it. If you came home tonight and told me you slept with another man, I would bathe you and make love to you so good that you would never want to sleep with another man again, baby." He got all teary-eyed, and the tears threatened to spill from his eyes. "That's how much I love you, Giselle. I would accept it like a man and move on. Because the only woman in this world that I want and have always wanted is you. And I will kill for you."

My cell phone vibrated on the nightstand. My heart sped up. Giovanni looked, then carried on as if he didn't hear the vibration. I tried to keep a normal expression on my face and to not look as anxious as I felt to check my phone to see if it was Bryce.

"I don't know what to do to make you not hate me, but, baby, I'm taking steps to restore your faith in me again. The day before yesterday, I went to see that specialist that I told you about before at Cedars-Sinai. They ran a few tests, and they are going to get back to me about why I have not been able to get you pregnant. I think it is a good idea for you to go as well. I know the last thing on your mind right now is a baby, but if you would at least think about it."

I nodded. Anything to get him out of my face. But as moments passed after I nodded, I realized that would be the positively worst thing that could happen. I had no intention at all of staying with my husband, so getting pregnant would be really, really bad. Also, as far as I was concerned, no baby was safe around someone like him. But I couldn't tell him this. I tried to keep the dread I felt at the thought of that happening off my face.

He bent over and kissed my lips before leaving the room.

As soon as the door to our bedroom closed, I snatched up my cell. I had a new text message. I read the text. It was from Bryce. It read:

If you can get away, meet me at Puddingstone in San Dimas

The thought of seeing Bryce excited me beyond measure and cheered me up. I couldn't wait. I missed being around Bryce all the time, like I used to be, before he sent me back to my husband. The perks of the mansion were no longer perks, and I would be perfectly content in the house Bryce had had me in. I was willing to take the risk to see him again, even if it was for a few hours.

I wasted no time. I rushed into our adjoining bathroom and took a quick shower. I dried off and then, naked, went into my walk-in closet. I chose a sexy, slinky black Prada dress and a pair of Gucci sling-back heels to match. I went to my panty drawer and pulled out a sexy hot pink thong and a matching polka-dot hot pink and white bra. I threw these on the bed, rubbed my body down with baby oil, and sprayed on some Chanel. Then I pulled my clothes on. I brushed my hair all the way back and placed it in a ponytail that hung at my nape. I put on my shoes, grabbed my purse and phone, and walked as fast as I could in my heels to the door.

I opened the door and damn near collided with my husband. I screamed.

"Are you okay?" he asked me, wrapping his arms around me.

I pulled away. "You scared me. And I thought you had left already."

"I was on the way outside, and the doctor called me, so I came back. Are you leaving?"

"Why are you questioning me?"

"You're my wife."

I thought of a lie. "I'm going to Burke Williams."

He started at me for a moment, like he didn't believe me. I didn't care if he did or not. But something about his eyes, and something about how silent he was, made me a little nervous. Then he gave me a smile and said, "Have a good time, baby. With all you have been through, you deserve to be pampered."

I sighed, relieved. Then in the same breath, I said, "What do you want?"

"I came back to tell you that I made us both appointments for Wednesday. They just want to take a few blood and urine samples from you and run a few tests. Is that okay, Giselle?"

"Fine." I was going to agree to whatever to get out of the house to see Bryce.

Before I could walk past him, he grabbed me and gave me a hug, saying, "I think a baby is just what we need to bring us close together, the way we used to be." Then he kissed me.

I kissed him back, playing along.

Once he released me, he said, "I'll walk with you, baby."

I huffed out an impatient breath as he followed me like a puppy dog.

Once we made it outside, Giovanni took my keys from me, kissed one of my hands, and gave the keys to the groundsman to bring out my Range. He parked it next to Giovanni's and had the engines running in both.

I nodded at the groundsman and hopped inside my truck as he held my door open for me.

"Have a good time, baby," Giovanni said as he got into his matching Range.

I ignored him and wasted no time. Once the groundsman closed my door, I drove to the gate. As I waited for the gate to open up, I pulled out my phone and called Bryce.

"What's up, baby?"

"I'm on my way to you, Bryce."

"Okay. We got number seventeen. Hurry up."

The gate opened, and I drove out.

"What are you going to do to me when I get there?"

He chuckled. His voice got husky, and he said, "I'm going to eat your cake like it's your birthday."

Sensations swept through my pussy. I couldn't get to him fast enough. I wanted to taste Bryce, and I wanted him to taste me. I turned on the iPod installed in my truck and tuned it to Musiq Soulchild's "So Beautiful."

I couldn't wait to see Bryce again.

Once I made it to Puddingstone, one of the staff escorted me to our hot tub. The moment I walked inside, Bryce came walking toward me. I threw myself in his arms and hugged him so close. Truly, I knew I loved him. He had all my love. My husband didn't have any more of it.

I kissed Bryce on the lips repeatedly. "It's so good to see you, baby."

He returned my kisses and said between them, "I know."

I pulled away and looked around the room. "What is all this, Bryce?" There was a bottle of Patrón sitting on top of the Jacuzzi. Rose petals were scattered around the room. And the Jacuzzi looked so damn inviting. Couldn't get better than this.

"Get undressed and get in," he said as he pulled off his white T-shirt.

"Okay." I pulled off my clothes until I was nude. I smiled as Bryce paused while taking off his own clothes to watch me.

I slowly walked over and slid into the Jacuzzi. I watched him pull off his shoes, which were a pair of Timberland boots, a pair of Seven blue jeans, and his boxers. I was reminded that Bryce had such a nice body. Big arms, a wide chest, and some serious abs. *Damn.* His dick was already hard and was bobbing into his stomach as he walked over and joined me in the Jacuzzi. Once he got in, we were some distance from one another.

He eyed my breasts, which were visible in the water.

I grabbed the Patrón and sipped from the bottle. The heat instantly swept through my throat when I swallowed the liquid. I then swam closer to him. He placed an arm around my shoulders, so that my head was resting on his chest.

"How you feeling?" he asked me.

The Patrón immediately started taking effect. I held the bottle up to his lips so he could take a sip.

Then I kissed him.

"This is nice," I told him, pulling away.

"After what you gave me a few weeks ago . . ."

I laughed. He was referring to my lap dance. I had actually taken a class to learn that, but I didn't want to tell Bryce that. I wanted him to think it was a talent I had.

"So any request tonight?" I asked.

"You taking requests?"

"I'd give you anything," I told him. When he looked in my eyes, they confirmed what I said. I meant it.

He bit his bottom lip and said, "I wanna see you play with yourself."

I kissed him on his lips and got out of the hot tub. I went over to the two chairs in the room. I positioned one of the chairs so it was in front of the Jacuzzi, facing Bryce.

I then sat in the chair and spread my legs apart so he got a full view of my pussy. I rubbed my hands down my chest and grabbed both my breasts in my hands, moaning loudly, as Bryce watched from the Jacuzzi. I licked my fingertips and rolled them around my nipples in a slow fashion, making them hard. While continuing to play with them, I took my free hand and ran it down my body, letting it rest in front of my pussy. I parted it and rubbed a finger along my clit in a circular motion, making myself so hot. I pinched my nipples more harshly, then began to stroke in and out of my pussy, all while rotating my hips in a circular motion. I did all of this while watching Bryce's actions. He was stroking his dick in the Jacuzzi and looking super turned on.

I continued in this fashion, driving myself and him crazy, until I heard, "Get over here."

I laughed and continued what I was doing, watching him as he stroked his dick with more urgency. I finger banged myself faster, making myself super-duper wet. "But I'm just getting started."

"Giselle, baby, please."

I continued until he again commanded, "Get over here."

When I stood and walked back over to the Jacuzzi, he reached out with his strong arms and yanked me in. Before I could move, he shoved me against the Jacuzzi wall, spread my legs open, and shoved his dick inside of me.

I moaned and closed my eyes as the pleasure of his dick engulfed my insides.

"You wanted to play with me." He started stroking harder inside of me and placed one of my legs over his shoulders.

I dug my fingers in his back as he dipped in and out of me. He started licking my nipples; then his mouth found mine. I used my tongue to lick around his lips.

He bit on my bottom lip gently before saying, "Giselle, I know I hurt you when I did this the last time, but I want to make up for that now, if you let me. If you trust me."

I knew what he was talking about.

I turned around, leaned over the rim of the Jacuzzi, and let him spread my butt cheeks.

He first kissed and licked my pussy from behind, making me cry out loudly, while at the same time sticking his finger in and out of my asshole, and I liked it. I anticipated what it would feel like to have him in there, inside of me.

Soon I felt him position his dick at my hole. It pinched a little as he put the tip of himself inside. He repeated this several times before I felt myself open up and him push himself farther inside. I moaned loudly at the sensations I felt. It was a pleasure beyond words. Bryce plunged in real slow. He gripped my breasts in his hands possessively. I turned my face so I could kiss him but found I was too weak with how good it felt to move my lips against his. His dick felt so fat, felt so big.

I could feel myself nutting and nutting. I moaned loudly. When Bryce released my breasts to play with my clit, all while fucking me in my ass, I started screaming as an orgasm that seemed unreal made me feel like I was floating and it made me squirt. It really had a hold of me. That shit wouldn't let me go.

After our session, we cleaned ourselves up. They had no shower, so we did the best we could. Bryce managed to make a pallet for us to lie on. He rested on his back, and I lay on my side with my head on his chest.

"This was really sweet. Thank you, Bryce."

"With the type of man I'm competing with to get your affection, your love, Giselle, a nigga like me is trying to step it up a notch."

Did he really think he had to compete with Giovanni? My husband meant nothing to me. It didn't matter how much more money he had in his possession. Didn't matter how much jewelry or how many bags he bought for me. That love I once had for Giovanni was gone.

So I told Bryce, "You don't ever have to compare yourself to him. That man is no longer a factor in my heart."

That had him smiling. "Then who is?"

"You don't know by now? You. I love you." It was the first time I had said those words to Bryce. I meant it. I really did. I was in love with Bryce. I thought about him all the time. I wondered what he was doing and if he was safe. I never wanted to leave his side. The thought of doing so always had me down. Yep. It was love.

He chuckled. "I never thought I'd hear you say that shit."

"And I never thought that I would. But that's what it is. It's love."

"I love you, too, baby."

I kissed his lips. There were other things that I wanted to say and ask him. Like how we were going to fix this situation. But before I could ask, Bryce started talking.

"I'm handling a few things. And if they work out, I'm retiring from this shit for good."

"That's good, Bryce. What made you decide to do that?"

"Funniest thing. Of all things to stop slanging dope for, I'm doing it for a woman. Her name is Giselle. She makes me feel like I got the potential to do better things."

I laughed, and he hugged me tighter against him.

"When everything dies down completely, and I finish up my business, you know you going to have to leave him, right?"

"And what am I supposed to do? I have no home or money of my own."

"That part you not going to have to worry about. Like I said, I'm working on a few things. I can't imagine this new life without you in it."

"What are you saying?"

"That I love you. More than I have ever loved any other woman. And it's starting to be a problem for me, sending you back to him. Not keeping you with me."

Jesus Christ, it felt good to hear that!

"Just give me a little time to get my shit together and you won't have to spend another night with that sick muthafucka. But for you to stay with me now and not go back, it would reopen that war with him, which I don't need for the shit I'm trying to do."

"What are—"

"Can't tell you that. Just trust me, baby."

I wished I could speed the process up by getting rid of Giovanni. I still wanted to go to Hank, and I wanted to see what DVD I could get out of Giovanni's office. But only Giovanni had a key to it. I hoped I was able to get it and Giovanni wouldn't be an issue. I smiled at Bryce, but truthfully, there were more questions that I wanted to ask. I had fears as well. How were we going to do this, and what about my brother? Would he be able to come with us? Were these *things* he was trying to do dangerous? But something about the way he held on to me and kissed me made me feel like Bryce had everything under control.

For the moment, I was just content having that day and lying in his arms . . . for the moment.

Chapter 20

I had washed up at the Puddingstone, but I knew I needed to take a shower. I still felt sticky between my thighs. This was where the dread came in. I always had a feeling of apprehension that my husband would discover I went to see Bryce on one of my outings. So I had to play it cool. Because I knew Giovanni would do something treacherous to Bryce and me if he found out.

As soon as Nisa opened the front door, I rushed past her, on a mission, and jumped when I saw my husband standing at the top of the spiral staircase. I regained my composure and walked up the stairs, not giving him any eye contact.

He had a very agitated look on his face. When I tried to walk past him, he said, "I called you eight times on your phone."

"The battery is dead," I lied. "So I had left it in the car."

"My parents are here. They brought us dinner from Morton's."

"Why didn't you tell me sooner?"

"I tried to. The eight times I attempted to call you."

I ran a hand through my hair. "Well, give me a few minutes to shower and freshen up." I rubbed the inside of my thigh with the other. *Sticky*. I hoped he couldn't smell Bryce on me.

"No. They have waited long enough for you."

I sighed, turned around, and stomped down the stairs. I walked past the living room and down the hall to the dining room. Bryce's mother and father were already seated, and by the looks of their plates, they had already eaten. So had Giovanni.

"Hi, Mom. Hi, Dad," I greeted.

I blew them both kisses before walking past them, sitting down, and tossing my purse on the arm of the chair. My husband sat next to me.

His mother looked surprised and said, "No kisses, Giselle? No hugs? We haven't seen you in, like, forever, since you decided you wanted to tour Italy."

Giovanni had mentioned that he didn't want them to worry. So he told them that I had been out of the country all this time. Despite hating Giovanni, I loved his parents.

"You know I love you guys. But you don't want this dragon breath on you," I revealed.

They both laughed and accepted that.

Giovanni looked infuriated.

The cook came out and sat a plate in front of me. It held a huge porterhouse steak, some mashed sweet potatoes, and asparagus tips. I was not hungry, so I picked at the food. Again, I hoped they couldn't smell Bryce. Or smell the after cum threatening to ooze out of me.

"Giovanni, what happened with your appointment?" his mother asked.

"Well, they called me this morning to have me come in for a follow-up. Giselle and I are going there on Wednesday to hear my results and to have some tests run on her."

Giovanni's mother looked at me. "Are you excited, Giselle?"

"Not really."

Giovanni's dad looked surprised by my comment, while his mother looked confused.

"Why not, honey?" she asked.

"Well, I'm not too sure that I want kids anymore." Truthfully, I wanted kids, just not with him.

Giovanni gripped one of my thighs under the table. "I think she means she doesn't know if she wants a girl or a boy."

I bit my lip to keep from commenting further.

"Oh, okay. Well, I cannot wait until you have a baby that I can spoil. Right, honey?" said Giovanni's mother.

Giovanni's father nodded. He never said much but always watched. It usually made me nervous, but today I didn't care.

My cell phone rang. It made my heart speed up, because Giovanni had caught me in a lie. I bit my bottom lip.

"Giselle, there is something different about you today. Baby, are you all right?" That was his mother.

"I'm fine."

"My wife is full of surprises today. I do know that," Giovanni said.

I rolled my eyes at him and said, "Mom, Dad, I'm feeling really beat. I'm going to go upstairs and get some rest. Maybe after we come back from the doctor tomorrow, you two can come over and we can have lunch. I will have the cook make us some goodies. Maybe some nice crab cakes, lobster ceviche, those little raspberry cheesecakes that I can't get enough of, and some blini. That sounds good! I'm just really beat right now."

I leaned away from Giovanni and rose from my seat. I blew two more kisses to both of his parents and walked out of the room.

I heard his mother say, "But wait! I want to know how Italy was!"

I ignored her and kept going.

When I got to my room, I threw off my clothes and went straight into the bathroom to jump into the shower. I stepped inside and immediately cupped my hands under my pussy. Despite the fact that I had washed up, there was still cream in my vagina, and it leaked into my hands. The aftershocks of sex. I chuckled, thinking about how good it was. Bryce had the ability to make me cum the way Giovanni had never done and probably never would. He had a magic about him that just drove me insane. I damn near pissed on myself when I saw Giovanni standing in front of the clear glass shower door.

He didn't say anything, so I played it off and turned on the shower. I grabbed the liquid jasmine soap and quickly poured some on myself using one of the folded washcloths that were neatly stacked in the cabinet that was built into the shower stall.

I looked out the corner of my eye and saw that he still stood there watching me.

I lathered up quickly and then rinsed off. I turned off the water and stepped out of the shower stall. I grabbed a towel and wrapped it around myself before exiting the bathroom. I was trying to get away from him.

As I dried off in the bedroom, I saw him come and stand in the middle of the room and watch me. I ignored him and pulled on my robe, tying the sash.

"So how was the spa?"

"What?"

"I asked how the spa was. You said that's where you went, right?"

"Yeah. It was fine."

"What type of massage did you get this time?"

I was silent, trying to figure out what to say. "It was the, uh, the deep tissue massage."

He just watched me, his arms crossed, standing in the center of the room. A few seconds later he said, "Don't ever in your life disrespect my parents. Do you understand me?"

"What are you talking about?"

"Giselle, I love you. And I'm sorry I have hurt you. But you are pushing me."

I almost dismissed him, until I saw the dangerous look in his eyes. It made me nervous. Should I tell him the truth? That I knew what he did and that I didn't love him, that I loved Bryce and wanted to be with him? *No,* I told myself. That would be signing my death warrant. I had to trust that Bryce would get me out of this. I also knew I had to bow down to my husband.

"All right. I'm sorry."

"Since you don't seem to care about spending quality time with your husband, I wanted to surprise you with a trip. I won't force you to go, but if you like, you can fly out to Vegas with me, Daryl, and Whitney for a couple days. We will be back in time for our appointment."

"Giovanni—"

"Now, I won't force you to go, baby. But I would like you to."

Two and a half months ago I would have jumped up and thrown myself in his arms and kissed him for a surprise excursion. When we went to Vegas, everything was always five-star. I had money to throw away, like it wasn't anything. I always had the flyest dresses, heels, and bags to show off, and I stayed on Giovanni's arm, making other bitches insane. Now I wasn't excited in the least bit. And I would be ashamed to be on his arm. I would much rather be in Bryce's arms.

So I told him, "I don't want to go. I'll stay home and see you on Wednesday for our appointment. Have fun."

He tried to smile at me, but I could tell he was disappointed that I didn't want to go. "If you don't want to, then I won't look at it as a bad thing. Maybe a few days apart is what we need."

"Maybe," I said.

"What is it going to take for you to love me again?"

I closed my eyes briefly. The truth was nothing would. I would never, ever love Giovanni or look at him the same way. It didn't matter what he did, because I knew that he was foul. "Just give me my space, Giovanni. You can't expect me to get over what you did this fast. You slept with my best friend."

He nodded. "Fair enough. But if you change your mind, call me. I can have you flown out at any time."

Just then someone knocked on the door. It was our maid Pillar. When Giovanni told her to come in, she quickly came into the room and went into the walk-in closet. When she came out a few minutes later, she had a small Gucci suitcase packed.

"Mr. Pride, I will take this downstairs for the driver. I started the shower for you. When you finish with your shower, I will come back and straighten up. I will set your change of clothes on the dresser. Mrs. Pride, do you need me to pack your bags, ma'am?"

"No thank you, Pillar. I'm not going."

Giovanni walked past her to the bathroom.

"Yes, ma'am." She walked out of the room.

Once Giovanni was fully dressed, he gave me a long tongue kiss, which I didn't even participate in. Then he was out the door, and I was happy to get him out of my hair for two days.

I stood up and went to grab my phone to call Bryce. I dialed his number quickly. When there was a knock on the door, I jumped. "Who is it?"

"Pillar, ma'am."

I hung up the phone quickly. "Come in."

She opened the door, walked in, and smiled at me. This was her normal routine—to ensure that our bedroom, bathroom, and closet stayed immaculate—and normally, it wouldn't bother me, but since I was trying to talk to Bryce, it agitated me. But I waited patiently while she straightened up the bathroom.

"Mrs. Pride?" She came out of the bathroom with a basket of dirty clothes and towels.

"Yes?"

"Mr. Pride left his keys here. They were in his pants pocket. I don't want them to get lost."

My breath caught in my throat. The keys were just what I needed to get into his cabinet. I tried to look normal.

"I'll hold on to them until he comes back," I told her.

She smiled and handed them to me.

As soon as she left, I sprang from the bed. I rushed out of the room and down the stairs. It took me a good ten minutes to get near the studio. Giovanni's office was down the hall. Luckily, it was late, so everyone was gone for the night.

I tried five different keys before one of them unlocked the door. I breathed a sigh of relief and closed and locked the door behind me.

I figured the smaller set of keys contained the ones that would open the cabinet he had. Once I was able to get the cabinet and then the correct drawer open, I gasped at all the DVDs in there. There were separated by year. They went back as far as 1997. I remembered that that was the year Giovanni said he started his company.

I braced myself and watched countless DVDs of Giovanni with young girls, very young girls, who looked around the same age as Bryce's little sister. When I slipped in a DVD that was filmed in 2011, I was disgusted beyond words. Although the little girl was a little older now, there was no mistaking who she was. The birthmark on her face said it all. It was Trinity, Lexi's cousin. I sobbed. Did Lexi know? I told myself that she didn't know. Who would willingly allow a grown man to do something like this to an innocent child? Seeing him victimize that young girl killed me softly. If Lexi knew about this, then she was sicker than I thought.

I ejected the DVD from the DVD player. I grabbed as many of them as I could and rushed back to my bedroom. I was not going to wait another day. Giovanni needed to be arrested for what he had done. All the pain he had inflicted on all these girls. He needed to be locked up for the rest of his life.

As I pulled on some jeans and a black T-shirt, I called Hank's home number. My husband had given me all the phone numbers of his friends and had said it was a way to show me that he was always accessible to me. First, I dialed him at home, and his wife, Vanna, answered. She told me he was still at work, doing paperwork.

I dialed the number for the Westwood Police Department. As soon as I was transferred to Hank, I didn't let him get his name out before I said, "Hank, it's me, Giselle! Listen to me carefully. I'm coming over there to show you something. Giovanni has been involved in a very serious crime. He has been sexually abusing underage girls and filming it. I have proof. He needs to be locked up. I'm bringing the DVDs to you right now."

"Giselle, are you sure about this?"

I went to my closet and pulled out a pair of tennis shoes. I cradled the phone with my ear and shoulder and yanked on the shoes. "Yes! Look, Giovanni is on his way to Vegas, so that gives us time. I'm on my way to bring you the DVDs now."

I grabbed my purse, tossed my cell inside, and rushed out of the house.

When I got outside, I tossed my keys to the grounds-man. "I need my car now!"

He rushed away, and a few minutes later he pulled my car up. I jumped in, pushed the gas pedal, and heard my tires squawk, but I didn't care. I was getting to that police station. Once the gates opened, I drove even faster.

Once I got there, I grabbed my purse and the DVDs. I rushed inside to the front desk. Before the police officer could say anything, I said quickly, "I'm here to see Hank Chisym. He knows who I am, and he is expecting me."

I was quickly escorted inside Hank's office. Then that officer left. I rushed up to Hank, hugged him, and said, "Thank you for helping me, Hank."

When I pulled away, I noticed there were two more cops in the room. Hank took a step back from me, nodded, and they both started coming toward me. I looked at them, confused.

"Hank, what's going on?"

I screamed when one of the cops twisted one of my arms behind my back. The other officer placed that wrist in handcuffs and my other arm was brought around and the cuffs were placed on that one as well.

"Hank, why are you doing this to me?"

He ran a hand through his blond hair, and his blue eyes pierced me angrily. "I'm sorry, Giselle, but I can't help you. Giovanni is my friend. You should have known better. You really are meddling in something that is not your place or your business. As good a husband as Giovanni is to you, I feel embarrassed for you for even trying to do something like this. You should, too."

I gasped at his words. I was shocked. Hank must have known all along what my husband was doing, and was okay with it. I was disgusted by the fact that he was okay with it. Fear that he must have told Giovanni I was coming there made me tremble.

"He needs to be put behind bars for the things he has done. You are the police chief. That overrides your friendship with him!"

He ignored me by casually tossing a hand in the air. "Take her home to her husband. He's waiting for her."

Was this all a setup? Had Giovanni really left, or had he set me up to dig a hole for myself?

"Wait, no! Hank, please don't do this to me Don't take me there."

He handed one of the officers a Post-it. "Take her home. The address is on here."

I sobbed as they pulled me by my arms out of the office. I was so scared. Hank had probably told Giovanni that I had tried to tell on him and get him locked up. And the cops were taking me straight to him! I realized then that what I did was dumb and reckless. Now I was going to pay for it. Dread consumed me as they stuffed me in the back of the police car. I bawled all the way to my house. I didn't know what Giovanni would do to me for this betrayal.

The police didn't stop until they brought me in the house and up the stairs, directly to our bedroom. It was like they were Giovanni's personal bodyguards.

Giovanni was seated on our bed, staring at me calmly as the officers took the cuffs off of me.

After the cuffs were off, Giovanni walked over to me and said to the officer holding the cuffs, "Tell Hank I'm borrowing these cuffs."

"No problem, sir," said the officer with the cuffs. He handed them to Giovanni. Then they both stood there, waiting for his next command.

"Ask your chief if we are still on for the shooting range on Saturday."

"Will do, sir," the other one said.

"All right, you two can go."

"Have a good night, Mr. Pride," they both said in unison. They walked out of the room.

I stood in the center of the room, scared as hell. The level of fear I had matched the fear I felt when I was first kidnapped and when I met Bryce. I didn't know what Giovanni was going to do, but I was scared as hell of whatever it was.

He stood in front of me and lifted my face so I could look him in his eyes.

"I planned this mock trip to see what you would do with me out of the house. Of all the crazy scenarios, I never thought it would be this. You thought you could go to my friend about me, huh?"

I ignored him.

"Answer me, you bitch!"

"I—"

"Not fast enough." He took the handcuffs and swung them like they were a bat right into my grill.

I screamed when one of my teeth flew and blood spilled from my mouth. I placed my hand over my mouth. I cried and dropped to my knees from the pain.

He crouched down in front of me. "Tell me something, sweet Giselle. I have given you every luxury known to man. Why would you betray me this way, huh?"

When I didn't respond, he gripped my hair tightly. I winced at the pain.

"Answer me, or I will pull every implant out of your fucking head!"

"I know about what you do. I know you rape young girls."

"Bitch!" He punched me dead in my face. I cried out again and fell backward. "You don't know any fucking thing. What I do is my business, mine! You are my wife. Those DVDs have nothing at all to do with you. That's my fetish. Everyone has one. Little girls just so happens to be mine. So what? It could be worse, bitch. It could be boys. It could be drugs or gambling. You should have played your part as my wife and stayed out of my business. You don't question anything about Giovanni Pride. I own you. The moment I wrote that check in my office, you became my property, and you will do as I say with my life and with yours. You should know by now I'm rich and money buys power. The police can't stop me. No one can."

I sobbed and kept my eyes closed as he spoke. I felt utterly powerless to stop his assault on me, because physically he was stronger and he was right. He had a lot of power because he had money. But still, he was more of a bitch than any man I had ever known.

He smoothed the hair out of my face. "Listen to me, baby. I don't want you to see this ugly side of me, but you gave me no choice. You had to be punished." He took a deep breath. "Here is what we are going to do. You are going to go and take a shower, get into bed, and go to sleep. From this point on, you are not going to leave this room—"

"Giovanni, no—"

His face turned ugly again. He grabbed me by my throat and said, "Shut up!"

I nodded fearfully.

"You are not to leave this room. Despite what you did, I still love you and you are my wife, and you will continue to be my wife until I feel or say differently. And we will move forward with seeing the specialist. I'm sure by then you will have come to your senses, anyway."

I sobbed and shook my head. I couldn't have a baby by this man. I couldn't. He was sicker than I'd thought. He didn't need to be the father to anyone. He shouldn't even own a pet.

He ignored me and stripped me out of my clothes.

"Just let me go," I begged. "I won't tell anyone about what you do if you just let me leave."

"Shh, baby." He dragged me to the bathroom, although I screamed for him to let me go. He dragged me inside the shower and came inside with me. "Wash the blood off of your face, Giselle."

"No!" I screamed. "Giovanni, just let me go!"

He started slapping me around in the shower. I slipped and fell down, hurting my side.

He lifted me back to my feet. "Stop, baby. See what you are making me do? Let me love you, baby. Let me be good and gentle to you."

I wanted him to just let me go. Dump me out on the street, ass buck naked if he had to, without a pot to piss in, but just let me go. I didn't want a baby, money, anything but my freedom, but it seemed that I had screwed that up. I regretted not being patient and letting Bryce handle this on his own. I'd screwed things up and made them worse. What were the chances of me being able to freely be with Bryce now?

Giovanni stood over me and drenched me with soap. It burned my eyes and nostrils. He took a washcloth and rubbed me down, despite my pleading for him to stop.

He kept repeating, "It's okay, baby." But then when I tried to fight him, he would punch me, then say, "Stop making me hurt you!"

I finally gave up and sat still, crying, as he rinsed the soap off of me and carried me, naked and soaking wet, toward the bed. Once he tossed me on it, I curled up in a ball and continued to cry.

He grabbed my purse, walked toward the door, stopped, and said, "I'm hurt by what you did today. But in time, unlike you, I will get over it and forgive you. But for now it's best you go to sleep. I will tell both the maids to resume their cleaning on another day. I don't want them to see the lady of the house this way, because you look a mess. I won't let anyone up to this wing of the house. Oh, and when time permits, I'll send you to our dentist to get that tooth replaced."

With that he left the room.

I leaped up from the bed to grab the phone and call Bryce. But Giovanni must have taken the cordless out of the bedroom, and there was not one in the bathroom, either. *Damn!* I had to get out of the house. I pulled on the first thing I saw, a dress and my flip-flops, and rushed to the door. I opened it and was surprised to see he had a guard planted outside the bedroom.

I squeezed out of the bedroom and started walking toward the stairs.

"Giselle."

When the guard called my name, I took off running. I was able to go down only four stairs when he grabbed me, lifted me in the air, and carried me back to the bedroom. He refused to put me down, despite me beating him on his back. I screamed, but no one came to my rescue. He finally put me down and headed to the door. I was a fucking prisoner again. I begged the security guard to let me go, but he wouldn't answer my pleas. They fell on deaf ears.

***

Déjà vu was the best way to describe my situation. I had definitely been there before. No one was allowed inside the bedroom, and security brought all my meals. I was totally isolated and cut off from the world. Only now I honestly felt that Percy was right when he told me I was a lot safer with Bryce than I was with Giovanni.

Giovanni came and went like we were still happily married. I was shocked beyond measure when he forced me that Wednesday to get dressed for the doctor's visit.

"Did you think I was done with you? You are my wife, and I want a child, and you have no choice in the matter, so shut the fuck up."

The ride was silent. My husband placed his hand over mine in the car. I ignored it and ached to snatch it away from him. But I was scared of what he would do to me. I was already bruised from the previous ass kicking, and I had lost a tooth.

Once there, we didn't have to wait long, and I knew that was because my husband had money. I mean, I had bruises on my face and one of my front teeth had been knocked out. Giovanni looked psychotic, with this crazy-looking smile planted on his face. But they overlooked all of that and saw only money. A fifty thousand dollar donation.

I filled out a questionnaire. They collected some urine and blood samples from me, did an ultrasound of my uterus, and told me they would pass my results to the doctor. Giovanni never left my side and even went into the room with the nurse and me as I gave my samples. Everything was expedited for us because we had money. Well, my husband did. They told me that my blood results would take about two days, though.

Once they were done, I was sent back out to my husband. In the twenty minutes we waited, I was so not interested. The last thing I wanted was to get pregnant by Giovanni. Someone like him should not be able to bring babies into the world. As sick as he was, who was to say he would not harm his own? He was, after all, a pedophile. I wished I could figure out a way to get myself out of this predicament. But at the moment I was lost. I needed to get away to call Bryce.

We were sent into the specialist's office to hear my husband's results and to get the results from my urine test.

"Hi. I'm Dr. Haro," the specialist said, shaking my hand before sitting down.

"Hello," I whispered.

"Good to see you again, Giovanni."

Giovanni nodded.

"So. How's life?" the doctor asked.

"Life is great, and I'll tell you, it would be even greater if my wife could get pregnant this month."

Dr. Haro grabbed a manila folder and opened it. "Let's see what we got here." He scanned the contents inside the folder and said, "Mr. Pride, I'll read your results first. Unfortunately, your results came back and show that you have Klinefelter's syndrome."

Before the doctor could finish, a nurse walked into the room and sat another file on the doctor's desk. Once she walked back out, he continued, "This is a genetic disorder that causes you to produce low amounts of sperm."

"What?"

"That's what your tests say, sir."

"Can it be treated?"

"In its early stages, when you are an adolescent, yes. Unfortunately, your parents should have had this treated with HCG. Over time Klinefelter's syndrome causes all active testicular structures to atrophy. Once testicular failure has occurred, improving fertility, I'm afraid, is impossible."

I gasped. God knew what he was doing when he made Giovanni sterile. There was no way anyone like him should be blessed with the ability to procreate. It made me feel a little better about my situation knowing that no matter how many times he raped me—because now sex with Giovanni would never be consensual—I could not get pregnant by him.

"Does that mean I can't have kids?" Giovanni asked.

"Yes, that's—"

My husband snatched me by my arm and stormed out of the office. I had to hurry to keep up with his pace.

"Mrs. Pride. Mrs. Pride! We're not done," called a nurse.

My husband stopped, and so did I. But if only I could have turned back time, kept going, and ignored her.

The nurse that had taken my samples rushed up to us. "Where are you going, Mrs. Pride? Doctor Haro didn't tell you?"

"Tell me what?"

"We need to get you on your prenatal vitamins."

"Excuse me?" I said, incredulous.

"Your pregnancy test came back positive."

Chapter 21

Okay. How am I going to get myself out of this one?
I thought. My husband was just informed that he could
not have kids. He was under the impression that I had
only been with him sexually, and here this nurse was
slinging prenatal pills in front of us.

My hands were shaking and my heart was pounding
super hard and hadn't stopped since the moment the
nurse told us that I was pregnant. And my husband, he
was shockingly silent. But that silence didn't last long.

As we walked in the parking lot toward his Range, I
struggled with some type of story to keep him from beating my ass or, worse, taking my life and even Bryce's.

He calmly asked, "Who are you fucking, and when
did you start this affair?"

I didn't want to give Bryce up. The way I figured,
whether I said it was consensual or rape, he would kill
Bryce. I couldn't let that happen.

So I quickly yelled, "No one! I never told you, because I was ashamed, but I was raped the first night I
was kidnapped by one of those men that attacked you
and took me that night at Morton's." I even squeezed
out some tears and added, "He didn't wear a condom."

He seemed convinced. Which relieved me. But I
knew that it was only for the moment. If he decided to
snoop in my purse and go through my phone, he would
see all the phone calls I had made to Bryce and a few
texts I had carelessly not deleted. I swallowed the lump
in my throat.

But when he asked, "So how many months along are you?"

I felt stuck. Truthfully, I didn't know the right number to say, because my brain went blank.

And before I could think, Giovanni said, "Let's find out." He dialed a number into his phone and said, "Yes, this is Mr. Pride. My wife and I were never told how far along in the pregnancy she is. Can someone please tell me? Quickly please."

Then the number of months came to me. I prayed she said I was three and a half months. Then my lie would not be exposed.

He waited a few seconds before saying, "Yeah, I'm here." I watched a look of rage come over my husband's face at whatever the nurse told him.

Out of nowhere a fist came down and punched me in my face. "You lying bitch! You're only two weeks pregnant. You are fucking someone else. All those days you went out alone, were leaving to see him. When I find out who it is, I'm going to kill him!"

I screamed. "No! I was raped. I was ashamed to tell you!"

He growled loudly in his throat. "Stop lying!"

He delivered more blows to my face. I stumbled backward, my vision clouded. But he continued to come toward me, with fury on his face. Punch after punch was delivered. Then a few slaps. Then he reverted back to punching. And after one more hit I was completely knocked out.

"Giselle, if you think that was something, wait until you see what I have in store for you, heartless bitch. That wasn't anything compared to what you are going to get."

I opened my eyes, and as soon as I did, my husband's fist came crashing down on my forehead. Before I could move, he grabbed me by my hair and dragged me from the car. He dumped me on the ground. I cringed inside due to the pain and looked up. We were home, in front of our mansion. He kneeled over me and dropped more blows with his fists, punching me as if I were not a woman. As if I weren't pregnant. I tried to get away from him by crawling and protecting my stomach. He then started kicking me in my back. At one point, after a few kicks, I lost my balance and thought smart by breaking my fall by landing on my side. It didn't stop him from attacking me. He didn't seem to care about my screams.

Our maids, Nisa and Pillar, ran outside, horrified, but they couldn't stop him—nor could any of his other staff—as he beat the fuck out of me.

Next, when it appeared he had used up all his energy, because he was breathing hard, he dragged me by my hair across the front lawn. The pain of him pulling my hair with all his might was excruciating. I closed my eyes, unable to get his hands out of my tresses.

He paused in front of me, cocked his foot back, and growled as he stomped me in my face. I screamed from the pain. He grabbed my hair again and dragged me to the front steps. The back of my head collided with each step, making the pain I was feeling more excruciating.

He did not take me upstairs to our wing, but instead took me to the wing that held the studio. There were a few female models standing by, shocked. He shoved them all out of the way, knocking one of them to the floor. "All you whores, go home. I only need one female working today." I looked at Nette's and Sean's surprised faces, as well as Rodney's, as they rushed out of the office because of the commotion. There was also a new security guard, who I didn't recognize, but he neither said nor did anything.

Giovanni walked past them, saying, "I need Poison, the Mandingo Brothers, Tank, and Adonis. Send the other whores home, and then get the fuck out of here. Don't come back until I tell you to. Filming will be temporarily shut down until I say different."

Rodney, the new guard, and Sean rushed away. But when Nette didn't move, Giovanni yelled, "Do it, bitch! Before I fire you!"

"Okay." She passed a pitiful look my way.

I kept my eyes closed in shame but could hear her scurrying off.

He continued to pull me into one of the rooms. Once inside he threw me on the bed.

Fearfully, I watched him turn on the film equipment. I prayed he wasn't going to do what I thought he was going to do.

"You wanted to be a whore, bitch. Now you're going to make me some money doing just that." He came toward me and tried to strip me of my clothes.

"Giovanni, please," I pleaded. "I'm your wife. You can't force me to do this."

"Don't say shit to me!" he raged. He slapped me again, so hard I flew back on the bed. He pulled every article of my clothes off. "You lied to me, you bitch. You have been running away to see and fuck someone, after all I have done for you. All the love I have shown you. If you had been raped, you would be farther long. Did you think you could lie to me and get away with it?"

At this point I could come up with the best lie in the world, but Giovanni, he would see right through it. "Please don't do this." He raised his hand toward my face. I jumped and said, "Just kill me."

"Kill you? Bitch, don't insult my intelligence. You're not getting off that easy."

He stepped out of the room. I stood and rushed up to the door. When I tried to turn the knob, I discovered that the door was locked from the outside.

"Get your ass in here!" I heard.

I hurried back to the bed, sobbing out of fear of what he was going to do to me. When he came back into the room, I was shocked out of my mind. He had brought Lexi. I gasped as she came into the room. I thought he had said she wasn't coming back.

She stood and gawked at me in an arrogant manner, as if to say, "I told you I was fucking him!"

I looked away. There was no need for her attitude; I believed her the first time she told me. I just didn't care about his end, but I'd always care about hers, because she betrayed me. There would never been a need to retaliate, because the best revenge was wiping her out of my life. Which I did. Couldn't say I didn't miss or need my best friend, but I had to question whether, if she did what she did, she was ever my best friend. It was possible, but only she could truly answer that. And she couldn't answer that now. I also wanted to know if she played a part in Giovanni assaulting her niece. Then I concluded that she had to have participated. How else would he even have known that Trinity existed if it wasn't for Lexi?

Giovanni stood with his feet shoulder-width apart and his arms crossed. "I tried to be a loyal husband to you. I treated you like you were a queen. You were my queen. And you betrayed me. Giselle, I loved and desired only you. Lexi, or Poison as she calls herself—and she truly is poison, though Vile would be a better name for her—never meant shit to me. She was just a way for me to take my mind off of what was happening to you. I'm a man. We men use pussy as a remedy for the flu.

"Giselle, you have to understand, the worst thing for a man—even worse than knowing another man is sleeping with their woman—is not knowing. It is a torture beyond words. You being gone with those men who took you, that kept me up at night, stopped me from eating, functioning. Then here comes Poison, a grown woman still looking for love in all the wrong places. Lexi was just a pussy with no face. My grief, and only that, caused me to fuck her. No lust, attraction, or passion. Who could care for something so trashy?"

I looked at Lexi's face as he talked about her like she was nothing. It was blank.

"Our affair . . . it was different. But you have the nerve to come back into my house, knowing you shared your body with another man. . . ."

I watched tears run down his face. I wondered what ever happened to his big speech about bathing and making love to me, should he ever find out that I was unfaithful. What ever happened to that? It was very interesting. My husband was the one who had slept with my best friend and numerous young girls. What could be worse than that? Men and their infidelity issues. It made me want to shake my head, but I was scared it would anger him. But Giovanni was a hypocrite at his best. I would have never even known that someone like Bryce existed if it wasn't for Giovanni's involvement in his sister being missing and turning up dead. If I had not discovered that he was this horrible person, I would have not fallen for another. Did he get that, or was he just plain delusional?

He turned to Lexi. "Bitch, take off your clothes and get on the bed," he ordered.

Lexi jumped like she had been burnt and stripped down to nothing. Giovanni went to stand behind the camera.

"Get on the bed!" he barked.

She climbed on the bed and sat next to me.

"Now, listen very carefully, Giselle, because if you don't, I'm going to fuck up that pretty face I used to love so much even more. Lexi, your best friend, who now hates you—and you hate her—and is now your enemy, is going to lie on her back, and you are going to eat her pussy. And I'm going to film it . . . bitch."

I sobbed silently and shook my head, pleading with him with my eyes not to make me do that. The thought of putting my mouth on her made me feel instant nausea, because I knew no matter how much I begged, he was going to make me do it.

He rushed toward me and punched me in my face. I fell back on the bed. When he balled up his fist again and aimed it toward my stomach, I feared that if my baby was still alive, he would kill it.

"Okay!" I closed my eyes briefly as Lexi lay back and parted her legs.

I got on my knees and inched toward her. Salty saliva filled my mouth, and I resisted the urge to vomit as I lowered my face toward Lexi's pussy.

"Giselle, you better do it," Giovanni ordered.

I kept my eyes closed and used my tongue to lick Lexi. Giovanni gave me specific instructions on exactly how to do it. It reminded me of the day I first came to the mansion and how Rodney had talked to me. If I could go back in time and reverse things, I would have never come. I would have somehow found another way for my brother and me to weather the storm. But it was too late to even dwell on this and think about alternate solutions. I should have thought about those in the moment. I was way past that moment. *Try years.*

The moment the flavor of Lexi's vagina hit my tongue, I gagged. I swallowed it down quickly, trying not to vomit as one of my hands clutched my belly, and obeyed my husband. I tried to be slick and simply keep my head over her pussy to obstruct his view, but he wanted to torture me, so he kept me down there for a while, saying, "Lick her pearl like the man licked yours, you fucking whore! Suck it. Suck it!"

My shoulders racked with sobs, but I did as he suggested, feeling like a piece of flesh was inside my mouth, and it was.

"Lick all of that cream off of her, you fucking bitch! Do it, bitch! Like you got yours licked. Did you enjoy it, you fucking slut? Suck. Her. Pussy!"

I tried. I did all that he wanted me to do and pretended this was a total out-of-body experience. I pretended I was somewhere with the people I loved, my brother, Bryce. I closed my eyes and pretended my brother and I were still at Roscoe's, catching up. Feeling loved. I pretended I was in Bryce's arms again. I thought back to when my mother and father were alive. Being in our home. How cozy and warm it always was. Hanging out in my bedroom, listening to music or watching BET with . . . Thoughts of Lexi brought me back to my predicament, making me gag again. And thank God Giovanni yelled, "Cut!"

Lexi rushed off the bed and scurried away from me.

There was a knock on the door. Giovanni opened it. Two men walked in the room. Alarm struck my face. They were huge. They had to be six foot four, and the fact that they were identical told me that they were twins. I shuddered to think what they were going to do to me. He was going to kill this baby, if he hadn't already done so.

Lexi hid in a corner of the room.

Both men took off their robes and joined me on the bed. Everything on them was huge. More tears slipped

from my eyes as my husband started filming again. Both
men looked at Giovanni as if they were a little lost.

"Whatever the scene was you were supposed to shoot
today, do it with her," he told both of them.

That was all it took. My lips trembled and tears ran
down my face at the realization that I was going to be
sexually assaulted by these two men. One of the men
yanked me on top of him. He positioned my legs by
grasping my thighs with both of his hands and spread-
ing them open so they straddled him, and without even
a moment's hesitation, he rammed his dick into my
pussy. The other man gripped my head and shoved
his dick into my mouth. I was forced to give him head
while the other invaded my insides. And the pain from
him yanking my hair and the other one going inside of
me was intense.

When my husband was convinced that he had had
enough of that position, we switched. I was riding one
guy like a cowgirl, while the other was letting his semen
spill on my face. My pussy was dry and burning, like
it was on fire. The guy I was forced to ride turned me
around so I was facing him. The other one came behind
me and, while the guy was still in my pussy, jammed
his dick into my ass. I screamed in pain, but he showed
me no mercy.

Giovanni made a call on his phone. Two more men
came into the room. They were also able to invade my
body. One more man came in. It became one big gang
bang, where I was forced to sex all five of them before
my husband's eyes. It got to the point where I stopped
crying and stopped begging my husband to stop what
he was allowing them to do to me. Lexi was still in the
room, watching me go through this. I looked her way
only once and could swear I saw her crying.

When all five men stood in front of me and sprayed me with their semen, getting it all in my hair, eyes, nose, and mouth, my husband finally said, "Enough. Get the fuck out. Nette will have your money tomorrow."

They all left the room.

My insides were so sore, and there was blood trickling down my legs. I used my hands to wipe the semen off my face while my body was curled in a fetal position. That was when I heard her. Lexi was sobbing.

I turned and looked at her face, then at Giovanni. His eyes were narrowed at her.

She sniffled and said, "I'm sorry, Giselle. So sorry for all of this. I have done some really, really horrible things on account of Giovanni. To you and to my family. I hate myself."

So she *had* done it. She had given him her cousin.

I looked at her tear-soaked face, her trembling shoulders. Despite the horrific truth of her character, I thought about how tight we used to be. I realized I still loved her; in that moment, I still did. Someway I figured out in that moment that all along Lexi had been a victim, because she never really had felt loved. And victims tended to victimize. I was not justifying what she did, but just figuring out why.

Giovanni saw how my face had softened toward her. It seemed to enrage him. He looked at Lexi and growled, "Oh, you're not mad at her anymore, Lexi? You no longer want her spot as my wife? With all the luxuries she got, and you don't have to sell your ass anymore without getting a fraction of what she got?"

Lexi shook her head.

He turned, looked at me, and said, "Giselle, you aren't mad anymore that she fucked your husband? You forgive this bitch? Do you accept her apology?"

I nodded, looking at her. Who knew what was going to happen to me at this point. If I was going to die, I didn't want to die hating her.

"Good. Giselle forgives you. Now maybe God will forgive you for being such a trifling piece of shit," he muttered.

Out of nowhere Giovanni pulled out a gun. He pointed it at Lexi. She looked horrified and scared. The color drained from her face, and she raised her hands, silently begging, because yeah, her lips were moving, but no words or even sounds came out of them. I had my hands over my mouth, horrified.

He pumped several bullets into her body, until she stopped moving.

Chapter 22

Giovanni dragged Lexi's limp body out of the room. He grabbed my clothes and said, "I'm going to leave you like the animal you are."

As he dragged her, I knew I needed to stop looking at her eyes, which just wouldn't close. But I couldn't. Yes, she had betrayed me, but she was the only friend that I had ever known and had. I sobbed in my arms on the bed. Giovanni closed and locked the door, making me once again someone's prisoner. I didn't know what Giovanni had in store for me next. The fear of it sickened me to no end. But I knew that when he was done with the torture, he was going to kill me.

As the hours drifted into night, I found myself unable to sleep, and I prayed my brother came soon, and I hoped he could get me out of this. I also prayed to God to get me out of this situation, and I hoped that my baby was still alive.

When I heard the door open, my breath caught in my throat. I sat up in the bed quickly, not knowing what my husband was going to do next.

I was surprised to see Mr. Pride, Giovanni's dad.

"Dad!" I cried.

"Giselle, what in the world?"

He took in my naked body, all the dried-up cum on me, the dried blood on my thighs, the bruises, and my missing teeth. But thank God I had stopped bleeding. I was just hoping the blood came from the penetration and not from me losing the baby. The blood was watery, so that gave me hope, because once Lexi had a miscarriage and she said the blood was thick, with clots in it. I didn't have that.

"It's Giovanni. Dad, he's turned into a monster. He killed my friend. You have to get me out of here before he kills me. And I need to get to the hospital before I lose my baby!"

He pulled a handkerchief and a bottle of hand sanitizer out of his suit pocket. Then he poured some of the sanitizer on the handkerchief and started wiping my face clean.

"Dad, get me out of here please. Giovanni had all those men rape me and . . ."

He looked surprised at my words. "What?"

Before I could respond, the handkerchief dropped from my face and his hand brushed against one of my breasts. I sighed as a look of lust came over my father-in-law's face. He dropped the handkerchief and the sanitizer.

Horrified, I begged, "Please no!"

He started unbuttoning his pants.

I jumped up and rushed up to the door. He grabbed me and tossed me back on the bed. I landed on my side.

Before I could get up, he pressed the full weight of his body on me so I couldn't get away and yanked down his pants.

"Get off of me please," I begged him.

He ignored me and took out his dick, slapping it against my ass. It instantly got hard. He completely flipped me onto my stomach and forced his dick in my pussy. I screamed. He shoved my face into the bed, muffling the sound. I was already in pain, raw and sore from the other men that had raped me earlier. It was like pouring bleach on a stab wound. That was the level of pain I was experiencing.

And in my mind, *repulsive* was the only word to describe being raped by my father-in-law. I was disgusted that he would do something like this to me. He saw I was weak and couldn't fight for myself, and he took the opportunity to sexually assault me.

As he rocked against me, he said, "Oh yeah. You got some good pussy. And I've wanted to try it from the first day I saw your pretty ass. I don't know what you did to my son, but don't worry. Giovanni said that it was okay." He was even stronger than his son, and I knew there was no way I could break the hold he had over me. So I lay limp and let him take it, since I couldn't overpower him.

I cried, though, all through the ordeal. Even when he flipped me over and continued to force himself inside of me. He placed a hand over my mouth and made a kiss face with his lips. I once again prayed to God that He get me out of this situation. That was all I wanted. After he ejaculated inside me, he shoved me away and rose from the bed.

He snuck out of the room, as if he had never even entered it and violated me.

I slept to block the images of Lexi's dead body and Giovanni's father and all those other men raping me.

I was awakened by someone coming into the room. It was Giovanni. He came with a dress and a pair of shoes for me to put on.

He tossed them at me. "Here you go, slut. Put this on now."

I donned the dress quickly and slipped my feet into the flats.

He yanked me by my arm out of the room. We went through the back of the house, and when we got outside, I noticed that Rodney had pulled up Giovanni's Range.

Rodney opened the door on my side of the truck, and Giovanni shoved me in before getting in on his side. He put his matching iPhone on the car charger and drove to the gates. When security took too long to open the gates, Giovanni leaned his head out the window and raged, "Open these motherfucking gates! You see me in the camera. You know who the fuck I am!"

They opened.

Giovanni sped out. As we hit the busy street, he said, "You know, I still can't believe you had the nerve to come into my home pregnant by another man."

"I'm so—"

"Shut up, bitch! You don't know the meaning of sorry yet. But you will! When I get done with you, you are going to be so humble. Back to the wife I knew and loved. I know you were fucking Bryce. Last night I went through your purse, went through your phone. I saw all the texts you sent him and the ones he sent you. You have been carrying on an affair with the piece of shit who took you. You lied to me. And what's more, bitch, you have been sneaking off to see him, deceiving me. Giving all your love to him. All those days you were leaving, you were going to see him. I should have had you followed and checked your phone. But you were my angel, and I never in a million years thought you would share your body with another man!"

One of his fists slammed into the steering wheel. "I'm going to have him killed just to let you know. Just like I killed his sister. Yeah, you heard me. I killed her. But first I'm going to get rid of the baby inside of you. The thought of the shit makes me sick to my goddamn stomach."

Alarm hit me. That was where we were going. He was taking me to get an abortion. I loved Bryce, and I did not want to lose our baby. The thought of aborting my baby had me teary-eyed and filled with anxiety.

"No! Please, Giovanni. Don't kill my baby."

He punched me in the side of my face, making my head bang on the car door. "Bitch, you're begging me to save another man's baby after what you've done to me? You should be begging me to spare your life!"

I sobbed as Giovanni stopped at a red light.

"How the fuck can you hurt me like this, Giselle? Maybe I should just kill you, instead of letting you make this right by killing that baby inside of you."

"If you kill this baby . . . you might as well kill me."

That did it. Giovanni went into full attack mode.

The light changed to green. Giovanni maneuvered the car with one hand, all the while punching me in my face several times with his other hand.

"Bitch!"

He took off his seat belt and continued to beat on me like I was a man, despite my begging him to stop. With that same hand he grabbed a handful of my hair and yanked it from my scalp. Then he fucked my face up with more punches.

I tried to fight him off, but the power of his fist was too much for me.

He swerved over to the right lane, toward the curb. Another fist closed down on my mouth, slamming into my teeth. I could feel my lip burst and blood fill my mouth. I also felt dizzy. Another punch landed in one of my eyes.

"I'm going to beat that baby out of you. Then there will be no need for a fucking abortion."

He resumed the hits, almost missing a stop sign. He struck me in my face again with a closed fist. Since his attention was barely on the road, he swerved and almost hit the car next to him. Then he slid over to another lane, never decreasing his speed. But when he saw that the car in front of him was not moving, due to the green light changing to yellow, he slammed on his brakes so hard that the truck jolted forward and he rear-ended the car in front of him. His head slammed down super hard on the steering wheel.

When Giovanni didn't immediately get up and resume kicking my ass, I assumed he had passed out, and I did not waste any time. I snatched his iPhone. I didn't take the time to see if he was okay. I unsnapped my seat belt, opened the car door, and jumped out of the car. I slipped past the car behind Giovanni's Range Rover and hit the sidewalk. I just ran for my life. I turned a corner and looked behind me. So far I didn't see Giovanni. So I was relieved but did not stop running. I ran down another busy street.

Not bringing attention to myself, I looked to see where I was. I was on Birch Street. I took a deep breath and slipped into Mountain Meadows Café. I went directly into the bathroom. I slipped into a stall.

I called Bryce and prayed he would answer. The first time I called, it went to voice mail. "Shit!" He probably thought it was Giovanni calling. I sent him a text saying:

It's Giselle. I have Giovanni's phone. Emergency!

Once it went through, I waited a few moments. I took a deep breath and dialed his number again. He picked up on the second ring. He must have assumed it was a trick, because silence was all I heard on the other end.

So I said quickly, "It's me, Giselle. I need you to come get me now!"

Chapter 23

Relief was what I felt when I saw a man's shoes underneath the bathroom stall.

I stood and unlocked the door. I knew I looked a mess with a black eye, a busted lip, missing teeth, and knots on my forehead, and with my hair wild and some of it gone.

When I saw Bryce's concerned face, I felt so weak and drained that I stood there, frozen. I raised my arms and then dropped them at my sides. I sobbed uncontrollably.

Bryce said nothing. He just took me in his arms and held me.

After I told Bryce what Giovanni had done to me, he rushed me to the hospital. In all the panic of trying to get away from Giovanni, I had forgotten about the baby. I sat in the hospital examining room, biting my bottom lip, while Bryce sat in the chair across from me with his head down, waiting to hear what the doctor would say.

The doctor came back into the room and said, "Well, I do have good news. The baby is fine."

I exhaled in relief. I looked at Bryce. He looked relieved as well. I silently thanked God for protecting my baby.

"You just need to be careful, and whoever that creep is who would physically assault a pregnant woman needs to be behind bars," said the doctor.

We were both silent.

"The nurse will give you your aftercare instructions, and you are free to go. Make sure you follow up with your ob-gyn."

"Thank you, Doctor," I said.

The ride from the hospital was silent. The first thing I wanted to do was call Brandon and tell him to stay away from Giovanni. But despite the many times I dialed his number, he would not pick up. I was so worried that my brother might be the next casualty. I wanted to go to his house, but Bryce said Giovanni might be casing the place, looking for us. He said it was too much of a risk. So I left Brandon several messages, and he never responded to any of them. I prayed that he was okay.

Bryce dumped his car and rented another one so we would go unnoticed in case Giovanni had some men watching us. I bit my lip as Bryce drove us to Moreno Valley. He said Percy was going to let us stay with him. I was concerned that Giovanni would find us there, but Bryce said that this was a new spot for Percy.

It was a small two-bedroom house.

Percy answered the door and escorted us inside. We all went to sit in his living room, but none of us said a word. It was an awkward silence.

Percy finally broke the silence. "How you holding up, Giselle?"

I offered a smile that was so forced. "I'm okay, Percy."

"You know, the day I left you with Bryce, it wasn't to punish you. Giselle, I knew that you would be okay."

I chuckled. "You leaving me with Bryce was the best thing that could have ever happened to me. I love him."

"What? Like that?" Percy said.

I looked from Bryce back to Percy. "You didn't know?"

"I knew. I'm fucking with you. I knew how Bryce felt. Before *he* even knew how he felt. Every time I turned around, he was blowing up my phone, bitching about you. You were getting under his skin, and you didn't even know it. And he kept bitching about you because he couldn't get you off his fucking mind."

Bryce busted up laughing.

"Who would have fucking known? Giselle and muth-afucking Bryce. Damn."

I smiled. "Who knew I would be carrying his baby?"

Percy's eyes got wide. "What?" He looked at Bryce for confirmation.

Bryce nodded.

"That's some crazy shit!"

"And all the reason to get the fuck out of Dodge." Bryce rubbed one of my thighs.

"Right. Right," Percy agreed. I couldn't help but notice the look of distress on Percy's face. He tried to look cool, but an expression of alarm was definitely there.

I said, "So where are we going from here? Better yet, what are you guys going to do to my husband?"

It was a simple question that seemed to complicate the conversation. The question took the ease away. It was replaced with tension.

When Bryce didn't answer, Percy gave him a look and said, "Listen, Giselle—"

Bryce cut him off, saying, "Hey, Percy, you still got your Superhawk?"

"Yeah, I got it."

"Let me take that shit out for a quick ride. I need to clear my mind and think on some things."

"All right. I'll get it out of the garage for you." Percy stood and walked toward a door in his living room, then disappeared through it. I assumed the door led to his garage.

Bryce looked at me and asked, "You hungry, baby?"
"No."

He rubbed my stomach. "You need to eat to feed the baby."

I nodded. "Okay." I wanted to ask him again about Giovanni, but I let it slide for the moment.

"What you want me to get you?"

I shrugged. "Doesn't matter."

He stood, leaned over me, and planted a deep kiss on my lips. "Why don't you go take a nap? I'll be right back."

He helped me to my feet and walked me to one of the bedrooms. Once there, I sat on the bed and he pulled off my shoes. I lay back, relaxed my head on the pillow, and closed my eyes. And for a few minutes, I could feel Bryce massaging my feet.

I guess when he saw that I was more at ease, he kissed me on my forehead and left the room.

When Bryce came back, I was still awake. He sat on the edge of the bed, and I could hear him fiddling with something. "I got you some fish tacos. They say it's good to eat fish while you're pregnant. Something about it being brain food. There's cabbage on these, too."

I sat up in the bed.

Bryce unwrapped one of the tacos, pulling back the white paper, and started feeding me.

I didn't have any interest at all in eating, but Bryce was right. I needed to feed the baby. I finished off one taco and washed my prenatal pill down with the apple juice he bought for me. Then I lay back down.

Bryce left the room with the leftover food and trash. When he came back, I watched him strip down to his boxers and wife beater and get into bed with me. He held me from behind and protectively placed a hand on my stomach.

"You good?"

I was silent before licking my dry lips and saying, "Bryce, what's the holdup? My husband is dangerous and wants to kill us both. What are we waiting for? Why don't we just leave?"

He sighed before saying, "Because I have a drop to make. I'm not some millionaire like your husband, baby. You know how I make my money. I need to make some more before we leave. I'm also in the process of selling the house in Paramount I held you at and the one in Chino. Plus, I have to make sure my mother is straight."

My body relaxed. It made sense. Money didn't fall out of trees, after all. "Where are we going?"

"Decatur, Georgia, will be the best bet. I mean, I ain't trying to live a fast life anymore. That country life may be just what you, I, and the baby need."

I had never thought about living in Georgia. I didn't know too much about it, except what I watched on TV about those housewives. I tried to have confidence that Bryce knew what the best choice for us was, the way I had always had confidence in my husband and had felt without a doubt that he knew what was best.

Bryce kissed me on my neck. "What do you want? A boy or a girl?" he asked me.

"I want a little boy. How about you?"

"Don't matter to me. I'll be happy either way."

With our current situation, it was so hard for me to bask in the joy of being pregnant. I mean, I was happy about having a growing life inside of me. But given the circumstances I was hella worried. We were hiding out. I was still married to my husband. He wanted us dead. It was all too much. To think about cribs, baby names, and what type of food I would serve at my baby shower . . . Nope, I couldn't do it.

"When are we leaving?" I asked, pressing.

"Tomorrow night." He started rubbing my nipples, turning me on. "Now, before I fuck the shit out of my pussy . . ." He flipped me onto my back and pulled up my dress and started sucking one of my nipples. I moaned, despite my racing thoughts. He pulled away from my nipple and said, "Do you have any more questions?"

I shook my head as one of his fingers dipped into my pussy. He rode me hard that night, making me scream so hard, I prayed that Percy didn't hear us. And as good as it was, and despite how tightly he held me, I still had my worries.

Chapter 24

The urge to pee woke me up. It was still dark, but I didn't know how late it was. Bryce wasn't in bed with me. I got up and walked out of the bedroom to the bathroom. After I peed, I washed my hands and left the bathroom.

The light was on in the living room, which I thought was weird, because it was late. I jumped when I saw a man sitting on the floor near the front door of the house. He was also holding a gun.

When I screamed, he stood and said, "It's okay."

It was Hog, the one who came with Angel the day I killed Bear. "Where are Bryce and Percy?" I asked.

"Can't tell you all that. Just relax, and go back to sleep."

I raced into the bedroom, calling, "Bryce! Bryce! Percy!" I went into the kitchen as well. They weren't there. I rushed back to the living room door. I was worried they had gone out and were preparing to do something stupid to get back at Giovanni.

Hog blocked me from going outside.

"Let me out, please."

"Naw. Go back to sleep."

"Let me the fuck out!" When he refused to move, I ran toward the door that led to the garage, opened it, and slipped inside the garage.

I saw Percy and Bryce seated at a table. There were guns scattered on the table. Bryce was pulling the safety off of one, while Percy was loading bullets in another one. Something was going down.

They didn't notice me standing there until I yelled, "Bryce! Percy! What are you about to do?"

Percy and Bryce froze at the sound of my voice.

Hog was behind me and said, "Aye, yo, I tried to stop her, but I didn't want to put my hands on her."

Bryce nodded at Hog. Bryce laid the gun on the table. He finally made eye contact with me.

"I knew you were keeping something from me. You said you had a drop. Bryce, tell me that that is the truth, because I don't believe you for shit!"

Bryce didn't respond. He just looked away. Percy was tight-lipped as well and looked at Bryce, refusing to make eye contact with me.

My suspicions were mounting, so I asked, "You guys are going to kill Giovanni, aren't you?"

Silence was the response I got.

Percy stood to his feet and walked toward me. Although I kept my eyes locked on Bryce, who wasn't looking at me, I felt Percy brush past me.

"Come on, Hog," Percy said.

"Bryce!" I yelled. "Answer me!"

Bryce shoved the table back and stood to his feet. "Yeah, and what you care for? Why are you concerned if I do plan on killing him? I mean, after what he did to you and to my family, Giselle, you should be happy!" He narrowed his eyes at me. "But you're not!"

"Baby, listen to me. You have no reason! No reason at all to feel jealous about Giovanni. I hate him. I love you! I want to be with you. But this is just too much. Like you told me before, this has gone too far already. We don't need any more bloodshed. No one else needs to die." I bit my lip before saying what my deepest fear was. I didn't want to say it, but I did. "Because what if the person that dies is you?"

He looked so insulted. Like I was saying he was a weaker man than Giovanni.

"I'm not saying Giovanni is a better man. He's not. Not by far. Despite your mistakes, they can't possibly add up to the ugliness of that man. But . . . I just don't think you can beat him."

"Giselle."

"Let's just go away, like you said. Let's just leave!"

"Giselle, I want this to be over, too. But this needs to be done. Do you know that I beat myself up every day for sending you back to him? I let my fear force me to do it, when all along I should have just deleted that fool and been done with it. But I thought he was more powerful than I was, instead of just taking my chances. I feel so stupid, because I could have lost you and my baby."

"But you didn't. I'm still here."

He took a deep breath. "You are just going to have to trust me."

"Bryce, don't do this. Leave the shit alone. Promise me you will."

I bit my bottom lip, felt the tears. Waited. And nothing. He refused to budge.

That was when I crumbled to the floor, sobbing, because I knew. I knew deep down there was nothing I could do or even say that would stop Bryce from doing what he had made his mind up to do.

Bryce rushed over to me, picked me up, and held me in his arms. "Stop crying, baby."

I buried my face in his neck. "I'm tired," I said between sobs. "So tired. I want this to be over."

He carried me back to our bedroom, saying, "It will be."

I woke up to Bryce's arms around me. I snuggled in his arms, taking a deep breath. The truth was, I didn't know how long I had been asleep or even if Bryce had left me again.

So I turned over in his arms and asked, "What time is it?"

"Five in the morning."

"Oh. Did you?"

"No. I just told Percy and Hog it was on hold. So they went over to some strip club to have some drinks and chill. Niggas still ain't back yet."

I snuggled closer at that.

"But it's still going down, so I don't want to talk about it. You just shut it down momentarily."

I yanked myself away from him, but he pulled me back into his arms. Why didn't he get it? What if he wasn't able to kill Giovanni? What if he got killed instead? I loved Bryce, really loved him. And what if I lost him?

"Baby? Baby?"

I wouldn't respond. I was too busy crying again, thinking about Giovanni killing him.

He chuckled, released me, and said, "I need to go take a piss."

I wiped the tears off my face with balled fists and watched him walk to the door.

Bryce opened the door, then turned back and looked at me. "I love you."

As he said this, I gasped as I saw something poke through the crack in the door. The more the door opened, the more I realized what it was.

"Bryce!"

But it was too late. By the time he turned around, a man had taken the butt of his weapon and bashed Bryce with the weight of it. I screamed as blood gushed out of his head and he went down. Next thing I knew, three more men rushed into the room with guns drawn. They all rushed Bryce and started beating him with fists, feet, and their guns. I screamed at the top of my lungs, hoping to alert someone. All that did was get the attention of one of the men. He came toward me with his gun aimed at my head.

"Bitch, shut the fuck up before I bust you in yo' muthafucking mouth." He kept his gun aimed at me.

I looked at Bryce and watched them continue to whip on him. One of the men was stomping him. Another took his gun and slammed it down on Bryce's head. I saw blood splatter on the carpet and on their shoes. I stood by, helpless, unable to help him as they beat him damn near to death. The way Giovanni was beaten when I was taken. When his body was limp and he wasn't moving at all, they stopped. My heart pounded as I bawled. Was he dead? I told myself no. I forced myself to believe he had just been knocked out. That was it. The three men snatched Bryce up and carried him out of the room.

The man with the gun on me grabbed me roughly, yelling, "Come on, bitch!" and pulled me after the other men and Bryce. Percy and Hog were lucky to have left the house. Not us.

Bryce was tossed into a huge black van, and I was forced into another black van. The men scattered to both the vans, but the one who had aimed a gun at me rode in the van I was forced into. I feared that these men had been sent by my husband. If they were taking me to my husband, I knew Bryce and I were going to die. I just knew it. And despite the fact that the man with the gun pointed at me had told me earlier to shut the fuck up, I couldn't stop crying.

Then he said, "Yo. What the fuck I tell you?"

The butt of his gun slammed into my temple. I was no longer crying, or doing anything, for that matter, because I was out.

Chapter 25

Okay. Here I was, back in a place I so did not want to be. And . . . just the mere thought of what was to come almost caused me to piss on myself.

I sat in a corner of the room, cowering and shaking, while my husband sat on a couch and stared at me. We were in the studio of the mansion, on the main set. I knew that no matter how much I screamed, no one would hear me. The studio was soundproof.

"So you decided to come home. No. Wait. You didn't come home. I found you. I told you this before, Giselle. Having money buys you all the information you need. You are stupid, and you insulted my intelligence by assuming I would not find you and that lousy hoodlum motherfucker." My husband gave a cold laugh. Before I could respond or beg for my life, which was what I wanted to do, my husband stood, came toward me, and gave me a hard punch in my face.

He held me by my hair and punched me in my face repeatedly. Then he took my head and slammed it against the wall. My head started pounding, but Giovanni didn't seem to care. He continued his assault, beating the fuck out of me. At one point, he punched me in my mouth so hard, I ended up spitting out blood, and I could feel where another one of my teeth was so loose, it was barely hanging on to a piece of my gum.

The men that had taken Bryce and me were standing around, laughing at me getting attacked. These were Giovanni's goons.

Despite my trying to get away, Giovanni continued to beat me. He was pulling plugs of my hair out of my head. One of my eyes was sealed shut, and both of my lips were busted. My nose started to bleed from a punch he had landed. Now he was kicking me all over as I lay curled up on the floor. All of my soft body parts were slammed into by his hard shoe. I screamed from the pain of it. But he continued until I was trying to slide my body away, because I was too weak to crawl or walk. All that did was make him angrier, and he continued beating me.

"Bring them in here."

The four men walked toward one of the filming rooms and went inside. Two of them brought Bryce out. I expected that. I knew they had him. They shoved him in a chair and shackled his wrists and feet with handcuffs. *Damn.* He couldn't help me. But the sight of the next person the other two men pulled out caused me to moan loudly. It was my brother. *Dear God, what have I done?* I had risked his life in this.

They shoved Brandon down to the floor. He was just as beat up as Bryce and I were. But they didn't put him in handcuffs.

"Here are the handcuff keys." One of the goons tossed a set of keys to Giovanni. He placed them in one of his pockets.

I looked back at Brandon. He was silent. And he looked scared, and there was nothing I could do about it. "Giselle!" he cried.

"Brandon," I sobbed.

"Brandon, let me tell you something about your sister. She is a fucking ungrateful bitch who allowed another man"—Giovanni pulled a gun out of the waistband of his pants and aimed it at Bryce—"that man to not only fuck her, but also to impregnate her. After all of this, I offered to forgive her if she aborted the bastard growing inside her, and I was going to take her back. I really was. As my wife. But the dumb whore ran off again to fuck him! The man who kidnapped her."

My brother's facial expression changed. Brandon stared Giovanni down like if he had a gun, he would shoot him.

"And, unfortunately, you are going to have to pay for her sins," Giovanni added.

My body grew numb. My mouth started moving, but not one sound came out. All I could hear was my own heartbeat. I ignored my pain. I rushed toward Giovanni, flung myself onto him as he aimed his gun at my brother, who dropped to his knees and had his hands up, begging him not to shoot him. Giovanni slapped me, causing me to fly back and drop to the floor. Bryce made a move, but three guns were aimed at him, and plus, he was shackled. I sprang to my feet again and ran in front of the gun to shield my brother. I could still hear only my own heartbeat . . . even though I was begging Giovanni. One of his goons snatched me up, dragged me away. I fought him with all the might in me. I punched him, bit one of his hands, and managed to escape.

I raced toward Giovanni to snatch away the gun and could feel my feet making progress. I had only a few more steps to take when I was grabbed from behind. My feet could no longer feel the floor, as they were in the air as I was being carried back. My arms shot out in front of me, and I continued to beg. That was when I heard it. The bullets going from my husband's gun into my little brother's body. Three of them. Each one felt like it was going into my body. I dug my fingers into my scalp and screamed at the top of my lungs as my brother's body jerked back and forth with the force of the bullets before he went down.

"Brandon!"

His body twitched.

I struggled to get away, but my captor held me in a full nelson.

"Brandon!"

I collapsed backward into the man's arms and cried loudly.

My heart was crushed. My brother was gone.

That was when I heard more gunshots ring out in the room. I looked up as two men came from nowhere. When the cloud of smoke momentarily cleared around their faces, I saw it was Percy and Hog. The guy holding me shoved me away and returned gunfire. I dropped to the floor, and all the men in the room, including Giovanni, were now firing at Percy and Hog. I rushed over to my brother and dragged his body to a corner of the room.

His eyes were cold and lifeless, the same way Lexi's were, which told me he was dead. Bullets whizzed past me, hitting walls and shattering windows. I watched one of Giovanni's men go down. I covered my head with my hands and stayed on my knees as more bullets flooded the room. Hog rushed farther into a room, firing like crazy at Giovanni's goons. Another one went down.

Giovanni's other two men and Giovanni fired back more fiercely. One of Giovanni's bullets hit Hog in his knee. He remained standing, even though blood gushed from it. Percy took another of the goons down, while at the same time Giovanni's last goon concentrated on firing at Hog. He continued to fire a stream of bullets into him, and Hog's body rocked back and forth with the impact.

A look of rage came over Percy's face. "Muthafucka!" He started firing like crazy at the last goon.

Giovanni ran and ducked behind a chair.

Two of the bullets connected with the goon's arm, making him drop his gun. It skidded on the floor and stopped a few inches from my brother. Another bullet got him in his leg. He spun around in a circle before falling to the floor.

"You punk bitch!" Percy kept firing and walking toward the goon. The bullets continued to hit him. The goon was laid out flat, and Percy was still firing bullets into him.

That was when I noticed Bryce yelling, "Percy, look out."

But it was too late. 'Cause as Percy inched toward the goon, my husband was inching toward Percy. And he had his gun drawn and aimed at Percy's head. And he fired, blowing the back of Percy's head off.

I looked at the hurt look on Bryce's face. He had lost someone else. His boy. More bloodshed. My brother was gone. Percy was gone. Bryce's brother and sister were gone. My best friend, Lexi, was gone. All on account of my husband. I knew I could not be weak. I had to be strong and get Bryce and myself out of this. I had to.

"One way or another, you are going to die, muthafucka," Bryce snarled.

Giovanni laughed and looked at Bryce. "Oh, really? And who is going to kill me? You?"

I took the distraction as an opportunity to pick up the gun near my brother. I tucked it into the back of my underwear.

"'Cause unless there is such a fucking thing as reincarnation, bitch, you won't be the one pulling any trig-

ger. I'm going to be pulling it on you." He walked closer
to Bryce, aiming the gun as he did.

"No! Don't shoot him please!" I begged. He had
taken my brother, my friend. He was not going to take
Bryce from me, too.

Giovanni froze and turned around to look at me, with
his gun still aimed at Bryce. I looked at my husband's
horrified face as he raised his gun to Bryce's head.

Bryce simply sat back, coughing and spitting up
blood. My husband looked from me to Bryce, then back
at me. The whole time his hand did not lower the gun.

"So what? You're in love with him, Giselle?"

I swallowed hard and tried to speak, with my arms
held wide, but nothing but inaudible sounds came out
of me. So I dropped my hands to my sides as moans
and sobs hit me.

My husband started sobbing, too. Huge sobs. Because he knew the truth. So why did he want to hear it?

Yes, I loved him. More than I had ever loved my
husband, more than I loved myself, and surely, more
than I loved my life. Which was pretty screwed up right
fucking now! I was staring at the man I had thought I
would love forever—a man I now loathed, hated, and
wished would die—and fearing that the man I wanted
to love forever was going to die.

"With all due respect, tell me, why did you kill my
sister?" Bryce muttered.

"What?" Giovanni said.

"I just want to know why you killed my sister, nigga!"

"You really want to hear this shit, huh? Before you
die? Okay, fine. Because she couldn't be paid off. With
the other ones, I could do what I wanted and could pay
them. That little bitch threatened to tell the police on
me and get her big brothers to come after me. Even
when I offered her money. So I beat her in the head un-

til her heart stopped beating. This is how she shook." I watched, horrified, as Giovanni imitated a person having a seizure.

Bryce gave him such a hateful look.

"She was just a little bitch on the way to being a fucking whore, anyway. I did the world a favor. She is one less scum, one less trick, to worry about."

Bryce's eyes were watery from what Giovanni was saying.

"Now you're going to join her."

"Pull the trigger, mufucka. Get this shit over with," Bryce said.

My husband yelled out in rage and rushed toward Bryce. "Shut the fuck up!" He started to beat Bryce in the head with his gun. "Don't make any fucking demands on me! You fucked my wife!"

"Yeah, and it was good, nigga!"

I rushed forward, threw myself on my husband's back, and pounded him with my fists anywhere I could hit him. "Get off of him! You took my brother from me! You are not going to take him!"

Giovanni easily tossed me off him. I flew and hit the floor with a loud thud, banging my knee as I did. My teeth clenched as pain shot into my leg.

My husband turned to me. He looked so hurt that I was protecting Bryce. "You want him, Giselle? Huh? You love him? Baby, just tell me the truth."

I closed my eyes briefly. Never in my wildest dreams did I think I would find myself in this situation. But it was my husband's bullshit that got me caught up with Bryce to begin with. Neither of us had planned for this. Too many lives had been lost. Shit, this has gone too far, and I wanted to end it. End the war. All the pain now. If I could. I wished I could tell him the truth and have it be okay. That I did love Bryce, and not him, and that he should just let us go. But I knew that there was no reasoning with him. Because I was looking at a straight monster with a gun. I closed my eyes at this harsh, harsh reality. I knew what I would have to do. But, damn, the shit was so fucking hard.

"Giselle."

I opened my eyes and stared at my husband. His lips were trembling, and his eyes were red.

"As much as this shit is going to hurt me to hear, baby, I need to know the truth." He took a deep breath. "Do you love this man?"

I took a deep breath and shook my head.

"Bitch! Do you hear me talking to you?"

"Yes. I love him!"

His whole face crumbled. "You were my baby." His voice lowered. "Sweet Giselle."

I started crying again. That voice. The way he said my name evoked so many memories. The first time he made love to me. The moment the pastor made me his wife and he kissed me. When he would hold me in his arms at night and tell me that my ever wish was his command. And it was. It was. He had kept his word. The way he said he adored me when we spooned in bed. . . . He would whisper it and bite me on my earlobe. Our vows came to mind. How he added at the end so many kind, sweet, endearing words. How much he would protect me and make sure no harm ever came my way. That my brother was his brother, and he had him as he had me. So many memories of what we were. And now . . . no matter how good those memories were . . . we just couldn't go back—ever.

I thought my husband was seeing the same things I was seeing. Recollecting all the beautiful moments we had shared. Then something brought him back to the present.

Suddenly my husband turned his focus back on Bryce. He aimed the gun. I tried to stand, despite the pain in my knee, and before I could stop him, he fired.

Bryce used the strength in his body to twist in the chair and make it fall backward, dodging the bullet. But Giovanni continued to fire. That was when I knew what I had to do. I had to end this. So I pulled the gun out of the band of my underwear. As he inched toward Bryce, I raised my gun, and without a moment's hesitation, I fired bullets into his back. I watched the gaping holes in his shirt. His blood immediately colored the shirt red. But my husband didn't fall. I started firing more rounds, until my husband turned and looked at me.

His eyes were wide.

I sobbed and waited. Slowly, he dropped to his knees, saying, "Giselle."

I shook my head as tears poured from my eyes. I kept my gun aimed at him, in case he decided to fire his. But instead slipped from his fingers.

I took a deep breath as he struggled to talk due to the blood spilling from his mouth.

"I love you, baby."

I raised the gun and fired one more shot into his head. His head split in half. I looked away as he fell forward.

And I didn't know how to feel. But all I knew was that he was dead.

"Giselle! Get the keys to the handcuffs."

I rushed up to Giovanni and rummaged through his pockets for the handcuff keys. Once I found them, I raced toward Bryce and unlocked the handcuffs on his wrists and ankles.

Once freed, Bryce stood to his feet.

I looked back at my brother. I ran back over to his body and threw myself on top of him and bawled. I still could not believe my brother was gone. I was supposed to protect him, and I had failed him. It was too much to bear. Bringing forth denial, I shook his body, praying he would wake up, come out of this. "Brandon. Brandon, baby, wake up, little brother." I shook his shoulders again. Tears spilled off my face onto his. "I love you, little brother. I love you so much."

Bryce's hand was on my back. "Come on, baby."

I knew we had to go. But I didn't want to leave my brother here. I closed his eyelids and kissed him on both his cheeks before Bryce damn near dragged me out of there.

Epilogue

"Ready, Brandon?"

"Ready. Okay, go!" he said.

I laughed at my son as he threw his hands in the air and went down his slide. I had just picked it up from Toys "R" Us with a gift card he got last week for his first birthday. I giggled at all the joy on his face as he raced to the steps to go down the slide again. And again, for the umpteenth time.

I just could not get over how much he looked like my brother, Brandon. It was obvious from the moment he was brought into the world. He had the same skin tone, same eyes, same lips. In fact, he was a replica of my brother when he was brought into the world. So that was why I named my precious son Brandon.

Looking back, I still could not believe Bryce and I were able to escape the horror that transpired almost two years ago. Considering all that we had lost, if we didn't have each other to help get past it, I don't think either one of us would have had the strength to function. He became my rock, and I became his. We relocated to Georgia, like Bryce had suggested. And that was just fine for me. All California represented to me was pain and memories. And frankly, I could do without both. . . . After all, everything that was familiar became unfamiliar because of how it was presented to me. I couldn't go anywhere without thinking of my loss. I knew Bryce felt the same way.

For example, say you took a simple walk down the street and it evoked memories of the person you last walked down that street with. Or the person you were going to see or you just left. Like visiting Santa Monica Pier and remembering that the last time you went, you were with your love. And now visiting the pier brought you down, because you no longer had that love, that person in your life, by your side. For me . . . it always came back to my brother and him not being there. And I . . . I just could not deal. I knew Bryce felt the same way. And he had to rid himself of all the grief, or lie down and die to escape it. And I knew Bryce was a fighter, so the best bet was to leave.

We set up shop in a small house in Decatur, on Clairemont Avenue. Bryce had some money to tide us over while he started and finished up plumbing school. What kept us going through all of this was the little life growing inside of me. To this day I still can't get over how he held on and how God kept that heart of his beating. Shortly after he was born, I was accepted to Agnes Scott College. I decided to study pre-law, and when I graduated, I was going to law school. I figured it was the best bet for me and my family. Bryce decided he didn't want to work for anyone, so he took the last of his savings and opened up his own plumbing business. For his birthday, I surprised him by renovating the garage and turning it into a makeshift art studio. That way, whenever he wanted to get away and sketch, he could.

We weren't living fancy. But at the end of the day, we were able to survive and we had everything we needed. Not the riches my husband had given me, the expensive clothes, bags, and jewelry, all the getaways. We had none of that. Yet life without that wasn't so bad. I loved Bryce. I was proud of the fact that he was able to leave that old life in his past and never reverted back. He came home sweaty, dirty, stinky, and proud, because he had earned his paycheck without causing misery or bringing grief to anyone. I loved it. And when he did come home, he always got a hug, a kiss, and a warm meal. Yep, he earned all of that.

Everything in our world centered on our son. We took trips to the park and the zoo, built sand castles on the beach, and my son had this thing for dinosaurs, so we visited the Fernbank Museum religiously. And once a month my neighbor would keep li'l Brandon so we could have a date night. It was more of a simple life. No Ranges, Prada, or Rolexes. We had no need for those things and no desire to keep up with the Joneses. We aspired to our own reality. And that was our life.

It wasn't easy at first. One day slipping into the next always brought my mind back to my brother. Crazy thing was that even though we were thousands of miles away from California, his spirit was right there with us in Decatur. When we first settled into our home, I could feel his presence lingering over me. It always felt like he had his arms wrapped around me. Or I heard a voice chanting his nickname for me, Gissy. I knew he was waiting, waiting to cross over, because he was watching over me, making sure I was able to go on without him. Then, after my son was born, I felt the presence no more. And I knew where he was. He had crossed over and had joined my parents. And as much as his death killed a part of my soul, which I knew I would never get back, as much as I missed my brother . . . I was okay with it. I really was. . . .

ORDER FORM
URBAN BOOKS, LLC
78 E. Industry Ct
Deer Park, NY 11729

Name:(please print):_____

Address: _____

City/State: _____

Zip: _____

QTY	TITLES	PRICE
	16 On The Block	$14.95
	A Girl From Flint	$14.95
	A Pimp's Life	$14.95
	Baltimore Chronicles	$14.95
	Baltimore Chronicles 2	$14.95
	Betrayal	$14.95
	Black Diamond	$14.95
	Black Diamond 2	$14.95
	Black Friday	$14.95
	Both Sides Of The Fence	$14.95
	Both Sides Of The Fence 2	$14.95
	California Connection	$14.95

Shipping and handling-add $3.50 for 1st book, then $1.75 for each additional book.

Please send a check payable to:

Urban Books, LLC

Please allow 4-6 weeks for delivery

ORDER FORM
URBAN BOOKS, LLC
78 E. Industry Ct
Deer Park, NY 11729

Name: (please print):_____

Address: _____

City/State: _____

Zip: _____

QTY	TITLES	PRICE
	California Connection 2	$14.95
	Cheesecake And Teardrops	$14.95
	Congratulations	$14.95
	Crazy In Love	$14.95
	Cyber Case	$14.95
	Denim Diaries	$14.95
	Diary Of A Mad First Lady	$14.95
	Diary Of A Stalker	$14.95
	Diary Of A Street Diva	$14.95
	Diary Of A Young Girl	$14.95
	Dirty Money	$14.95
	Dirty To The Grave	$14.95

Shipping and handling-add $3.50 for 1st book, then $1.75 for each additional book.

Please send a check payable to:
Urban Books, LLC
Please allow 4-6 weeks for delivery

ORDER FORM
URBAN BOOKS, LLC
78 E. Industry Ct
Deer Park, NY 11729

Name: (please print):_____

Address:　　　_____

City/State:　　_____

Zip:　　　_____

QTY	TITLES	PRICE
	Gunz And Roses	$14.95
	Happily Ever Now	$14.95
	Hell Has No Fury	$14.95
	Hush	$14.95
	If It Isn't love	$14.95
	Kiss Kiss Bang Bang	$14.95
	Last Breath	$14.95
	Little Black Girl Lost	$14.95
	Little Black Girl Lost 2	$14.95
	Little Black Girl Lost 3	$14.95
	Little Black Girl Lost 4	$14.95
	Little Black Girl Lost 5	$14.95

Shipping and handling-add $3.50 for 1st book, then $1.75 for each additional book.
Please send a check payable to:
Urban Books, LLC
Please allow 4-6 weeks for delivery